MURDER
at the
CHARITY BALL

BOOKS BY HELENA DIXON

HELENA DIXON

MURDER
at the
CHARITY BALL

bookouture

Published by Bookouture in 2023

An imprint of Storyfire Ltd.
Carmelite House
50 Victoria Embankment
London EC4Y 0DZ

www.bookouture.com

ISBN: 978-1-80314-301-9
eBook ISBN: 978-1-80314-300-2

Murder at the Charity Ball is dedicated to all of the unsung heroes of the charity world. Having worked in that field I know how tiring, time-consuming and what hard work it can be to raise funds and give support. There are so many tiny little charities doing wonderful work, week in, week out, in difficult conditions and for little thanks or reward. I see you, you are all heroes.

PROLOGUE

TORBAY HERALD
SATURDAY, DECEMBER 15TH 1934

The cream of Torbay society is expected to be in attendance this evening for the annual festive charity ball hosted by Lady Eliza Foxley and her sister, Mrs Lillie Trentham. The much-anticipated event, a highlight of the social calendar, is in aid of the Seafarers' Widows and Orphans Fund. A worthy cause founded by Mrs Trentham in memory of her late husband, Mr Hubert Trentham, to support families whose loved ones have perished at sea. This is indeed a cause dear to Mrs Trentham's heart since the tragic loss at sea of her own beloved husband some years ago. Lady Foxley and Mrs Trentham are very recently arrived back from New York and the ball this year has been organised on their behalf by Mrs Millicent Craven, former mayoress of Dartmouth.

The ball, held at Lady Foxley's beautiful home, Villa Lamora, in Torquay, regularly raises a considerable sum of money for the charity. The event has been sold out for several weeks, such is the demand for tickets.

CHAPTER ONE

The thick winter velvet curtains were drawn in the first-floor bay window of Kitty's grandmother's salon at the ancient Dolphin Hotel in Dartmouth. A fire crackled cheerily in the grate of the marble fireplace and the lamps were lit. A Christmas tree stood on the table in the curtained bay and greetings cards were strung above the fireplace.

Pine scented the air and strands of tinsel sparkled against the greenery. Despite the festive gaiety, however, the atmosphere in the room held the same chill as the night air outside on the embankment.

'I'll be perfectly honest, Kitty, I thought your father had lost the knack to surprise me with his shenanigans but really, this time he has taken the biscuit.' Mrs Treadwell's shoulders were rigid with disapproval beneath her dark-blue silk evening gown.

Kitty, however, was seldom surprised by her father. Edgar Underhay was not known for his reliability. 'Perhaps we shall learn more when we arrive at the ball. I think Mr Potter's taxi should be here for us in a moment.' She glanced at her fiancé for support.

'Yes, I rather think we should gather our coats. It was quite chilly out this evening when I arrived.' Matt, tall and handsome in his evening attire, gave her a smile.

'Well, I think it very thoughtless. It's just over a week to your wedding and for your father to go changing the arrangement of things willy-nilly on a whim. Well, words fail me.' Kitty's grandmother huffed as Matt assisted her with her thick woollen fur-trimmed black evening stole.

Kitty suppressed a sigh. Her father's ship had been late docking at Plymouth after encountering some bad weather during the crossing from America. This had meant she had not been able to go to meet him as she had intended.

She had booked him a room at the Imperial Hotel in Torquay for the duration of his visit. Both her father and her grandmother had been in rare agreement that them being under the same roof at the Dolphin would not be a good idea. Indeed, being in the same town would have been a stretch. It was far better that her father stayed in Torquay for the duration of his visit. At least, that had been the plan.

A message had just been received to say that the reservation at the Imperial had now been cancelled and instead her father would be staying at Villa Lamora, home of Lady Eliza Foxley, whose acquaintance he had apparently made on board the ship from America. Lady Foxley was also the hostess for this evening's ball, organised on her behalf by Mrs Craven, Kitty's grandmother's particular friend.

The black Bakelite telephone on the bureau rang and Kitty picked up the receiver.

'Thank you, we will be right down.' She replaced the handset.

'I take it that Mr Potter has arrived?' Matt assisted her with her own winter evening coat. The gauzy red chiffon of her dress wouldn't have offered much protection against the winter cold.

'Yes, let's go and enjoy ourselves at the ball.' Kitty collected her silver evening purse and accompanied her fiancé out of the suite, with her grandmother following behind still fussing with her fur-trimmed leather gloves.

Kitty and her grandmother took the rear seat of the taxi while Matt hopped in the front to sit beside Mr Potter. He liked to have the window cracked open to allow a little air into the motor car, a legacy from his time at the front during the war. Mindful of Kitty's grandmother's dislike of the cold though, it was better that he sat beside Mr Potter.

Mrs Treadwell spread one of the tartan woollen travel rugs that the taxi driver had thoughtfully provided for the comfort of his passengers over her knees and shivered dramatically.

'I do hope that Lady Foxley has good fires.' She settled into her seat.

'I take it that Mrs Craven must know Lady Foxley quite well as she's organised the ball for her this evening?' Kitty asked as their driver steered his car onto the ferry to cross the river.

'I believe it's her sister, Mrs Trentham, who is Millicent's acquaintance. They both serve on the board for the Seafarers' Widows and Orphans Fund. Lady Foxley is a very different character to her sister.' Mrs Treadwell gave a slight sniff of disapproval to accompany the last part of her statement.

'Mrs Trentham is a widow?' Kitty asked. She had heard a little of Lady Foxley's reputation but knew very little about Mrs Trentham.

'Oh yes, my dear, it was terribly sad. Her husband drowned in a shipping accident, leaving her with a young daughter. Caroline, a sweet little thing, was only six when it happened. It was quite a few years ago, so I rather think the girl must be at least fifteen or sixteen by now. Mrs Trentham set up the charity to aid the families of the sailors who lost their lives in the same tragedy. Since then, she has expanded it to help others and save them from destitution.' Kitty's grandmother drew her stole more closely around her as the car made its way up the hill through Kingswear and on towards Paignton and Torquay.

'And Lady Foxley allows her home to be used to host the ball each year?' Kitty was keen to discover as much as she could about her father's hostess before she met her.

'As I said, Lady Foxley is a very different character to her sister. She married Lord Foxley when she had scarcely left school and he was old enough to be her grandfather. Naturally enough it ended in scandal and divorce, although she kept the title, her diamonds and a considerable portfolio of stock. He died shortly after the divorce, or was it just before? When poor Lillie Trentham was widowed, her sister offered her and the child a home and they have been there ever since.' Her grandmother glanced at her. 'I'm rather afraid, my dear, that Lady Foxley and your father are not dissimilar in habits.'

Kitty pressed her lips together to refrain from answering and gazed out of the window as the darkness of the countryside gave way to the street lamps in the town. Her father was sadly quite a disreputable character. He had been absent for most of her life, leaving for America at the start of the Great War and only returning to England for the first time a year ago.

Kitty had hoped that he had now settled down and started to put his somewhat colourful past behind him. Although she acknowledged that this was probably more hope than expectation on her part. He had insisted that he wished to return for her wedding to Matt, to give her away. While she was delighted that he was back in Torbay she couldn't help but be a little worried that his stay might prove to be rather trying.

The taxi had swung away from the seafront road and was now heading inland up towards the area with the better addresses on the edge of the town. After a moment Mr Potter drove them through a grey stone portal, guarded by a magnificent pair of stone lions, and onto a gravel drive. Ahead of them, the large cream-painted walls of Villa Lamora could plainly be seen. Electric lights blazed at every window and in front of the carved stone portico several impressive motor cars were already parked.

Mr Potter pulled the car to a stop and the sound of the engine was replaced by the faint strains of jazz music emanating from the house.

Matt and the taxi driver got out and opened the doors of the car for Kitty and her grandmother, and assisted them out.

'What time would you like me to return, Mrs Treadwell?' Mr Potter asked as he closed the rear door of the car.

Kitty's gaze locked with her grandmother's. She suspected her darling Grams would quite happily have climbed back in the car right there and then.

'Shall we say midnight?' Kitty suggested.

'Very good, miss.' Mr Potter touched the brim of his flat cap and returned to the driver's seat.

'Well, this all looks very gay. Shall we?' Matt offered Kitty and her grandmother his arms and they entered the house together.

An elderly, grey-haired butler met them at the door and, after checking their tickets, directed a maid, smart in a dark grey and white uniform, to take their outdoor things. The volume of the music was louder inside the house. Kitty looked around her with interest while they got their bearings.

The hall was spacious and square with a black and white chequerboard tile floor. Kitty blinked when she realised that the large picture in the gilt frame at the foot of the stairs was that of a somewhat scantily clad Lady Foxley. Blonde-haired and swathed in barely there diaphanous material, Eliza looked out from the canvas. There was a glint of devilment in her bold blue gaze and scarlet-lipped pout.

'Kitty, my darling girl!' She was swooped upon by her father, immaculate but slightly roguish in his evening attire. He kissed her cheeks and held the tops of her arms as he studied her face. 'As beautiful as I remember and so much like your mother. Congratulations, my dear, I'm looking forward to the wedding.' He turned to Matt and shook his hand. 'Captain Bryant, Matthew, I see you have been taking good care of my girl. This is all rather splendid, isn't it?' He waved his hand generally in the direction of the house.

Kitty's grandmother gave a discreet cough.

'Where are my manners? My dear mother-in-law, looking as well as ever.' Edgar Underhay refrained from kissing or shaking hands with Kitty's grandmother, who was fixing him with a glacial stare.

'Edgar, looking as worthless as ever.' Mrs Treadwell gave him an icy nod while Kitty's father pretended not to have heard her.

'Grams, you promised,' Kitty reminded her quietly in her ear.

'Very well, just keep him away from me as much as possible,' her grandmother murmured back.

'You must come and meet Eliza. She's the most wonderful sport. We hit it off straight away and got to know one another well on board the ship.' Edgar took Kitty's arm in his and led their small party along the hall towards a large room at the rear of the house.

A wave of chatter and music hit them as soon as they entered. A jazz quartet was playing at the far end of the ballroom, with a female vocalist singing one of the latest songs. The air was thick with cigarette smoke and chandeliers glittered above their heads.

Edgar made his way through the crush towards a small group of people standing near the partly open French doors. On the way there he liberated glasses of champagne for them all from the tray of a passing waiter.

'Eliza, darling, here is my daughter, Kitty, and her fiancé, Captain Matthew Bryant. Kitty, Matt, Lady Eliza Foxley. Oh, and this is my mother-in-law, Mrs Treadwell, Mrs Treadwell, Lady Foxley.' Edgar beamed as he made the introductions.

Kitty was relieved to find that Lady Foxley was wearing slightly more clothing than she had worn for her portrait in the hall. Her blonde hair was artfully waved, and diamonds glittered in her ears. Her evening gown, however, made Kitty feel quite matronly in comparison. The dazzling scarlet sheath was fitted to her slender figure and both back and front were cut daringly low.

'I'm delighted to meet you, Kitty. Edgar has told me so much about you.' Lady Foxley smiled. 'And, Mrs Treadwell, you look divine. Darling Millicent has said what a dear friend you are. I believe she is over there talking to my sister.' Lady Eliza waved a scarlet nail-tipped hand in the direction of a group on the far side of the room.

Kitty looked across and recognised the feathery plumes of Mrs Craven's favourite evening headpiece waggling above the crowd.

'Thank you, Lady Foxley, if you'll excuse me, I'll just let her know I'm here.' Kitty's grandmother slipped away into the crowd.

'Your father tells me that your wedding is on Christmas Eve morning?' Lady Foxley said as she captured a waiter, setting her empty glass down on his tray and replacing it with a full one.

'Yes, at Saint Saviour's in Dartmouth,' Kitty responded politely, before taking a sip from her own glass.

'How marvellous, such a quaint church. I was married at St Paul's in London, terrible mistake, darling. I hope the two of you will be much happier than I was with poor dear Barty.' Lady Foxley giggled and took a large swig of champagne from her glass.

A plain-looking dark-haired young girl dressed in blue velvet appeared at Lady Foxley's side. 'Aunt Eliza, Mummy has said that I am not to drink.'

Kitty assumed this must be Mrs Trentham's daughter, Caroline, as she seemed to be the right sort of age.

'Well, Caro, darling, I can hardly tell you to defy your mother's wishes, can I? And you are only sixteen.' Lady Foxley looked at her niece. 'I had enough trouble persuading her to let you come.'

The girl huffed and stormed away.

'Oh dear, Caroline is at such a difficult age. Left to myself I don't really see the harm in a small glass or two, but Lillie is terribly strict. I have advised her to send the dear child to finishing school as I fear her social skills could use some improvement.' Lady Foxley gave a slight shrug of her elegant shoulders as if the girl's behaviour seemed to bear out the advisability of her suggestion.

As Caroline stalked away a tall, distinguished-looking man with silver hair took the girl's place. 'Oh, darlings, let me introduce you, Sir Stanford King, my financial advisor, Miss Kitty Underhay and her fiancé, Captain Matthew Bryant. Kitty is Edgar here's daughter.' Lady Foxley placed a proprietary hand on Kitty's father's sleeve.

A gesture that Kitty saw did not go unnoticed by Sir Stanford, who did not appear to be too pleased by it.

'I'm delighted to meet you both.' He bowed his head a little stiffly towards them.

'Darling Stanford is always so solicitous of me.' Lady Eliza bestowed a dazzling smile on him as he procured her another glass of champagne to replace the one that had miraculously emptied itself during the course of their conversation.

'One does one's best,' Sir Stanford agreed.

'Which reminds me, darling, we need to go over my portfolio tomorrow. Perhaps after lunch? I'll ask Phillip to have everything ready.' She looked at Sir Stanford and took another sip from her glass.

'I'm sorry, did you just call, Lady Foxley?' A thin, rather

anxious bespectacled young man who Kitty had noticed loitering nearby came to join them.

'Yes, Phillip, I was telling Stanford that we would review my investments tomorrow afternoon. Perhaps you can be at hand and have the papers ready.' Lady Eliza's tone sounded a little sharp to Kitty.

'Yes, yes, of course, I'll be sure to have everything ready in your study.' Phillip's cheeks flushed red in his anxious rush to reply. 'I'll just go now and check.' He disappeared back into the crowd.

Lady Foxley sighed. 'My secretary, Phillip Peters. Sadly, he doesn't seem to be the brightest of sparks, but he does try I suppose.' She looked past Matt and signalled to a large older woman dressed in such deep black Kitty at first thought she must be in mourning.

'Tiny, darling, please can you keep an eye on Caro? I rather think she intends to try the champagne and you know that if she does Lillie will blame me.'

The woman nodded and set off towards the dance floor.

'Miss Morrow was Lillie's and my nurse when we were children and she has looked after Caro too ever since she was a baby. Such a treasure.' Lady Eliza finished her drink and bestowed another of her dazzling smiles on Kitty's father. 'Edgar, darling, can I tear you away from your lovely daughter? Only this music is so divine, I really must dance.'

'Kitty, my dear, would you mind?' he asked.

Kitty smiled her assent, and her father promptly took his leave to escort Lady Eliza towards the dance floor.

CHAPTER TWO

Sir Stanford also excused himself to head towards the bar, leaving Kitty and Matt alone with their drinks.

'Phew, that was all rather intense, wasn't it?' Kitty remarked.

Matt looked around at the crowded room. 'It was rather.' He was quite glad they were standing near the open window. The room was over warm, and the air was quite muggy.

He wondered if Kitty had noticed Lady Eliza's proprietary air towards her father. Clearly the two of them seemed to have become quite close for such a short acquaintance.

'I hope my father will be able to tear himself away from his new friend in order to give me away at our wedding,' Kitty remarked a trifle ruefully.

'I think we can see why he decided to accept Lady Foxley's offer of hospitality.' Matt placed his arm around his fiancée's waist and gave her a gentle hug. 'Never mind, old thing. I expect you'll have lots of time to talk to him before the big day.' He was aware that Kitty had hoped to spend some time getting to know her father better in the run up to their nuptials.

'She is quite lovely,' Kitty said. Matt followed Kitty's gaze to where Lady Foxley was dancing with Edgar. Her scarlet figure cut quite the dash in Edgar's arms as they whirled about the dance floor.

'Not as lovely as you.' Matt stole a kiss and chuckled as Kitty blushed.

'Now then, you two lovebirds!' a familiar female voice chided him, and he felt a gentle smack from a folded fan on his knuckles.

'Mrs C, the ball appears to be a roaring success.'

Mrs Craven, Kitty's grandmother's closest friend, had come to join them, resplendent in peacock-blue shot satin with a rather peculiar peacock-feathered hair ornament bobbing above her head.

'One cannot take all the credit, Matthew, but of course I do have considerable experience at organising social occasions, as you know,' Mrs Craven replied. 'Please allow me to introduce you both to Mrs Lillie Trentham. Lillie my dear, Captain Matthew Bryant and his fiancée, Miss Kitty Underhay, Mrs Treadwell's granddaughter.'

Lillie Trentham bore no resemblance to her sister. If Mrs Craven had not told him who she was Matt would not have thought them to be related. Where Eliza Foxley was lithe, blonde and glamorous. Lillie was dark haired and dressed in a somewhat shapeless gown that he suspected was not the latest fashion. There was an air of frailty and gentility about her slender form.

'I'm delighted you could both come. It must be such a busy time for you both with your wedding so close.' Lillie had a quiet, well-modulated voice that was a little difficult to hear over the hubbub in the room.

'Oh, we are having a very small, simple wedding. Neither of us wanted any fuss and, of course, this is in aid of such a good cause,' Kitty assured her.

'Well, it sounds very romantic, getting married on Christmas Eve,' Lillie said.

A rather bluff, ruddy-faced gentleman in his late forties came to join their group carrying two glasses of champagne. 'Lillie my dear, I wondered where you had gone.' He handed a glass to Mrs Trentham, who performed the introductions.

'Captain Bryant, Miss Underhay, may I introduce Roger Hemmings. He was a fellow passenger on our journey. He is staying at the Grand Hotel in Torquay.'

Matt wondered that Lady Foxley had not extended the same invitation to Roger Hemmings to stay at the house that she had issued to Kitty's father. Then again, perhaps this Hemmings chap was more Lillie's friend than Eliza's.

'Pleased to meet you.' Hemmings shook hands with them both. Mrs Craven's attention had been claimed by another acquaintance.

'It's a splendid ball. It should raise a lot of money for your charity,' Kitty said to Lillie.

'Oh yes, dear Mrs Craven has been a marvel. I'm so very grateful she was able to help. With us all being stuck in America the ball would have had to be cancelled if Mrs Craven had not responded to my urgent telegrams for help. Such wonderful generosity from the local businesses donating prizes for the raffle too,' Lillie agreed.

'Very good cause,' Roger Hemmings concurred with them. 'So, Captain Bryant, what is it you do?'

'I'm a private investigator,' Matt answered and took a sip of his champagne. Often he found people were slightly disparaging when he gave his profession, assuming he dealt with divorce cases and other less salubrious work. Or they suddenly became more guarded, leaving him to wonder what they were afraid he might discover. 'And you?'

Roger seemed to freeze for a fraction of a second. 'Splendid,

that sounds fascinating, well, my line of work will sound much
more mundane compared to you.'

'Roger is in valves,' Lillie said.

Her tone as she replied made Matt wonder how long Roger
might have bored her on the subject.

* * *

Kitty often wondered why people always asked what Matt did
but never appeared to think that she too might have employ-
ment beyond the home.

'Kitty is a hotelier, she and her grandmother own the
Dolphin Hotel in Dartmouth.' Matt appeared to read her mind
and he gave her a cheeky wink.

'How interesting. The Dolphin is such a lovely hotel. I
didn't realise you were a private investigator, Captain Bryant.
Tell me, is there enough crime in our sleepy bay to keep you
occupied?' Lillie asked.

'Unfortunately, there is rather more than you might imagine, Mrs Trentham,' Matt answered with a smile.

Kitty caught a glimpse of Caroline Trentham on the edge of
the dance floor laughing with a group of young people who all
appeared a little older than her. A young man in the group
pressed a glass of champagne into the girl's hand. Caroline
immediately drank half of it straight away.

'Please excuse me.' Lillie Trentham had evidently spotted
her daughter at the same time as Kitty, as she immediately
plunged away into the crowd in the direction of the dance floor
and the errant Caroline.

With Lillie gone, Roger Hemmings also made his excuses.
Matt relieved Kitty of her empty glass and set it down beside his
own on a nearby marble-topped side table.

'Now then, darling, this is a ball after all, and we should

make the most of the evening.' He offered her his hand and looked towards the dance floor. 'Shall we?'

The next hour or so was spent in the most delightful fashion, dancing and eating from the delicious silver trays of canapés that were pressed upon them by the attentive waiters. Kitty caught glimpses of her grandmother seated at a table talking to a group of her friends, while Mrs Craven was busy circulating around the room, and other members of Lady Foxley's party were either dancing, talking or eating.

Kitty's father also appeared from time to time, and she even managed a couple of dances with him while Matt escorted Mrs Craven around the floor.

'I haven't seen Lady Foxley for a while,' she remarked to her father as they took their second dance together.

'Oh, I think Eliza may have gone to powder her nose. She's probably talking to one of her friends somewhere. She's a very popular lady,' Edgar replied.

'Did you know her well before the voyage?' Kitty asked. She was curious about the friendship. There seemed a depth of familiarity that spoke of a longer acquaintance than a mere Atlantic crossing.

'We have met a few times before in New York at various events,' her father said carelessly. 'You know how it is with those things. You always run into the same crowd.'

'Hmm.' Kitty could see that her father clearly appeared smitten by the dazzling Eliza. 'Her sister is a rather different character?'

'Oh Lillie, yes. Totally wrapped up in that girl of hers, Caroline. Rather a sad story, being widowed at such a young age. A terrible tragedy.' Edgar whirled Kitty around.

The music stopped and the crowd applauded before the band restarted and a male singer took over.

'I suppose I should go and look for Eliza. I had expected her to return before now,' Edgar said as he handed Kitty back to

Matt. 'Most unlike her to miss the fun, and I think the raffle is being drawn soon.'

'Time for a drink?' Matt led Kitty from the dance floor so she could catch her breath.

'A cocktail would be rather fabulous,' she agreed. She had seen various people at the small corner bar where the drinks were being dispensed enjoying a variety of intriguing concoctions.

'Take a seat and rest your feet for a moment, I'll be right back.' Matt indicated a vacant gilt-backed chair at the side of the room next to a large potted palm.

Kitty was quite glad to take him up on his suggestion. The high-heeled red satin shoes that matched her evening gown were making her feet ache. She took a seat and wondered if anyone would notice if she slipped them off for a moment.

'Gin Fizz, darling.' Matt returned and handed her a glass before taking a seat from a nearby table and sitting down next to her.

'Delicious.' Kitty licked her lips after taking a sip.

Matt leaned across and chinked his glass against hers. 'Cheers.'

Kitty laughed. 'It is rather nice to come out like this and have some fun. I can't believe it's only nine days to our wedding. Lucy and Rupert will be arriving in a few days' time. It's a shame my aunt and uncle couldn't get away earlier to arrive with them.' She had prepared rooms at the Dolphin for all the expected members of the wedding party.

'It will be nice to see them again. I presume Lucy will be accompanied by Muffy?' Matt asked.

Muffy was her cousin's little dog and went with Lucy everywhere she went. Lucy was to be Kitty's matron of honour.

'Your parents are due to arrive at around the same time, I think.' Kitty was not looking forward to her prospective in-laws arrival quite so much.

'Oh yes, Mother is wittering away about the arrangements as usual. Aunt Euphemia is looking forward to it all.' Matt grinned at her. His parents were old friends of her grandmother.

She had met his formidable aunt Effie before in Yorkshire when Kitty had been a bridesmaid for Lucy at her wedding. Matt's aunt had been dispatched to assess Kitty's suitability before handing over the family heirloom engagement ring that now graced Kitty's finger.

'I do rather like your aunt Effie.' She smiled back at him. She preferred the straight-talking Effie to Matt's parents, conscious that although friends of her grandmother, they did not really approve the match.

Matt had been married before, to Edith, a woman a few years older than him who, along with her baby daughter, Betty, had been killed during the war. It comforted her slightly that his parents had also not approved of Matt's first wife either. It had taken a long time for Matt to recover from their deaths and Kitty was always sensitive to his loss and his memories.

She took another sip from her drink and settled back in her chair, glad of a few moments respite to look around her. A huge Christmas tree covered with silver strands stood at the side of the stage area where the band were playing. Green festive garlands adorned the tops of the window frames and holly wreaths were hung on the walls. Everywhere was full of glitter and sparkle.

Her happy reverie was soon broken.

'Captain Bryant, we need your assistance. I must beg you to please come with me, it's most urgent.' Lillie Trentham stood before them; her face so pale Kitty thought her about to faint.

Matt leapt to his feet with Kitty following suit.

'What's wrong? Has something happened?' Matt asked.

'You look most unwell,' Kitty added, preparing to insist Lillie take a seat on one of their freshly vacated chairs.

To her astonishment Lillie seemed unwilling to meet her gaze. 'Something dreadful, really dreadful. Please, you must come, I can't explain here.' She turned abruptly, and they had little choice except to follow her.

Kitty downed the last of her cocktail en route and left her empty glass with a waiter at the door of the ballroom. She had no idea what could have occurred to cause Lillie such distress, but she sensed that whatever it was she might need fortification.

Instead of heading back towards the main entrance hall Lillie took them towards the very rear of the villa and through the green baize door into the servants' area. Kitty's sense of bewilderment increased as they were led up the plain wooden service stairs and then out onto the main landing area.

'It is better to be discreet, although under the circumstances...' Kitty was unsure if Lillie was talking to them or to herself.

A door stood open spilling light out onto the large unlit gallery landing.

'I can't go back in there.' Lillie stopped so abruptly just before the open door that Matt almost tripped over her.

He went around Lillie and Kitty went to follow him, only for Lillie to catch hold of her arm.

'Miss Underhay, it may be better if you remain here. I have instructed my butler to call the police and a doctor.' Lillie's grip was surprisingly strong, her fingers digging into Kitty's flesh.

Kitty could hear the murmur of male voices inside the room, and she itched to enter and see for herself what was going on.

'Lillie, whatever has happened?' Kitty asked.

The older woman appeared to take a breath and squared her shoulders before meeting Kitty's gaze. 'My sister is dead. Murdered and I... I... fear your father is responsible.'

Kitty stared at her for a moment unable to comprehend what Lillie was telling her.

'Impossible.' She wrenched her arm free of Lillie's grasp and hurried through the open door.

The room clearly belonged to Lady Foxley. Luxuriously appointed in shades of pink the vista was marred by the sprawled body of Lady Eliza on the bed. The crimson of her dress clashed with the dusky-pink silk of her eiderdown.

Edgar Underhay was seated in a white leather and cane seat beside the window, his head in his hands. Matt was engaged in cautiously examining Lady Eliza's body.

'Matt, what's happened? Papa?' She looked from her fiancé to her father, desperate to understand what could have occurred within the room.

'It appears Lady Foxley has been strangled, with one of her own stockings,' Matt said.

Kitty saw that the top drawer of the inlaid walnut dressing table was partially open, revealing a glimpse of stockings and mounds of delicate lace lingerie. Her legs were surprisingly wobbly as she approached the bed to stand beside Matt.

As she drew nearer, she saw what appeared to be a new stocking on the counterpane next to Lady Foxley's body.

'It looks as if she had laddered her stocking and had returned to her bedroom to change when the killer struck.' Kitty looked at Matt for confirmation.

'That would be my guess,' Matt agreed.

'And your father killed her. Driven mad by lust, I suppose.'

Kitty and Matt turned to discover the woman they had briefly met earlier, the one Lady Foxley had called Tiny was standing in the doorway. Her round face was dark with fury, and she had one massive, meaty arm around Lillie's delicate shoulders.

'I did no such thing. I merely came to find Eliza as she had been gone from the party for a while. And God help me, I found her like this,' Edgar protested, seemingly aroused from his stupor by the ferocity of the woman's accusation.

'We shall see what the police have to say about this. My poor Eliza.' The woman's face crumpled, and a huge sob wracked her frame.

Kitty looked around the room. Lady Eliza's jewel box seemed undisturbed and there were no indications that the room had been searched for any valuables. The only items out of place were the partly opened dressing table drawer and Eliza's discarded high-heeled patent evening shoe on the white fur rug at the end of the bed.

Lady Foxley was still wearing her diamond bracelet and Kitty could see the glitter of diamonds around her neck under the knot of the stocking used to murder her. Her earrings were also still in her ears.

'There are no signs of robbery,' Kitty murmured to Matt.

'I noticed,' Matt agreed.

Kitty crossed the room to kneel beside her father. 'Tell us what happened.'

Her father groaned. 'I came to look for Eliza as she had been gone for a while. I thought perhaps she might be unwell. She had drunk rather a lot of champagne. When I arrived upstairs her bedroom door was open, and I could see a light. I called her name and knocked on the door first.'

'Lies,' Tiny said between sobs as Lillie pressed a restraining hand on the companion's arm.

Edgar stared ahead as if attempting to evade the memory of his discovery. 'She didn't answer so I gave the door a push to open it a little further and saw her lying on the bed. I came inside thinking perhaps she was just lying down for a brief rest before rejoining the ball. Then, when I got closer, I saw...' He paused and swallowed. 'I saw the stocking around her throat. I checked her pulse in case there was any chance that she might merely be unconscious, but I knew it was too late.'

He turned his head and looked at Lillie. 'That was when Mrs Trentham appeared. I asked her to get help. To call for the police and to get you, Matthew. I can see how it must look but I swear on Kitty's life I never harmed Eliza. She was already dead when I found her.' Edgar's hands were trembling, and Kitty took them in her own.

'Did you see or hear anyone else up here when you came upstairs?' she asked.

Her father shook his head. 'No one.'

CHAPTER THREE

Matt was relieved to see the familiar figure of Inspector Greville arriving in the doorway of the bedroom at that very moment, accompanied by a uniformed constable.

'Now we shall see. Officer, arrest that man for murder!' Tiny raised a trembling hand and pointed an accusatory finger at Kitty's father.

'Now then... Miss?' Inspector Greville took out his notebook and a pen and looked enquiringly at Tiny.

'Miss Morrow, I am Miss Caroline Trentham's governess.' Tiny sniffed and drew herself up to her considerable height, easily matching the inspector.

'Thank you. Perhaps if you and this other lady...' the inspector said.

'I am Mrs Lillie Trentham. The victim is my sister, Lady Eliza Foxley,' Lillie interjected.

'As I was saying, if you ladies might care to find a quiet place to wait. Perhaps a cup of tea or a drop of brandy might help with the shock, and I shall be along to see you both in a few minutes. Constable, perhaps you could accompany them?' the inspector suggested.

Tiny kept her arm about Lillie's shoulders as they left the room after throwing another ferocious glance at Kitty's father on their way out.

'Righto then, Captain Bryant, Miss Underhay, perhaps you could enlighten me?' the inspector said as he stepped further into the room and snapped on the glass-shaded overhead light, throwing the scene into stark brightness.

The inspector bent to make his own examination of Lady Foxley. Matt provided a succinct summary of all they had seen and heard since Lillie had come to fetch them from the ballroom.

Once his examination of Lady Foxley was complete, the inspector turned his attention to Kitty's father.

'Now then, sir, you say that you found the body?'

Kitty's father leaned back in his chair, the stark overhead light revealing the haggard expression on his face. 'Yes, it was exactly as Matthew described it. I came upstairs about forty-five minutes or so ago, I saw no one else on my way to the room and I was about to go for help when Lillie, Mrs Trentham, entered the room and saw me here.'

The inspector scribbled frantically in his notebook. 'How long have you known Lady Foxley, sir?'

'I suppose it must be some four to six months. We met a few times in New York but became more closely acquainted on our passage back to Plymouth. She invited me to stay with her here at her home instead of taking up my reservation at the Imperial.' Edgar glanced apologetically at Kitty and Matt saw him tenderly squeeze her fingers.

'Thank you, Mr Underhay, and do you know of any reason why anyone would wish to harm Lady Foxley?' the inspector asked.

A frown crinkled Kitty's father's brow. 'I personally have no reason at all to harm Eliza. We were on very good terms, and I appreciated her great kindness in offering me hospitality at her home. I know she and her sister often had disagreements, as sisters do, but nothing that would lead Lillie to harm her I wouldn't think. The main bone of contention between them seemed to be Caroline, Lillie's daughter. Then there were a few quarrels during our passage between Eliza and Sir Stanford King. I believe she was unhappy with the performance of some of her investments, but again I don't think he would harm her in any way.'

'I see, sir, thank you. That's much appreciated, background information is always useful,' Inspector Greville remarked. Matt noted a certain stiffness in the policeman's tone when he addressed Edgar.

'I suppose, though, that any one of the other guests could have come upstairs from the ball and harmed Lady Foxley,' Kitty said.

The inspector stroked his moustache. 'It would have seemed that way, however I spoke to the butler on my way upstairs and it doesn't appear to have been the case. He has been at his post in the hall for the entire evening and anyone who is not a member of the household is not permitted upstairs.'

'What about the servants' stairs? Lillie led us up that way?' Matt asked.

'Again, there were people around that area all evening and it would have to be someone very familiar with the house who would have entered that way without attracting notice. We shall check, of course, but I think it unlikely,' Inspector Greville said.

'But possible, surely?' Kitty's father looked at the inspector.

'Possible yes, sir, but as I said, unlikely. Nothing appears to have been taken from this room. Lady Foxley is still wearing some very valuable jewellery and her room is otherwise undisturbed, so I doubt that robbery was a motive. The lady herself also appears to be unmolested.' The inspector's cheeks flushed slightly, and he coughed.

Matt could see what the inspector was driving at. 'So, the

motive for her death would seem to be more personal, meaning it's more likely to have been committed by someone close to her?'

'Exactly. A spontaneous act of rage or malice seems the most likely explanation,' the inspector agreed.

There was a light tap on the open door of the room and the chubby cheery face of Doctor Carter appeared.

'Inspector, Captain Bryant and Miss Underhay, when shall we three meet again, eh? Over another body it seems.' He stepped into the room clutching his black leather medical bag.

He glanced at Kitty's father.

'Doctor Carter, I believe you may remember my father, Edgar Underhay,' Kitty said.

The doctor offered his hand to Edgar to shake. 'Dear me, yes, Saint Saviour's Church, wasn't it? Not long until we are gathering there again, for a happier occasion this time.' The doctor beamed at them. 'Now then, let the dog see the rabbit, eh.'

He moved the inspector and Matt out of his way and began a meticulous examination of Lady Foxley's body.

'Perhaps we should adjourn to wherever Mrs Trentham and Miss Morrow have gone to while Doctor Carter concludes his preliminary examination. It sounds as if the party is still in full swing downstairs.' Inspector Greville led the way out onto the landing where the faint sounds of jazz and conversation greeted them.

Kitty walked with her father while Matt fell into step beside the inspector as they headed down the main staircase into the hallway. It felt surreal that everyone else was still unwittingly enjoying themselves whilst their hostess lay dead upstairs.

'Mrs Trentham and Miss Morrow have gone to the study, sir,' the butler informed them discreetly when they reached the hall. He indicated a door just along the corridor.

'Thank you, Mr Hedges. Could you ask the rest of the

family and the house guests to join us? Obviously continue to be discreet, we have no desire to alarm the party guests at this point. If anyone leaves the house my other constable should be outside to take their details. Any problems, please come and find me,' the inspector instructed.

'Of course, sir.' The butler nodded and Matt could see that despite his apparent professional composure that the man was quite rattled by news of his mistress' death.

* * *

Kitty followed behind Matt and the inspector as they entered the study. She had her arm linked with her father's offering her silent support in what was clearly a very difficult situation.

A green glass-shaded brass desk lamp was on along with a pair of red and gold Chinese-style silk-shaded side lamps. The room was quite large for a study, with an imposing oak desk at its centre. Mrs Trentham and Miss Morrow were seated on black leather chairs at the side of the room. They each had a large cut-crystal brandy goblet in their hands and had obviously helped themselves from the decanter that stood on the gilt and onyx trolley next to them.

Miss Morrow glared at Edgar when he entered the room.

'Ladies, I appreciate that the death of Lady Foxley must be most distressing to both of you. I have asked the servants to send the rest of the family and house guests to this room so that we might ascertain when Lady Foxley was last seen alive,' Inspector Greville explained as he took his seat at the desk.

'I wouldn't have thought there would be much need for that, considering as how Lillie caught the culprit red-handed.' Miss Morrow glowered meaningfully at Kitty's father.

'And why do you think that Mr Underhay may have murdered Lady Foxley?' the inspector asked in a mild tone as

Edgar sank down on a vacant chair on the opposite side of the room from his accuser. Kitty remained at his side.

'Well, it's obvious, isn't it? He's a man and Eliza was an attractive woman. He was sniffing around her all the voyage over. No doubt she spurned his advances, and he killed her in a fit of rage.' Miss Morrow dabbed fiercely at her eyes with a large white-cotton handkerchief.

'I did not kill Eliza. I had no reason at all to harm a hair on her head.' Edgar seemed to be recovering his usual composure now the initial shock of his grisly discovery had faded.

The inspector held up his hand to stop the squabble. 'Perhaps, Mrs Trentham, you can tell us what you witnessed?'

Lillie still appeared pale and shaken. 'I too noticed Eliza was missing from the ballroom. My daughter had also vanished. Tiny, that is, Miss Morrow, had been looking for Caroline and I suddenly thought that she might be with Eliza.' She paused to wipe a tear from her cheek with the corner of a lace-edged handkerchief. 'They often got into mischief together. I... I suspected they were hatching some sort of prank. I came upstairs to look for them and saw the door to Eliza's room was ajar.'

She paused again and looked at Kitty's father. 'I called Eliza's name and went in. She was lying on the bed. I saw her red dress.' She stopped once more, and a shiver seemed to run through her body. 'I saw Mr Underhay bending over her. There was something not right about the scene, the position of how she was lying on the bed. Before I could speak Mr Underhay said, "Call the police, Eliza is dead."' More tears coursed down her cheeks.

'There, there, my pet, don't you take on so,' Tiny comforted Lillie whilst sending a look of pure hatred at Edgar.

Lillie sniffed and wiped her nose. 'I asked, "Is she hurt?" And he said, "Someone has killed her. Fetch Captain Bryant, he will know what to do." I was so shocked I came to fetch Captain

Bryant and I asked my butler to telephone for the police. Tiny saw me in the hallway and could see I was upset.' Lillie stopped once more and shook her head as if unable to believe what had happened.

'What time was this?' Inspector Greville asked.

Lillie shrugged helplessly. 'I don't know. I suppose it must have been an hour or so ago now.'

'Not long after Mr Underhay said that he too came upstairs and found your sister?' Inspector Greville asked.

'Yes, I suppose so,' Lillie agreed.

Kitty glanced at the tiny gold evening watch on her wrist. It was eleven thirty now and Mr Potter would be calling for them at midnight. By the timings her father and Lillie had given to the inspector Eliza must have been killed shortly before ten o'clock. She tried to remember when she had last seen her on the dance floor.

It must have been just after nine because she remembered looking at her watch shortly after Mrs Craven had left them.

There was a knock at the door of the room and Sir Stanford King entered.

'My dear Lillie, I have just heard the news. Shocking, just shocking. How could such a thing happen in a house full of people?' Sir Stanford appeared quite pale as he approached Lillie.

'Sorry, sir, you are?' Inspector Greville asked.

'Sir Stanford King, I'm Lady Foxley's financial advisor and a family friend.' The man turned to face the inspector.

'Thank you, sir. I'm Inspector Greville and will be conducting the investigation. May I ask, sir, when you last saw Lady Foxley this evening?'

Sir Stanford blinked and stood for a moment, his hand resting lightly on the back of Lillie's chair. 'I think I saw Eliza on the dance floor at about nine fifteen. Yes, around nine fifteen. I remember because Phillip Peters, her secretary, met me near the bar to tell me he had prepared everything for my meeting with Eliza tomorrow afternoon. I noticed the time on the clock above the bar as I was annoyed that he was interrupting the ball with business matters.'

'And you did not see Lady Foxley again after that time?' Inspector Greville asked as he made his notes.

Sir Stanford shook his head. 'No. I danced a couple of dances with Lillie and then went outside to the terrace for a breath of air. The room had grown a little muggy by then and I was warm from my exertions. I am not much of a dancer.'

'You did not venture upstairs for any reason during the course of the evening?' the inspector asked.

Sir Stanford shook his head once more. 'Not that I recall, I don't think so.'

There was another tap at the door and Phillip Peters came into the room. 'I say, is it true? I was just told that Lady Foxley has been murdered?' He blinked at them all through his blackmetal round-framed spectacles like a bewildered owl.

Kitty thought how young he looked, not much older than her friend, Alice.

'Unfortunately, yes,' Inspector Greville confirmed.

The colour seemed to leach from the secretary's anxious face, and he sank down on a nearby seat. 'I don't believe it. How?'

'Perhaps a drop of brandy, Mr Peters?' Tiny suggested and poured a measure into a glass before pressing it into the man's hand.

'I take it that you are Phillip Peters? Lady Foxley's secretary?' Inspector Greville asked after checking his notes.

'Yes, sir.' The man took a sip of the drink. Kitty could see his hand was trembling and he pressed the glass hard as if trying to stop himself from shaking.

'When did you last see Lady Foxley this evening, Mr Peters?' Inspector Greville asked.

'I? Well, when I saw her in conversation with Sir Stanford and the lady and gentleman over there.' He inclined his head in Kitty and Matt's direction. 'She wished to have a meeting tomorrow afternoon with Sir Stanford. I had prepared some papers for her during our voyage and she wished to compare them to the documents she had in the safe here at the house. I took it upon myself to check that everything was ready.' A tinge of pink had started to creep back into his cheeks.

'You didn't see her afterwards?' the inspector asked.

'No, sir. I looked for her, but I didn't see her. I saw Sir Stanford at the bar and told him I had checked that everything was ready. I thought it best to be prepared. Lady Foxley was very sharp when it came to her business affairs.' Phillip's composure seemed to be returning and he took another tentative sip of brandy.

'And this would be at around nine fifteen?' Inspector Greville looked at his notes.

'Well, I didn't notice the time, but I suppose it must have been around then, yes,' Phillip agreed.

'And did you return upstairs for any reason during the course of this evening?' Inspector Greville asked.

'Upstairs?' the secretary asked.

'Yes, sir. Did you perhaps go to fetch something or to find Lady Foxley at all during the ball?' The inspector regarded him with a level gaze. Phillip ran the tip of his tongue over his lower lip as if his mouth had suddenly dried.

Kitty wondered what he was so concerned about.

'Er, no, I, um, don't think I did,' Phillip responded.

Kitty could tell from his demeanour that there was something he wasn't saying. Had he been upstairs? Was he the person who had murdered Lady Foxley?

Lillie jumped to her feet. 'Where on earth has Caroline gone? I assume, Inspector, that she too would have been sent for? She will be extremely distressed when she learns about her aunt. She and Eliza were very close.'

Inspector Greville's brows raised. 'I'm sure Miss Caroline will be here shortly. I asked for all the family and guests staying at the house to come here.'

He had scarcely finished speaking when the door opened once more allowing a blast of music and Caroline Trentham to enter.

'Caro, where have you been?' Lillie pounced on her daughter.

Kitty glanced at Matt. It was apparent from the girl's rosy cheeks and slightly glazed expression that she had managed to imbibe some of the champagne her mother had been keen to keep from her.

'What's going on? Why is everyone in here instead of at the party?' The girl looked around the room, a puzzled frown wrinkling her forehead.

'Oh, darling, something terrible has happened.' Lillie attempted to gather her daughter to her, but Caroline pushed her away.

'What's happened? Where is Aunt Eliza?' Caroline looked about her as if expecting to see her aunt's slender scarlet-clad figure.

'Oh my poor little duck, it's your aunt Eliza. She's been murdered,' Tiny blurted out.

Caroline looked around her as if trying to tell if Tiny was telling her the truth or if it was all some frightful prank.

'No, that can't be right.' Caro shook her head causing some of her short dark hair to come free of the diamanté barrettes adorning her head.

'I'm so sorry, darling. The police are here, and they will work out who did it and what happened,' Lillie attempted to console the girl while looking at Inspector Greville for guidance.

'I'm very sorry, Miss Trentham, but I'm afraid that Lady Foxley was killed earlier this evening,' Inspector Greville confirmed the truth.

Caroline gasped and before anyone could catch her, she fell to the floor in a dead faint.

CHAPTER FOUR

A hubbub broke out in the room as everyone rushed to the girl's aid. Matt picked Caro up and carried her across to a small black leather-covered sofa where he set her down. Lillie chafed her daughter's hands as Tiny delved into the depths of her black chiffon-covered bosom to produce a tiny bottle of smelling salts.

After uncorking the stopper and wafting them under Caro's nose the girl came round, coughing and spluttering.

'There, there, my love, it was a terrible shock,' Tiny soothed as she re-stoppered the small blue-glass bottle and returned it to its hiding place.

'I don't understand. That's impossible. What's happened to Aunt Eliza?' The girl extracted her fingers from her mother's grasp and pushed herself into a sitting position.

'Lady Foxley was killed in her bedroom during the course of the ball.' Inspector Greville seemed to choose his words carefully.

'But she was dancing and drinking and... just being Aunt Eliza.' The girl's lower lip wobbled, and tears brimmed in her eyes.

'Can you recall when you last saw your aunt?' Inspector Greville asked.

'Um, she was on the dance floor, and someone brushed past her. She looked down and there was the most enormous ladder in her stocking. She was quite cross, so I think she planned to slip away and change it.' Caro sniffed and Sir Stanford took the pocket square from his jacket and handed it to her to dry her eyes.

'Do you know roughly what time this might have been?' the inspector asked.

Caroline shook her head. 'It was after Mummy embarrassed me by taking my glass away in front of everyone, but I didn't look at the time.' She glared at her mother.

'I see, thank you. Did you see your aunt again after that time or did you go upstairs at all this evening?' Inspector Greville asked.

'No, that was the last time I saw her. I did go part the way up the stairs because I knew that Mummy had asked Tiny to stay with me and I didn't want to be chaperoned like a little girl. So, I slipped past Hedges, our butler, and hid behind the floor-length curtain on the first-floor half landing until Tiny had given up looking for me.'

Matt's gaze met Kitty's and she knew he too appreciated the significance of Caro's words.

'Did anyone else come past you on the landing while you were hiding?' Inspector Greville asked.

Kitty could almost feel the tension building in the room as the inspector asked his question.

Caroline's frown deepened. 'I wasn't there long. I thought I heard footsteps but didn't peep out as I didn't want to be caught. Then I heard more footsteps and when I looked I saw Tiny at the top of the stairs, so when she had gone out of sight I came back down to the party.'

Everyone turned their attention to Miss Morrow.

'So that's why you wanted to point the finger at me. You went to see Eliza.' Kitty's father trembled with rage.

'Nonsense. I was looking for Miss Caroline.' Tiny's round face had flushed a dark red.

'Miss Morrow, I would remind you that this is a murder enquiry. You have heard me ask every person here if they went upstairs before Lady Foxley's body was discovered and you did not disclose that you yourself had done so.' Inspector Greville's voice was cold and angry.

Tiny seemed to shrink a little at the look he gave her.

'It didn't seem important, especially after Lillie said as how she found Mr Underhay with Eliza's body. I thought he must have done it so my going upstairs was of no matter,' the woman protested.

'Did you see Lady Foxley? Enter her room?' Inspector Greville persisted.

'The landing was dark, so I knocked on her door. I thought as Caro might have gone upstairs with her aunt. She called me to come in, she was hunting in her drawer after a stocking. I asked her if she'd seen Caro and she laughed and said she was probably hiding under a table somewhere getting drunk.' Miss Morrow's lips pursed.

'I take it she didn't take Caroline evading you very seriously?' Inspector Greville said.

'No, she did not. She'd had quite a fair bit of champagne herself too, I could tell.' Miss Morrow huffed. 'Well, I'm ashamed to say it after what's happened to her, but one word begot another.'

'You argued?' Inspector Greville made more notes in his book.

'Yes, and I'm proper ashamed of that now but she were alive and well and set to change her stocking when I left her,' Miss Morrow finished, lifting her chin as if to defy anyone present to disagree with her.

'You didn't see anyone else upstairs?' the inspector asked. 'Or note the time of your altercation?'

'I didn't see anyone, no, but the landing was dark. It must have been about twenty minutes or so after I left her when I bumped into Mrs Trentham in the hall, and she was all of a fluster,' Miss Morrow said.

A shiver ran down Kitty's spine and she wondered what Tiny and Eliza had quarrelled about. The woman was easily large and strong enough to have killed Lady Foxley. Or had there been yet another person lurking in the shadows on the landing waiting for Miss Morrow to leave?

There was another knock on the door of the room and this time it was the constable who entered.

'Begging your pardon, sir, but Miss Underhay and Captain Bryant are wanted.'

Kitty glanced at her watch and realised it was after midnight. Her grandmother must have been searching for them and wondering what had happened. It really was most vexing. There were lots of questions she wished to ask and yet she knew she must head back to Dartmouth.

'You go with your grandmother, Kitty, and I'll stay with Edgar. He can return home with me later,' Matt assured her.

Kitty would definitely feel happier knowing that her father was staying at Matt's house. She couldn't see Lillie or Tiny being terribly pleased if he continued his stay at Villa Lamora considering the circumstances. Left with little choice in the matter she kissed her father's cheek and pressed Matt's hand, before making a polite and swift goodnight to Inspector Greville and the rest of Lady Foxley's party.

Her grandmother was waiting for her in the entrance hall accompanied by Mrs Craven.

'Kitty, where have you been? Where is Matthew? Mr Potter has been waiting outside for us for at least ten minutes.' Her grandmother looked around for a maid to collect Kitty's evening coat from the cloakroom.

'Matt is returning home later. Something has come up and Mrs Trentham requires his assistance,' Kitty explained and gave her ticket to the maid so her coat could be retrieved.

'I thought I saw a constable here a moment ago.' The feathers in Mrs Craven's headdress waggled accusingly at Kitty.

Kitty took her coat from the maid. 'I really can't say.'

'It's not your father, is it? Oh, Kitty, please don't tell me he's managed to get himself arrested. Who will give you away?' Her grandmother shared a look with Mrs Craven.

'Father hasn't done anything. The constable's presence has nothing to do with him.' Kitty stretched the truth a little in her response, but she knew that if Mrs Craven learned what had happened to Lady Foxley then she would haunt poor Inspector Greville and Lillie Trentham.

'Well, that's a relief. Let us hope he manages to keep himself out of mischief at least until after the wedding. Now, my dear, we must hurry or we shall miss the ferry back across the river.' Mrs Treadwell took Kitty's arm ready to leave.

'I shall stop by tomorrow,' Mrs Craven called after them as they made their exit from the house.

Mr Potter was waiting patiently in the taxi. He jumped out to come around and open the rear passenger door to assist Kitty's grandmother inside the car.

'No Captain Bryant, Miss Kitty?' he asked.

'Unfortunately, he has to stay later, so we will go straight to the Dolphin,' Kitty explained.

'Off home, Miss Underhay?' Doctor Carter hailed her in a cheery voice from the other side of the driveway where he was clearly about to set off in his own rather more sporty motor.

'Yes, Matt is staying for a while longer to assist.' Kitty hoped her grandmother wouldn't hear too much of the conversation since she was already inside the taxi arranging the travel rug over her knees.

'Jolly good. I'm all done here now so I'm off too. Good to see you both. My wife and I are looking forward to the wedding.' He gave her a wave and started his car. The throaty rumble of the engine drowning out any possibility of further conversation.

Kitty slid onto the back seat next to her grandmother. She would have liked to ask the doctor if he had found anything significant to aid the investigation. It simply was too frustrating to be sidelined when there were so many things she wanted to know.

'Really, Kitty. You've let all the cold air in,' her grandmother complained as Mr Potter closed the door and resumed his seat behind the steering wheel. 'Was that Doctor Carter you were talking to? I didn't see him at the party? And Mrs Carter not with him this evening?' She settled back in her seat and pulled her fur collar closer to her neck.

'I don't think so. He was just saying they were looking forward to the wedding.' Kitty occupied herself with settling a corner of the tartan travel rug over her own legs and avoided her grandmother's gaze.

Nothing more was said on the matter as her grandmother was quickly diverted into reminding Kitty of all the outstanding tasks that needed to be done in time for the wedding.

'Don't forget you must attend church with me this morning,' her grandmother reminded her as she kissed her goodnight in the lobby of the hotel.

'I won't,' Kitty promised. Her grandmother ascended the stairs to her suite while Kitty went to the hotel kitchen in search of hot chocolate to help settle her mind before she went to bed.

As she waited for the milk to heat in the small, enamelled pan on top of the stove she wondered how Matt and her father were faring. Perhaps Matt would learn more about why Miss Morrow had quarrelled with Lady Foxley. Or if Phillip Peters had been telling the truth about not having ventured back upstairs.

Kitty poured the milk into her favourite thick blue-and-white striped crockery mug and stirred in the chocolate powder. She washed the pan and her spoon in the sink and returned them to their proper places as she didn't wish to cause work for her staff.

Sir Stanford had seemed a little uncomfortable too, now that she thought about it. Eliza had said that she wanted to discuss her investments with him, and it must have been something urgent to wish to do so on a Sunday afternoon.

She carried her drink to the top floor of the hotel where she had a tiny suite of her own. Mr Lutterworth, their new hotel manager, was to move from his temporary room into her accommodation once she moved out after the wedding.

After switching on her bedside lamp with its slightly faded rose-pink silk shade, she looked around her room at all her familiar possessions. Her cuckoo clock from the Black Forest, one of the few things she possessed that had been her mother's, showed the time. It was one thirty already.

Matt had suggested that after their marriage they should retain separate rooms. He had engaged a carpenter and a connecting door had been fitted between his room and what was to be her suite in his house in Churston.

Matt often slept poorly and when stressed he would have terrible nightmares. The arrangement with the rooms was for her protection as Matt was concerned that he had no control over his dreams. In the past he had destroyed items in his room, smashing things only to wake the next morning with no memory of what had happened. It was yet another legacy from his time on the battlefield.

Mickey, the hotel maintenance man, had already begun to find some boxes so that she could pack her things ready for the move. Some of her possessions had already gone to Matt's home.

She had chosen the colours for the walls and ordered new bed linen to match.

A small silver-framed picture of her mother stood next to her bed ready to be packed, and Kitty stroked it tenderly with the tip of her finger.

'Oh, Mum, let's hope the inspector discovers who murdered poor Lady Foxley or Papa might find it difficult to clear his name.' She finished her drink and turned out the lights.

The hot drink must have done the trick because by the time her friend, Alice, one of the hotel chambermaids, knocked on the door a dull light was already creeping around the edges of her bedroom curtains.

'Morning, Miss Kitty, how was the ball? Did you see your dad?' Alice knew that both Kitty and her grandmother had been discomfited by Edgar's sudden change of heart about his accommodation plans.

Kitty rubbed her eyes and pushed herself up into a sitting position as Alice placed a laden breakfast tray on her bedside table. 'I thought you had a day off today, Alice?'

'Half day, miss. Your grandmother asked if I'd mind helping get things ready for Captain Bryant's parents to stay. I think Captain Bryant's aunt is coming here too she said.' Alice whisked open the rose-patterned curtains letting more of the grey wintry light into the room.

Kitty groaned as she settled herself against her pillows. 'I think they are due to arrive on Wednesday. Lucy and Rupert are arriving the same day for the dress fittings. My aunt and uncle are travelling here next Saturday. They had hoped to come with Lucy and Rupert but my uncle has work commitments.'

Alice placed a metal tea strainer over a dainty china cup

and poured Kitty's tea, before producing a thicker crockery cup from the pocket of her apron and pouring one for herself.

'It'll be lovely to see Miss Lucy again. I wonder if she'll have a picture of Miss Daisy's baby when she comes. I sent her a little white matinee jacket that I'd knit for him,' Alice said as she settled herself on the edge of the bed for a chat with her friend.

Daisy was Rupert's sister and had recently delivered a healthy baby boy, much to everyone's relief and delight. She and her husband had an apartment at Rupert's ancestral home and Daisy was a good friend to Lucy and also to Kitty.

'That was kind,' Kitty said.

'Sent me a lovely thank you note, she did. Anyways, how was your dad? How come he didn't go to stay at the Imperial like you'd arranged?' Alice asked.

Kitty told her friend everything that had happened the previous evening. The maid's eyes grew wider and her tea cooler as she learned more about the night's events.

'Merciful heavens, Miss Kitty. I expect Captain Bryant will be telephoning you in a bit to tell you what's gone on. Your dad wouldn't have wanted to stay on there. Do you think as he's gone back to Captain Bryant's house?' Alice asked.

'I hope so. Perhaps then he can take up his original room at the hotel later today. I think it best he distances himself from Mrs Trentham's household until Lady Foxley's killer is caught. Grams and Mrs Craven know nothing of any of this yet, but you know they will think the worst when they do find out.' Kitty finished her tea and set the cup back down on its dainty floral-patterned saucer.

Alice finished her own drink, her brow creased in a frown. 'That Lady Foxley had a bit of a reputation, you know.' The girl blushed, her cheeks turning a similar shade to her red hair. 'Fast, she were. She liked the company of gentlemen,' she said primly. 'Not like her sister. Mrs Trentham is the model of decorum. Our Betty says as they used to have dreadful rows.'

'Betty? Has Betty worked for them?' Kitty wondered why she was surprised. Alice's slightly older cousin Betty hopped around from job to job and had probably worked for most people in the bay at some time or other.

'Yes, a few months ago just before they went to America. She said as she could hardly believe it with Mrs Trentham always being so quiet and polite and all,' Alice assured her.

'Did Betty say what the arguments were about?' Kitty's curiosity was roused. It might not have anything to do with Lady Foxley's murder but it was interesting information all the same.

Alice's nose wrinkled as she tried to recall what her cousin had told her. 'I think it were mostly about the girl, Miss Caroline. Oh, and money. Miss Trentham isn't terribly well off and Lady Foxley held the purse strings.'

'Hmm, interesting.' Kitty suddenly caught sight of the time on the clock. 'Heavens, I am to accompany Grams to church this morning.'

Alice jumped up from the bed and placed everything back neatly on the tray. 'You'd best fly then, miss. Shall I get your things out ready?'

'Oh, would you, Alice? That would be so kind.' Kitty scrambled out of bed and hurried off to the bathroom, leaving her friend to pull her Sunday best frock from her wardrobe and find her black patent shoes.

CHAPTER FIVE

Matt poured some more coffee from the tall silver jug into his cup before checking the time on his watch. His unexpected guest was still upstairs asleep, seemingly untroubled by the events of the previous night.

He wanted to talk to Kitty to share what he had learned the previous evening and to hear her thoughts on Lady Foxley's murder. He knew though that Mrs Treadwell was very keen that her granddaughter should accompany her to church since it was almost Christmas, and the wedding was rapidly approaching.

A creak on the stairs told him that his guest was finally awake and about to join him for a belated breakfast. Matt's blue roan cocker spaniel, Bertie, lifted his head and thumped his tail in welcome against the floor of the dining room.

'Good morning.' Edgar Underhay, dapper and unruffled as ever in a paisley silk dressing gown and navy silk pyjamas, entered and took the seat opposite him at the breakfast table.

'Good morning. There is some coffee still in the pot and steamed milk in the jug. Would you care for some toast?' Matt asked as he surveyed his future father-in-law. Bertie, who had been lying under the table hoping for bacon bits, lifted his head to sniff interestedly at Edgar's leather slippers.

'Just coffee will be most welcome,' Edgar said as he helped himself to the beverage.

'How did you sleep?' Matt made polite conversation, curious to know if Edgar had been troubled by Lady Foxley's death.

Edgar set the milk jug down on the table and added sugar to his cup. 'Jolly well, all things considered. Most comfortable bed and I have to say, despite poor Eliza's death, I dropped off quite quickly.'

Matt took a sip from his own cup of coffee. 'You are most welcome to stay here as my guest if you prefer, or I believe you may be able to take up the reservation at the Imperial. I rather think there are only the larger hotels open this close to Christmas.'

'That's very kind of you to offer to host me, dear boy, but I think perhaps it might be better if I remove myself to the Imperial. My darling mother-in-law will get quite squint eyed at me if she thinks that I'm getting under yours and Kitty's feet. I appreciate there is a lot to do before Monday.' Edgar waved a careless hand.

The dog looked up hopefully at this sudden movement. He then seemed to realise that no more bacon would be coming his way and settled back down with a disgruntled sigh.

'I think Kitty and her grandmother have the wedding arrangements well in hand. Mrs Craven has been most helpful.' Matt hid a slight smile behind his cup as he recalled Kitty's exasperation with Mrs C's many well-intentioned helpful suggestions.

'Ah yes, I believe I met the Craven woman last night. Bossy lady, reminded me of one of those geese that chase you away from the edge of ponds. Feathery and hissy and more than a little frightening.' Edgar plucked his silver monogramed cigarette case from the pocket of his dressing gown. 'Mind if I smoke, dear boy?'

Matt chuckled at his future father-in-law's description of Kitty's bête noire and nodded his permission for Edgar to light up. He refused the offer of a cigarette for himself. Lately he only tended to smoke when he was under pressure or stressed in some way.

'That sounds like Mrs C. It seems to me that unless there is someone else who was at the ball who had a particular grudge against her, that it must be someone who was close to Lady Foxley who murdered her.' Matt chose his words carefully.

Edgar lit his cigarette and settled back in his chair to consider what Matt had said. 'Yes, I see what you mean. The butler chappie, Hedges, would have prevented any old Tom, Dick or Harry from going upstairs by the main stairs and you would have to know the house well to find the servants' stairs and get past without someone seeing you. It's a bit of a maze in that part of the house.'

'Hmm, that seems to fit with what the inspector said.' Matt sipped his coffee. He could see Edgar turning the matter over in his mind as he smoked his cigarette.

'I suppose there is always that other chappie. He was there last night, I saw him dancing with Lillie. I wonder if the inspector has spoken to him,' Edgar mused as he blew out a thin stream of pale blue smoke.

'Which chap?' Matt asked curiously.

'Hemmings, Roger Hemmings, hanging round Lillie like a bad smell on the boat over. I think he was rather put out that Eliza didn't invite him to stay at the house. Lord knows he dropped enough hints about it.'

It took Matt a second to recall who Edgar meant. 'Oh, the valve man?'

'That's the one, rather a bore but seems very sweet on Lillie.

Eliza wasn't keen. She said he was dull, and Caro got rather cross when he kept monopolising her mother's attention.' Edgar gave a little chuckle at this. 'I rather think he and Eliza had an argument just before we disembarked. I only caught the tail end of it, mind you, but I have to say that he looked quite put out. I heard Eliza say, "I can manage my own affairs and my sister's perfectly well, thank you."'

'Did he say anything else to Lady Foxley?' Matt asked.

'He said something like, "I'm warning you for your own good." They stopped talking when they realised I was walking towards them.' Edgar looked around for an ashtray before leaning back in his seat to reach for a small onyx one from the side table.

'Odd. Any idea what it was he may have been warning her about?' Matt thought it seemed a rather queer conversation.

Edgar extinguished his cigarette. 'No idea at all I'm afraid, dear boy. I thought it a little strange, but Hemmings is a bit of a dogmatic type of chap and Eliza doesn't – or rather didn't – like being told what to do.' A sad expression passed fleetingly across his face. 'Eliza was rather lovely, you know. Warm hearted, vivacious and generous to a fault. I shall miss her.'

'Mrs Trentham seems a very different character to her sister.' Matt set his empty coffee cup back on its saucer.

'Oh yes. Eliza was terribly protective of Lillie, and of Caro too, for that matter. I think sometimes Lillie resented Caroline's closeness with her aunt. Lillie tends to baby the girl rather, lets her have her own way. Eliza thought it would do Caro good to go to finishing school. Switzerland or Paris or somewhere I think, but Lillie didn't like the idea and, funnily enough, Caro wasn't keen either. Yet I thought she wanted to escape her mother and dear Miss Morrow too, of course.' Edgar picked up his coffee and finished his drink. 'Well, I suppose I had better telephone the hotel.'

'There is a telephone in the sitting room if you wish to call. I was going to telephone Kitty, but I think she'd promised to attend church this morning with her grandmother.' Matt checked the time on his watch. Kitty would be in the morning service by now.

Edgar's brows rose slightly at this information. 'I see, well I'll telephone the Imperial and then go and dress. Do you know if Kitty is free this afternoon? I could take you both to tea somewhere if you fancy it?'

'Thank you, sir, I'll ask her when I call her. She should be back at the Dolphin before twelve I should think. I daresay she will wish to know what happened after she left us last night,' Matt said.

A broad smile lit up Edgar's face. 'Of course she will. She is her mother's daughter. Elowed was unendingly curious about everything. Kitty is very like her.' The sad expression from earlier returned and flickered across his face before he headed off to make his telephone call.

* * *

Kitty wrapped up warmly in her winter coat and pushed her best dark-green felt hat down firmly over her short blonde curls. The wind was blowing in today along the estuary and her grandmother had decided the short walk to St Saviour's through the town would do them both good.

Mr Lutterworth, the hotel manager, was accompanying them. His tall, thin frame was smartly clad as usual in a grey pinstripe suit and a thick black woollen overcoat. His trademark rosebud was pinned to the lapel. He offered her grandmother his arm to assist her on the steep areas as they walked.

As they made their way through the town and along the cobbled street up the hill towards the ancient church Kitty wondered how she would feel in just over a week's time, approaching it as a bride.

Her uncle had offered the use of his Rolls Royce and chauffeur to take her and her father to the church, while Matt's parents had said they would bring her aunt and uncle and Matt's aunt Effie. Mr Potter was to transport her grandmother and great-aunt Livvy, and then return for Lucy as her matron of honour. Matt and Rupert, who was to be best man, were going to walk. Alice had declined to be a bridesmaid, stating it wouldn't be right for her to stand up for Kitty next to a titled lady. No amount of persuasion would move her on this, so Lucy was to be Kitty's only attendant.

Mrs Craven was standing outside the old, open door of the church. She waved a fur-trimmed gloved hand at their approach.

'Oh, my dear, I'm so glad I caught you before the service. Have you heard the news? I almost telephoned you last night but, of course, it was after midnight,' Mrs Craven burst into speech as soon as they approached.

'Millicent, whatever has happened?' Kitty's grandmother released Mr Lutterworth's arm.

'Lady Foxley is dead. Murdered last night during the ball.' Mrs Craven dropped her voice to a dramatic whisper as a small group passed them to enter the church.

'Oh dear, how dreadful,' Mr Lutterworth said.

'Indeed,' Mrs Craven concurred; her eyes gleaming.

'So that was why Doctor Carter was at the house last night. Kitty, did you know about this?' Her grandmother turned to her.

Kitty's shoulders slumped. Trust Mrs Craven to discover what had happened. 'Yes, Grams, that was why Matt stayed behind. He was assisting Inspector Greville.'

The church bell tolled above their heads.

'We had better go inside and take our places,' Mr Lutterworth suggested.

'Yes, and you, Kitty, can tell us everything after the service,' Mrs Craven added in a meaningful tone.

Mr Lutterworth escorted them to their places. Mrs Craven had a seat on one of the front pews while Kitty, her grandmother and Mr Lutterworth sat further back. The church was already decorated for Christmas. The carved and painted nativity set was in place under the huge evergreen Christmas tree awaiting the imminent arrival of baby Jesus.

The church smelt of greenery and wax. The painted woodwork glowed in green, gold and scarlet. Creamy-coloured Christmas roses were arranged in artistic displays with pine and holly. Kitty could see that it would all make a very lovely setting for her wedding.

The soothing tones of the elderly vicar and the choristers' renditions of old seasonal favourites did much to settle her suddenly frazzled nerves. It really was too bad of Eliza Foxley to get herself murdered right before Kitty's wedding. As if she didn't have enough to think about with packing up her rooms, dress fittings, catering and coping with her future in-laws.

She just hoped that her father would be quickly exonerated from the investigation. The last thing she needed was the possibility of him being arrested before he could give her away. She knew he was no stranger to the inside of a prison cell and hoped this wouldn't influence the police investigation.

The service was over before she knew it and she barely had time to shake hands with the vicar before Mrs Craven was at her elbow.

'I thought we might call in for coffee at the tea room by the Butterwalk. They are open today. You can tell us what happened over a nice piece of cake,' Mrs Craven suggested, looking at Kitty's grandmother and Mr Lutterworth for agreement.

Kitty could see from their expressions that she had little choice except to give in gracefully, so they followed Mrs Craven to a small tea room that opened on Sundays, usually for the holiday trade.

Once ensconced around a table with their order for a large pot of coffee and slices of Victoria sponge given to the uniformed waitress, Mrs Craven drew off her gloves. 'Now then, Kitty, tell us what happened.'

'There is not much that I can say,' Kitty protested. She was certain Inspector Greville wouldn't wish her to be going around Dartmouth telling everyone about the nature of Lady Foxley's demise.

Her grandmother tucked her own brown leather gloves inside her handbag. 'I knew something dire was bound to happen if your father was involved. Please tell me he is not caught up in this matter?'

All three of her companions turned their gaze on Kitty and she fidgeted uncomfortably under their scrutiny.

'I knew it. Trouble follows Edgar Underhay everywhere he goes.' Her grandmother shook her head.

'I'm sure Father has nothing to do with Lady Foxley's murder.' Kitty's tone was rather sharp.

There was a pause in the conversation when the waitress arrived with a trolley and set out their coffee and cake.

'Hmm.' Mrs Treadwell looked unconvinced as Mr Lutterworth took it upon himself to pour coffee for them all.

'Lillie Trentham was in a dreadful state last night when I left. I'd wondered why neither she nor Lady Foxley had appeared to announce the raffle winners or to close the ball before the carriages arrived. Obviously, I tried to find them, and I ran into that secretary. Phillip somebody. I needed to give the takings over and to take my leave. He told me then what had happened,' Mrs Craven explained as she stirred her coffee.

'It must have been most distressing for you, Millicent. We saw Doctor Carter in his car as we were leaving, and I did remark on his being there to Kitty at the time. I should have known then that something was wrong.' Kitty's grandmother gave Kitty a baleful look.

'Well, after that secretary told me that Lady Foxley had been murdered, I insisted on seeing Lillie. I had to make sure she was all right. Inspector Greville was there, of course, poking around and eating some of the leftover canapés. I didn't see Matthew or your father though, Kitty,' Mrs Craven said.

'I expect they had left by then. I believe Matt was going to take Papa to stay at his house.' Kitty sipped her coffee.

'That was probably a good idea under the circumstances. I do hope your father won't take advantage of his hospitality though. You know what your father is like, Kitty. Give him an inch and he takes a mile. You and Matthew have so much to do still to get the house ready for after the wedding.' Her grandmother attacked her piece of sponge with a cake fork.

'I expect Papa will go to the Imperial as planned. It was all rather late last night, and I think he was very upset about Lady Foxley's death.' Kitty thought Lady Eliza's death had distressed everyone. Poor Caroline had fainted with the shock.

'I wonder what will happen to Mrs Trentham and her daughter now? They were completely dependent – money-wise you know – on Lady Foxley. Dear Lillie was left very badly off when her husband died. That was one of the main reasons she started the charity. She didn't want other women to find themselves in as much financial trouble as she was after the accident.' Mrs Craven took a mouthful of cake and chewed thoughtfully.

'Such a shocking thing to happen though, with the house full of guests for the ball.' Mr Lutterworth dabbed at the corners of his lips with a cream linen napkin.

'Exactly. I've said it before and I'll say it again, the world is becoming a frightfully dangerous place. I expect some lunatic saw all the cars and lights and poor Lady Foxley probably surprised the villain about to make off with her diamonds or something.' Mrs Craven glanced down at her own diamond brooch twinkling on her lapel and shuddered at the thought of its loss.

Kitty said nothing. Mrs Craven's idea might have had some merit, except there was no evidence that anything had been disturbed and Mrs Trentham had seemed quite certain that it would be difficult for a stranger to make his way upstairs unnoticed.

CHAPTER SIX

A message from Matt awaited Kitty in the lobby on her return to the Dolphin.

'Papa has invited Matt and I out to tea.' She read the note aloud to her grandmother.

'You had better take your purse then, Kitty dear. No doubt he will have forgotten his wallet when the bill arrives,' her grandmother muttered.

Mr Lutterworth's brows raised, and he gave Kitty a sympathetic smile. 'I have organised luncheon for one o'clock. I hope that is acceptable?' he asked.

'Of course, thank you, Cyril.' Kitty smiled back at him, and he left them in the lobby to check on the kitchen staff.

'Really, Grams, you are far too harsh on Papa sometimes,' Kitty reproved her grandmother as they ascended the stairs together.

Her grandmother sighed. 'Perhaps I am, my dear, but sadly there is one thing your father is good at. He never fails to disappoint, and I don't wish to see you as unhappy as your mother.'

Kitty knew her grandmother worried about her father's reappearance in her life after being gone for so long. She also knew that under his pleasant and charming manners her father was not reliable. Despite his many shortcomings, however, she refused to believe that he was involved in any way with Lady Foxley's murder.

'I shall see you shortly for luncheon then, my dear, and then I suppose you shall drive to Matthew's house?' They had paused on the landing near the door to her grandmother's suite.

'Yes, it will be nice to have a quiet talk with Papa. Last night was so busy and with that dreadful murder...' Kitty shivered.

'So long as you remember that you are getting married in eight days' time. You have a dress fitting tomorrow for a start. There is no time for you to involve yourself in asking questions and gallivanting about investigating Lady Foxley's death. Leave it to the police and Inspector Greville for once. It is his job after all,' her grandmother warned.

'Yes, Grams.' Kitty kissed her grandmother's soft cheek and made good her escape up another flight of stairs to her own room. It might well be her wedding soon, but if a cloud of suspicion was hanging over her father's head, as she feared it might be, well, she was duty-bound to look into matters.

* * *

Matt walked Bertie, then took Edgar to dine at the golf club for luncheon. Kitty's father had been successful in his telephone call to the Imperial, and he had also telephoned Villa Lamora to arrange to have his trunk removed to the hotel, having only packed an overnight bag for his stay with Matt.

They had not been back at the house for long when Bertie leapt to his feet to run into the hall. Matt guessed the dog must have heard Kitty pulling her little red motor car onto the driveway at the side of the house.

Sure enough he heard the sound of Kitty inserting her

brand-new house key in the door, followed by her laughter as she greeted the enthusiastic Bertie.

'We're in the sitting room, darling,' he called through to the hall.

A moment later Bertie rushed back into the room, his plumed tail wagging happily as he retook his spot on the hearthrug near the fire crackling in the grate. Matt and Edgar both rose to greet Kitty as she entered the room, her cheeks pink from the chill outside air.

'Come and sit by the fire.' Matt showed her to a seat and he and Edgar sat back down. Edgar folded the newspaper he had been perusing and stowed it in the chrome paper rack next to his chair.

'Well, what news?' Kitty asked, smoothing the navy serge material of her best Sunday frock over her knees. She looked expectantly from Matt to her father.

'I presume you mean the investigation into Eliza's murder,' her father said. 'There is not much to tell you, I'm afraid.'

Kitty told them what she had learned from Alice and from Mrs Craven. 'What do you think, Papa? How were things between Eliza and Lillie? You saw them together during the voyage.'

Her father frowned. 'They did argue from time to time, as all siblings do. You only have to consider my own relationship with your aunt Hortense to understand that. There was an underscore of tension, I suppose. I had not, I confess, given it much thought. I assumed it was because Eliza controlled the purse strings, and she did interfere a great deal with Lillie's plans regarding Caroline.'

Matt could see the cogs turning in his fiancée's mind. 'And did Inspector Greville discover what Lady Foxley and Miss Morrow had been arguing about?' Kitty asked.

'Miss Morrow appeared reluctant to say, but it seems it was

to do with her role in the household once Caroline went to finishing school,' Matt said.

'I suppose she would be redundant as Lady Foxley would not require her services and I expect Lillie could not afford them if her sister usually paid the bills,' Kitty said thoughtfully.

'Exactly that. You have hit the nail squarely on the head, my dear. Miss Morrow wished for Caroline to remain at home for another couple of years before making her society debut, rather than attending a school.' Kitty's father looked approvingly at his daughter.

'Why was Lady Foxley so keen on sending Caroline away, if both the girl and her mother were opposed to it?' Matt asked.

Edgar gave a slight shrug. 'Eliza loved Caro, but she felt that it would be good for her to see more of the world. To obtain poise and polish before making her way in society. Something Miss Morrow could not provide. You've both met Tiny, she is quite a homely soul.'

Matt told Kitty about her father's thoughts regarding Roger Hemmings.

'You say Lady Foxley was not encouraging about the friendship between him and her sister?' Kitty looked at her father.

'She thought Hemmings dull and suburban. Thinking about things now it may also have been because he was clearly interested in Lillie. Eliza, I think, rather enjoyed her control over her sister and I suppose Hemmings could have threatened that if they had fallen in love.' Edgar's brow creased in concentration as he appeared to consider the idea.

The logs in the fire shifted, sending a small shower of sparks ascending up the chimney. Bertie huffed and shuffled a little further away from the heat.

A sudden knock at the door startled all of them and sent Bertie into a frenzy of barks as Matt went to see who could be calling at this time on a Sunday afternoon. He shushed Bertie as he opened the door to discover Inspector Greville and a uniformed constable on his doorstep.

'Inspector, this is a surprise, do come in.' Matt stepped back to allow both the inspector and the constable to enter the hall. The presence of the uniformed man triggered a sense of unease.

'We are all in the sitting room. Can I get you both a drink?' Matt offered.

'I'm afraid not, Captain Bryant, thank you. We are here on official business.' The inspector's expression was unusually grave.

'Then do go on through. Mr Underhay and Kitty are both in there.' Matt indicated the door to the sitting room.

He followed the inspector in through the sitting room door while the constable stationed himself in the hall outside the room.

'Inspector Greville, has something happened? Do you have whoever did it?' Kitty asked as the inspector removed his hat and undid his overcoat, before taking a seat on the sofa.

Bertie resumed his position on the rug after determining the inspector was not in possession of any tasty titbits in his pockets.

'I'm afraid, Miss Underhay, that I am here to ask some more questions of your father.' The inspector looked at Edgar who seemed quite unruffled by the appearance of the police.

'Of course, Inspector, I will be happy to answer any questions you might have for me,' Edgar replied.

He took out his cigarette case and offered it to the inspector.

'No, thank you, sir,' Inspector Greville declined the offer. Edgar shrugged and returned the case to his pocket, before lighting his own cigarette and settling back in his chair, ready to answer the policeman's questions.

'Should my father have a solicitor present?' Kitty asked, her brow creased with worry.

'It's quite all right, dear girl. I'm sure I can answer anything the inspector wishes to know,' her father assured her.

Matt met Kitty's gaze and could see the fear lurking in her eyes.

Inspector Greville felt inside the breast pocket of his jacket and brought out his small black notebook and pen. 'Now then, sir, you said that when Mrs Trentham discovered you leaning over the body of Lady Foxley you had just discovered her and were checking to see if she was still alive?'

Edgar nodded. 'Yes, that's correct. I thought at first she had fainted or fallen asleep.'

'Can you remind me, sir, why you were upstairs?' Inspector Greville's tone was mild, but Matt thought he sensed a hidden meaning behind the question.

'Eliza had been gone from the ball for some time. I thought at first she might have been talking somewhere but when I didn't see here downstairs, I went to look for her. She'd had quite a few glasses of champagne, so I was concerned.' Edgar flicked some ash into the onyx ashtray on the side table.

Inspector Greville flicked back through the pages of his notebook as if looking for something.

'I see, sir, and can you recall when this was?'

Edgar stubbed out his cigarette in the ashtray. 'I'm not sure, ten, ten fifteen, perhaps. I know it must have been about forty-five minutes before you yourself arrived. I didn't look at my watch.'

'Are you certain that was the time you went upstairs, sir? It is very important,' Inspector Greville asked.

'What are you driving at, Inspector?' Kitty asked. 'My father has already told you he didn't check his watch.'

'The point is, Miss Underhay, that Mr Hedges, Lady Foxley's butler, insists that your father ascended upstairs some twenty minutes or so before Mrs Trentham went upstairs and discovered him in Lady Foxley's room. I would like Mr Underhay to account for his movements during that time.' The inspector looked at Kitty's father.

Kitty gasped in surprise. 'Papa, what does he mean?' Her tone held a warning note.

'It's nothing, my dear. I told you, Inspector, I can't be certain of the time. I noticed Eliza was missing and went to look for her. This butler fellow must be mistaken,' Edgar said.

'His testimony is backed up by the maid, who was assisting him with the coats. They noted the time particularly since they were anxious about serving the hot canapés. Lady Foxley had given them explicit instructions about the timing for the evening and Mr Hedges checked the time on the hall clock.' Inspector Greville's eyes were flinty as he regarded Kitty's father.

'Papa?' Kitty's eyes were almost as stony as the inspector's.

Edgar Underhay sighed. 'Oh, very well. Yes, I went upstairs a little earlier than I said. The landing was dark, and all the doors were closed. I went into my own room first to collect my lighter. I had rather stupidly left it there when I dressed earlier in the evening. When I came out from my room, however, Eliza's door was ajar and the light was on. I thought she must have come upstairs so I went over as I said to see if she was all right.'

'You say the doors were all closed when you went upstairs. You didn't put on the landing light?' Inspector Greville asked.

'No, my room was the first door as you entered the gallery, so I didn't bother. It took me a while to find my lighter as I thought I'd left it on the dresser, but it had fallen off and jammed itself under the bed. I checked all my pockets and everything before I recalled hearing something fall when I got my cufflinks from my bag.' Edgar met the inspector's gaze without flinching.

The inspector made a series of notes in his notebook.

'I see, sir, thank you for clearing that up for us. Now, just one more small point.'

Matt could see that Kitty was becoming annoyed at the direction of the inspector's questions.

'Really, Inspector Greville, what more can my father possibly tell you that he hasn't told you already?'

'I think, Miss Underhay, that you will agree that your father has been less than frank with us in his original answers.' The inspector's moustache twitched in reproof, and Kitty blushed.

'Now then, Mr Underhay, you said in your original statement that you had no reason to harm Lady Foxley. You were grateful for her hospitality?' The inspector glanced up from his notebook and looked to Edgar for confirmation.

'That's true, Inspector. Eliza was a generous soul, and I enjoyed her company greatly. I had no reason to wish her harm.' Kitty's father appeared unruffled, but Matt noticed he had tightened his grip on the black leather arm of the chair.

'I have a witness that said you quarrelled with Lady Foxley shortly before she left the ballroom.'

Matt saw Kitty's face pale at the implication of the inspector's words. She looked at her father for an explanation.

Edgar was very still in his seat. 'I see. Your witness must be mistaken. Eliza and I would frequently verbally spar with one another. She shared my sense of humour.'

Inspector Greville's eyebrows lifted, and he turned back a couple of pages in his notebook.

'The following conversation was overheard on the dance floor.' The inspector cleared his throat. '"I'm sorry, Edgar, the answer is no." This was Lady Foxley. You were heard to say, "Then you leave me no choice." Lady Foxley said, "Do what you will, I don't care." You then said, "For two pins I could strangle you, Eliza."'

There was a moment's silence in the room broken only by the crackle of the fire in the hearth and Bertie's gentle snores.

Edgar put his head in his hands.

'Papa?' Kitty went to kneel by her father's side.

'It's not what it sounds like, darling. I swear I never harmed Eliza. She was dead when I found her. Someone else wrapped that stocking about her throat, it wasn't me,' Edgar reassured his daughter.

'Constable,' Inspector Greville called to the policeman outside the door. 'I'm very sorry, Miss Underhay.' He returned his notebook to his pocket and placed his hat back on his head as the constable entered the room.

'Edgar Underhay, I am arresting you for the murder of Lady Eliza Foxley.' He placed a hand on Edgar's shoulder.

'There must be some mistake. Inspector Greville, surely you don't believe my father killed Eliza?' Kitty rose to her feet.

Matt rushed to his fiancée's side as the constable led her father from the room and out to the waiting police car.

'I'm very sorry, Miss Underhay.' The inspector's face was grim as he tipped his hat to Kitty and nodded to Matt in farewell. 'I have my duty to do.'

CHAPTER SEVEN

The police car had barely pulled away before Kitty broke down in Matt's arms. 'Oh, Matt, what are we to do? He didn't kill Eliza Foxley. I know he didn't.' She hiccoughed to a halt and fumbled for her handkerchief.

Bertie, concerned by her distress, pushed against her legs and attempted to lick her hands.

'Come and sit down, old thing. It's been the most frightful shock.' Matt guided her back to the sofa where Bertie stationed himself at her feet, his head on her knee.

She dried her eyes and blew her nose while Matt poured a shot of brandy for each of them into a crystal glass.

'Drink this.' He pressed the glass into her hand. Her fingers were shaking, and she struggled to grip it. 'Careful, darling.'

He guided it to her lips, and she sipped obediently. The liquid burned on the tip of her tongue, warming her as it slipped down her throat. She was numb with shock.

She had anticipated that suspicion might fall on her father since he had been discovered in such a compromising position with Lady Foxley's body. But to be arrested for murder? How could this have happened? And what was her father not revealing about the circumstances surrounding Lady Eliza's death?

'Take another sip,' Matt instructed.

'What shall we do? We have to find the real murderer.' Kitty turned to Matt who had taken a seat beside her. 'Papa is giving me away a week tomorrow!'

Matt took a sip from his own glass. 'I'm afraid it does look rather bad at the moment, old girl. Edgar didn't answer the inspector's last question, did he?'

'I wonder who that witness was?' Kitty said thoughtfully. It could have been someone with a grudge against her father. Miss Morrow certainly seemed to dislike him. The more she thought about it, the more it seemed to her that it wasn't just that Lillie had discovered him with Lady Foxley's body. It might suit a good many people if her father were convicted of Eliza's death.

'It could have been anyone. Perhaps someone came forward when they heard what had happened,' Matt said.

Kitty frowned. 'I'm not so certain. It had to be someone who could have identified him. He hasn't lived in England for many years now so it's unlikely to be someone who knew him in the past. Edgar is a fairly common name so the name itself would mean very little. No, I think it had to be either a servant or even a member of the household.' Perhaps they had spoken up after Matt and her father had left the ball.

'Your father suggested Roger Hemmings as a suspect this morning when we were talking over breakfast.' Matt finished his brandy and set the glass down on the table.

'He was the man from the ship, wasn't he? The valve man who was sweet on Lillie?' Kitty's eyes brightened. 'I wonder if Inspector Greville has spoken to him.'

'It's all rather a mess, isn't it?' Matt gave her a faint sympathetic smile.

'My father is many things, but he is not a murderer. Of that

I'm certain.' Kitty grimaced as she swallowed the last of her brandy.

Matt took hold of her free hand and squeezed her fingers. 'I wish we knew what he quarrelled with Lady Foxley about, and what he was really doing in those twenty minutes or so before he found her body.'

Kitty blinked. Of course Matt was right, her father's tale of looking for his missing cigarette lighter was rather thin. 'We need to go back to Villa Lamora and speak to everyone.'

Matt sighed. 'Will they wish to speak to us though? Especially once word gets around that your father has been arrested.' He leaned forward and kissed her cheek. 'There is also the small matter of our marriage being only a week away.'

'Oh no, the wedding! My aunt and uncle will be furious with Father. You know what Aunt Hortense is like. Not to mention your parents and your aunt Effie. Oh, Matt, whatever shall we do?' Kitty could see that all the plans for their nice quiet wedding were being thrown into chaos. Not to mention that her father could be facing the noose. It all felt like a dreadful dream that she couldn't escape from.

'Chin up. One thing at a time. Listen, we'll get your father a solicitor tomorrow and see if Inspector Greville really intends to charge him formally. In the meantime, let's head over to Villa Lamora. We can always say we are there to check if your father's trunk has gone ahead to the Imperial. You never know, they may agree to see us.' Matt jumped to his feet.

Kitty could see the sense in his suggestion and followed suit. At least it would feel as if they were doing something to assist her father. She tidied her face and put on her outdoor things while Matt secured Bertie in the kitchen.

'He is much better behaved these days, but he has chewed a hole in the rug behind the sofa,' Matt said as he collected his coat and hat.

'Oh dear.' She hoped that Bertie's destructive habits would

stop. Keeping a dog was proving very expensive. Kitty tugged on her scarlet-leather driving gloves, a gift last Christmas from Matt, and they hurried out to her car.

While they had been inside the house a dull, grey mist had descended over the common, swirling about in front of Kitty's car as they made their way towards Torquay and Villa Lamora.

When they arrived the lamps on either side of the front door of the house were lit, casting a soft yellow light into the bleak afternoon. The front of the house, which had been so busy with vehicles the previous evening, was now empty. Kitty pulled her car to a halt near the front door. A chill ran along her spine as she studied the gloomy frontage of the villa.

Matt looked across at her from under the brim of his hat as she switched off the engine. 'Courage, old thing. We'll get to the bottom of this.'

She managed a tight smile and they headed towards the dark-green painted front door. The house was ominously silent after the music and chatter of just a few hours previous. It felt to Kitty as if Eliza's death had extinguished all other life from the house in its wake.

Matt pressed the brass button on the wall. From inside the house, they heard the faint distant chime of the bell. The mist seemed to permeate Kitty's thick woollen coat and the skin on her face was chilled.

She was about to push the bell pull again when the door was finally answered by a solemn-faced uniformed maid.

'We would like to see Mrs Trentham if she is receiving.' Matt gave the girl his card and she permitted them to enter the hall to wait while she went to let Lillie know they had called.

Matt placed his hand on Kitty's waist as they stood at the foot of the stairs looking at Eliza's portrait.

'She was frightfully pretty, wasn't she?' A voice above them made them turn and look up to see Caroline coming down the dark oak staircase towards them.

'Yes, she was. I'm so very sorry, you must already miss her terribly,' Kitty said.

The girl looked pale in her dark-grey flannel dress and black stockings.

'Yes, I do. She always treated me like a grown-up.' Caro looked at the portrait. 'Tiny says this picture is in poor taste, but I think it's rather lovely.'

'I think the artist certainly captured your aunt's spirit,' Matt agreed. 'You say Lady Foxley treated you like a grown-up but yet she wanted you to go away to school?'

Caro turned her attention from the portrait to study Matt carefully. 'Yes, she thought I'd like it.'

'And would you? Like to go abroad to school?' Kitty asked.

Caro shrugged. 'I don't know. I've always been perfectly happy here. I don't suppose it matters now anyway, Mummy won't send me.'

Her tone was flat, and Kitty couldn't decide if the girl was pleased about this or not. Everyone had said that she hadn't wished to go, but perhaps they were mistaken.

Caro looked at Kitty. 'Tiny says your father killed Aunt Eliza.'

Kitty swallowed. 'Well, Miss Morrow is mistaken. He discovered your aunt and asked for help to try to save her.'

'Who do you think might have wished to harm your aunt?' Matt asked.

Caro turned back towards Matt. 'I don't know. If it wasn't Mr Underhay, then perhaps Sir Stanford? Aunt Eliza was quite cross with him on the boat. Something to do with her money. I heard her telling Mummy that she intended to have it out with him when we returned here, and she could check her papers.'

The sound of the maid coming back towards them echoed on the tiled floor.

'I should go,' Caro said and slipped away through a nearby door.

The maid halted in the hall and offered Matt his card back. 'I'm very sorry, sir, miss, but Mrs Trentham is not at home to visitors today.'

Kitty exchanged a glance with Matt before they followed the maid over to the door where she was preparing to let them out.

'Thank you. Please send our regards to Mrs Trentham with our apologies for disturbing her and tell her we shall be in touch again soon,' Matt said as they ventured back out into the wintry afternoon air.

'Well, that was rather vexing,' Kitty remarked as the door clicked shut behind them.

'At least we managed to speak to Caroline,' Matt said as they walked the short distance to Kitty's car.

She glanced back at Villa Lamora and thought she caught a glimpse of a pale face looking out at them from an upstairs window. Whoever it was though vanished before she had the chance to identify them.

'What shall we do now?' She couldn't help feeling rather despondent as she opened her car door and slid behind the wheel.

Matt took his seat beside her. 'This is a bit of a long shot, but are you up for a spot of tea?'

Kitty looked at him in bewilderment. 'Tea?'

Matt grinned and a dimple quirked in his cheek. 'It's a horrid day, let's head for the Grand and take tea. We might just happen to find a certain Mr Hemmings there if we are lucky. The weather may have deterred him from venturing out.'

Kitty brightened at the suggestion. Unusually for her she didn't feel hungry, but they had nothing to lose and there was every chance that on a dull Sunday afternoon Mr Hemmings might well be in one of the public rooms.

. . .

The Grand Hotel stood just slightly back from Torquay seafront, a large white-painted building with a square tower at each end. It was highly regarded and, like the Dolphin and the Imperial, it catered to guests at the higher end of the social scale.

The mist was still thick as Kitty drove past Torre Abbey and into the grounds of the hotel. The headlamps of her little car made a poor impression in the fog as she ventured past the smart wrought-iron railings guarding the top of the red stone garden wall.

'Ugh, I do hope this fog lifts a little before we drive back. It's getting quite dark now as well. Grams will start to fret.' She knew her grandmother would do more than fret when she learned that Kitty's father had been arrested for murder.

'It will be all right if you take it steadily. You know how this can be patchy in some places and clearer in others. It may lift a little while we are at tea,' Matt reassured her. 'Now, let us go inside, see if we can get some refreshments and spy Mr Hemmings anywhere.'

The lobby of the Grand Hotel was considerably larger than that of the Dolphin and the hotelier side of Kitty couldn't help but admire the elegant plasterwork. It was fitted out in the latest style and had clearly been updated from its earlier more ornate roots.

Matt enquired at the desk about afternoon tea, and they were directed to one of the smaller public lounges. Kitty looked around with approval as they entered the comfortably appointed room and chose a table near the window with a some-what foggy view of the bay. Fortuitously, however, it provided an excellent view of anyone coming or going in both that room and the adjoining one.

A steward approached them, and Matt ordered afternoon tea for two. Kitty took off her driving gloves and placed them on top of her bag before unfastening her coat.

'It's fairly quiet in here. I don't suppose they are terribly busy. They usually fill up just before Christmas Day as they have a wonderful party here on New Year's Eve,' Kitty observed.

There was a family also taking tea at a table a little further away from them, a man, woman and two small boys in navy sailor suits with white collars. An elderly lady was knitting peacefully at another table and an older man was snoring discreetly in the corner, a newspaper open across his knees.

Her spirits dipped when she realised there was no sign of Roger Hemmings. The steward returned after a short time with a trolley containing a curved deco-style silver stand laden with finger sandwiches of cucumber, crab and cheese and a selection of pastries.

He placed them on the table along with a round silver teapot with a bone handle and elegant geometric-shaped china.

'Thank you.' Kitty's appetite, which had been firmly squashed by her father's arrest, suddenly reappeared at the sight of such a delectable tea. She only wished her father had been with them to enjoy it. No doubt he would be receiving one of the desk sergeant's teas in a chipped enamel mug instead.

She poured tea for herself and Matt and settled in her seat. Outside the window the mist swirled and obscured what must, on a fine day, be a glorious view of the sea. Lost in her own thoughts about the wedding, what she would tell her grandmother, and worrying about who could have been responsible for Eliza's death, she forgot to look for Hemmings.

'Kitty, I've just seen him,' Matt's urgent whisper called her from her daydream.

'Mr Hemmings.' Matt had sprung from his seat and gone to greet the man, leading him back to join them at their table.

'Captain Bryant and Miss Underhay, isn't it? I've just returned from Cockington. An old friend of my mother's lives there so I had to make a duty call. It's a filthy evening out there.'

He accepted a seat and Matt summoned the steward to bring a fresh pot of tea and an extra cup.

'We just called at Villa Lamora. We were concerned about Mrs Trentham after what happened yesterday.' Kitty carefully omitted their real reasons for calling. The less people who knew that her father had been arrested the better.

'Poor Lillie. I telephoned her, you know, just before lunch to offer my support and to see if there was anything I could do.' Roger Hemmings helped himself to a sandwich as the steward placed a cup and saucer in front of him.

'It's a bad business. I suppose, though, Sir Stanford and Lady Foxley's secretary will be able to assist her. She at least has Miss Morrow to help look after Caroline,' Kitty remarked as she stirred the fresh pot of tea before pouring some into his cup.

'Thank you, Miss Underhay, most kind of you. Yes, I suppose so, although I'm not sure how Lillie feels about the secretary chap. Bit ineffectual, I think.' Roger picked up his cup and took an appreciative gulp.

'Did you know Lady Foxley or Mrs Trentham before the voyage?' Kitty asked.

Roger scratched the side of his nose. 'I had seen Lady Foxley at a couple of events in New York, but I didn't really know her. I met Lillie on board. I got roped in for a game of quoits, you know as one does. A charming lady, you wouldn't have thought she and Eliza were sisters.'

'Yes, they seemed very different,' Matt agreed. 'Of course, Lady Foxley appeared to be the one in charge.'

Roger helped himself to a slice of sponge cake. 'Yes, absolutely. Lillie was completely dependent upon her, I believe. Sir Stanford helped Eliza with her finances, advising and investing on her behalf, although I rather think that arrangement may have been about to end.'

'Oh?' Kitty asked, trying not to sound too interested.

'Yes, I think she was unhappy about some arrangements

he'd made. Only my impression, of course, not really my business. Although I did try to mention a couple of things.' Roger popped a piece of cake into his mouth and munched happily.

'I take it that was what you were warning her about on the ship before you disembarked?' Kitty said as she poured more tea into their cups.

Roger fixed his attention on her. His pale blue eyes suddenly shrewd. 'I see, ha ha, um, I'd caught a glimpse of some papers Sir Stanford had left lying around just the day before. I noticed one of the investments and I was surprised as it was one a cousin of mine had been warned to steer well clear of just before we set off. I thought I should mention it to Lady Foxley. Just a friendly hint.'

'Of course,' Kitty agreed.

Roger pushed his chair back from the table and dabbed at the corners of his mouth with his linen napkin. 'Well, thank you for the tea. If you'll excuse me, I'd better go and change. I'm still a little damp from my journey back. Nice to run into you both.'

Kitty watched him stroll away in the direction of the bedrooms. 'Well, what do you make of that? Is he telling the truth do you think?' There was something about Hemmings and his explanation that didn't quite ring true for Kitty. Although she couldn't say for certain what it was that made her feel that way.

He was just a little bit too bluff, too full of bonhomie.

'I don't know. There is something about him, isn't there? He was very quick to take his leave when we started asking questions. I expect Inspector Greville will be making enquiries into Mr Hemmings and his valve company.' Matt drained the last of his tea.

'I wish I shared your confidence. I'm horribly afraid that our friend thinks he has already captured Lady Foxley's killer.' She was deeply troubled by that thought.

'Then we have to keep digging. There seem to be plenty of

people with a motive for murdering Lady Eliza and they would have had ample opportunity to slip up the servants' stairs. It has to be someone familiar with the house who knew which was her room,' Matt said.

'Yes, you're right. Father really doesn't have a motive to kill her. That weak story about an argument and a jocular threat is a far cry from actually committing such a violent crime.' Kitty picked up her bag and pulled on her gloves while Matt called for the bill.

'I had better get back to Bertie before he wreaks too much destruction in the kitchen. Chin up, old thing, we'll work this out,' Matt assured her.

CHAPTER EIGHT

Kitty was glad of Matt's company on the slow drive back to his house at Churston. The mist had closed in even further whilst they had been at tea. It was difficult to see more than a few feet in front of her and the last of the daylight had faded from the sky.

'Darling, why don't you come in and wait it out? See if this awful weather will lift?' Matt suggested as they halted on the drive beside his house.

As he spoke, they heard the distant boom of the foghorn in the bay warning shipping of the conditions. It was a tempting offer, but she knew if she didn't continue now then she might not get across the river should the ferries stop running.

'No, I should go. You know how much Grams worries when I am out in this kind of weather. I need to speak to her too, the sooner she knows what's happened to Papa the better. Otherwise, Mrs Craven or someone will beat me to it.' She wasn't looking forward to informing her grandmother of her father's arrest.

'Are you sure, darling?' His expression betrayed his worries for her.

'I'll be very careful. I only have to drive down the hill to Kingswear and I'll be home in no time. I'll telephone you to say I'm back.' Kitty appreciated his concern for her safety. It had been on a night like this on the same stretch of road that she had almost met her end.

He kissed her lips, sending her heart rate soaring. 'Make sure you do.'

She waved as she pulled back out onto the road. She suspected that memories of that dreadful crash she had sustained earlier in the year were the root of his concerns. Mindful of the risks of her narrow tyres on the wet and slippery road surface she crawled down the steep hill towards the bright lights of the station at the bottom.

It was a relief to find the ferry was still operating.

'Just in time, Miss Underhay. We're going to stop running in half an hour. Conditions is bad tonight,' the ferryman told her as he guided her on board.

Mr Lutterworth was at the reception desk when she entered the lobby. 'Kitty, your grandmother will be pleased to see you. She had started to fret.'

'I must just telephone Matt to let him know that I'm back, and then I'll go up to her.' Kitty smiled at her hotel manager and let herself into the small office behind the reception desk to make her call.

Matt answered on the first ring, leading her to believe he had been waiting by the telephone. 'I'm glad you are safe, and don't worry about your father. I know a good solicitor and I'll contact him tomorrow. Goodnight, my dear.'

Kitty replaced the receiver of the black Bakelite telephone back in its cradle and returned to the lobby.

'Did you have a pleasant afternoon with your father?' Cyril asked.

Kitty's shoulders drooped. 'Unfortunately, no. My father

has been arrested by Inspector Greville. He believes he killed Lady Foxley.'

Mr Lutterworth's expression betrayed his shock. 'Dear me, how dreadful.'

'Of course, Papa didn't do it. My father may be many things, but he is not a murderer.' Kitty appreciated her hotel manager's calm and unflappable nature.

'Then I am sure the inspector will realise his mistake. He is an intelligent man,' Mr Lutterworth assured her in a bracing tone.

'He is, however he does have some form for arresting the wrong person. He arrested Matt a little while ago on suspicion of murder.' Kitty decided that Inspector Greville really needed to start being more careful about the people he arrested.

After all, he had locked up Matt and now her father, but Esther Hammett, who had committed a multitude of crimes, including attempting to kill Kitty in the past, kept getting off scot-free.

'Then let us hope that he realises his error speedily with the wedding so close at hand,' Mr Lutterworth agreed.

Kitty trailed somewhat dispiritedly up the broad oak staircase towards her grandmother's salon. Her grandmother was seated beside the fire listening to a programme of festive music on the radio when she entered.

'Oh, Kitty, my dear, I'm glad you're back. I was becoming quite anxious with the way the fog has come down over the bay.'

Kitty hung her hat and coat on the peg by the door and came to warm her legs beside the fire.

'I know, it's a ghastly night out there.'

'And how was Edgar? Did he pay for tea?' Her grandmother arched an immaculately pencilled eyebrow as she asked her question.

Kitty perched herself on the edge of the chenille covered

armchair opposite her grandmother. For two pins she wanted to just burst into tears and have her darling Grams rub her back like she had when she was small.

Everything suddenly felt all too much. Lady Foxley's murder, her father being arrested and her grandmother and Edgar's constant sniping at each other.

'Matt and I had tea at the Grand in Torquay. Father couldn't come.' Kitty's voice wobbled.

Her grandmother frowned. 'Oh, darling, whatever is wrong? Did he let you down?' Concern filled the elderly woman's voice as she studied Kitty's face.

'Inspector Greville has arrested him for the murder of Lady Foxley.'

Mrs Treadwell gasped and placed her hand on her throat. 'Oh, Kitty, but what evidence does he have? I mean, I know you told me how your father had discovered Lady Foxley but he surely must have some other reason for this arrest?'

'It all seems to be circumstantial and based on hearsay.' Kitty gave a faint shrug of her shoulders. 'Matt is contacting a solicitor he knows tomorrow. It may be the one who helped him when *he* was arrested.' She gave a wry smile.

'This is preposterous. Even I struggle to believe Edgar capable of murder. Many other things, but not that. Whatever shall we do if he is not released in time for the wedding? Surely, he won't have to spend Christmas in jail?' Mrs Treadwell sounded aghast at the thought. 'Whatever will we tell people?'

Kitty didn't know whether to laugh or cry. 'Matt and I will simply have to find the real murderer before Christmas Eve.'

'It's a week until your marriage. You have a dress fitting tomorrow and Lucy and Rupert and Matthew's family are due to arrive on Wednesday. I knew your father would do something to complicate matters.' Her grandmother's blue eyes were warm with concern.

Kitty hoped the solicitor Matt had mentioned might at least

be able to persuade the inspector to release her father from custody. She looked around her grandmother's cosy room at the replies to the wedding invitations nestled next to the Christmas cards and sighed.

The faint niggling concern at the back of her mind up till now had been that Esther Hammett might resurface and attempt to derail the wedding in some way. After all, Esther's son had kidnapped her only a few weeks earlier and Esther herself had made numerous threats and attempted to kill Kitty previously. What Kitty had not anticipated was that her father would manage to get himself arrested for murder.

* * *

Matt telephoned the solicitor first thing the following morning and apprised him of Edgar's case. He then promptly telephoned the police station and asked to speak to Inspector Greville.

'Good morning, Captain Bryant.' Matt detected the note of caution in the inspector's greeting.

'Good morning, Inspector. I thought I should let you know that Mr Shillingford will arrive at the station shortly before lunchtime to meet Mr Underhay. He will be acting on Mr Underhay's behalf.' Matt knew the solicitor would no doubt contact the station himself, but he wished to be courteous and forewarn the inspector. He also hoped he might obtain some information that could be useful to their case if they kept the inspector on their side.

'I see, thank you. I will inform my desk sergeant to expect him. I hope Miss Underhay appreciates that I had little choice in the matter of making the arrest?'

Matt felt this was a somewhat optimistic statement, but until another stronger suspect could be found then he could see the policeman's dilemma. He told the inspector of their conversation with Caroline and with Roger Hemmings.

'I see, thank you, we are continuing to look into Lady Foxley's affairs,' Inspector Greville responded.

'Do we know much about this Roger Hemmings?' Matt asked. 'There is just something that feels a little off about him but neither Kitty nor I can quite put our finger on it.'

'I have cabled to his company in New York asking for background. Of course, it will probably be this evening before I get a response due to the time difference and the office being closed yesterday,' the inspector assured him.

'And, forgive me, Inspector, do we know the terms of Lady Foxley's will yet?' Matt was curious to discover if anyone could have had a financial motive for killing Eliza.

'Yes, there was a copy in her safe. The secretary, that Peters chap, found it out. Bulk of her estate goes to her sister, Mrs Trentham. A large lump sum to the niece, Caroline, when she attains her majority or on her marriage. An annuity to Miss Morrow and various sums to other long-standing servants. Nothing out of the ordinary,' the inspector said. 'I have a meeting at Lady Foxley's bank this morning to assess her accounts, look through any unusual payments et cetera. Then I intend to talk to Sir Stanford about his role in managing her stocks and other investments.'

Matt felt more reassured that the inspector was clearly being very thorough in looking at motives for Eliza's murder. 'Thank you for being so frank, Inspector. I'm sure you'll appreciate that Kitty and I are anxious for the matter to be resolved and her father released from custody as soon as possible.'

'I can understand Miss Underhay's anxiety on the matter. However, our new acting chief constable is keen to see results. You know how it is. He wishes to impress, and it will look bad in the press that a noted local socialite was murdered in her own home when it was full of the great and the good of Torbay.'

Matt understood the inspector's meaning. 'Then it seems

we are both working to the same ends, Inspector, to catch the real culprit and put them behind bars as soon as possible.'

* * *

Kitty had slept badly. Her dreams punctuated with visions of her father standing trial, culminating with the bewigged judge in his robes reaching for his black cap to pronounce sentence. When Alice tapped on her door, she was already awake and sitting up trying to shake the horrible feeling of foreboding hanging over her.

'Morning, Miss Kitty, I brought your tea and some toast.' Alice set the tray down as usual on the bedside table and opened the curtains. A pale wintry light filled the room and Kitty could see that the fog of the previous evening had cleared.

'Are you feeling all right, miss? You look as pale as your sheets,' Alice observed as she poured Kitty a cup of tea before producing her own mug and pouring one for herself.

'Oh, Alice.' Kitty made room for her friend to sit beside her as she told her everything that had happened.

The maid's eyes were as round and wide as the saucer under Kitty's cup by the time she had finished.

'Oh dear me, what a thing to happen. I do wonder at that Inspector Greville sometimes.' Alice shook her head in despair causing a stray lock of her auburn hair to escape from under her cap. 'Whatever are you and Captain Bryant going to do about it?' she asked.

'Matt is appointing a solicitor to act for Father. I must confess though, Alice, I'm not sure who we should be questioning or where to find a lead to the real culprit. If Mrs Trentham will not admit us to the house, then it will be very difficult to talk to her or Sir Stanford.' Kitty looked at her friend.

Alice sipped her tea and considered the problem. 'There's them other two as well, the secretary and that Miss Morrow.'

'Yes, you're right, any of them might have a motive for killing Eliza. Lillie was dependant on her sister for money. Sir Stanford seemed uneasy about Lady Foxley wishing to discuss her investments. Caro didn't wish to be sent away to school – or so we are led to believe – and Miss Morrow would have lost her position. Phillip Peters did not appear to be a terribly good secretary in Eliza's opinion, so I suppose there might be something there.' Kitty picked up a knife and spread marmalade thickly on a slice of toast.

'Here, don't you be getting that on the bed sheets,' Alice chided as she quickly spread a thick linen napkin under Kitty's plate.

'Sorry, Alice.' Kitty hastily licked a blob of butter from the side of her thumb.

'And you and Captain Bryant think as that Mr Hemmings isn't all he should be, neither?' Alice asked.

Kitty munched on her toast. 'No, there's just something not quite right about him, but I don't know quite what it is.'

The maid looked at her. 'You probably won't care for what I'm about to say, Miss Kitty, but I think if you wants to help your father then you'll have to bite the bullet.'

Kitty had a horrid feeling that she knew what Alice was about to suggest. She placed the last piece of her toast back down on her plate, her appetite suddenly diminished. 'Mrs Craven?'

Alice nodded. 'She's friends with Mrs Trentham and she has to see her to wrap up all the work as she's been doing for Mrs Trentham's charity. If anyone can get you or Captain Bryant into that house so as you can poke about, then it's her.'

Kitty knew that her friend was right. It was very hard for people to refuse Mrs Craven anything. The woman had the hide of a rhinoceros and could insert herself anywhere. The problem was that she loved to play detective and often flattered herself that Kitty could not manage to solve cases without her assistance.

To ask for her aid this time would play right into her hands and would involve Kitty having to swallow a great deal of pride if she wished to exonerate her father. Her expression must have betrayed her feelings on the matter as Alice chuckled.

'Never mind, Miss Kitty, you look as if you've lost a crown and found a sixpence. You could call on Mrs Craven after you've had your dress fitting.' The maid smiled at her and drained her cup.

'You are a regular Job's comforter this morning.' Kitty finished her own tea and set the things back on the tray as Alice jumped off the bed ready to clear everything away.

'You know as Mrs Craven will be happy to help, even if she don't like your father much,' Alice remarked as she collected the tray.

Mrs Craven's views on Edgar Underhay had been fixed ever since his last visit when she had been assaulted in her own garden by someone searching for an item her father had hidden years before.

'That's true, Alice. She does like to be *helpful*, even if it is my father,' Kitty agreed.

Her friend's grin widened as she whisked out of the room bearing the breakfast tray to allow Kitty to dress.

Once ready for the day Kitty telephoned Matt to let him know her plan to call on Mrs Craven. He told her of his conversation with Inspector Greville.

'I'm glad he isn't just resting on his laurels and is still looking at the other people in the household,' Kitty said.

'Yes, I felt more reassured. I've arranged to go with Mr Shillingford to see your father. He called me back after he had spoken to the inspector. I'm hoping Edgar can recall something useful to get him off the hook,' Matt said.

'We can only hope,' Kitty agreed. Her father might even be able to account for that missing twenty minutes.

'Try to put this from your mind and enjoy your dress fitting. I'll speak to you later and we can compare notes.' Matt rang off and Kitty went downstairs to see her grandmother.

'I'm sure Millicent will be delighted to help you,' her grandmother replied briskly when Kitty explained her plan. 'I shall telephone her now and then we really must set off for Torquay or we shall be late for your fitting.'

Kitty resigned herself to accepting Mrs Craven's assistance and put on her hat and coat.

'There, it is all arranged, my dear.' Her grandmother replaced the handset on the telephone. 'She is free after lunch.'

The drive to Torquay and the dressmaker's atelier was much pleasanter now that the fog had dissipated. Her grandmother was an uneasy passenger and her relief showed plainly on her face as they drew to a halt outside the shiny black-fronted shop with its elegant gold lettering.

The plate glass windows on either side of the shop door displayed glamorous evening gowns ideal for seasonal balls and parties. There was an air of gaiety and expectation in the busy street as shoppers walked purposefully in search of the perfect gifts for under the tree.

The large brass bell on its curved spring tinkled above their heads as they entered the shop. The young shop assistant in her smart plain-black dress was occupied with a customer. Kitty amused herself by looking at the display of evening purses in the cabinet while she waited for Mademoiselle Desmoine to come down from her workshop.

She had remembered to bring the ivory satin shoes she had purchased to wear for her wedding so that the hem could be finished to the correct length. Kitty often found that being barely five foot two even custom-made garments required careful measurements if they were to fit her correctly.

'Miss Underhay, Madame Treadwell, please to ascend.'
The small French dressmaker emerged from behind the curtain leading to her workshop on the first floor and greeted them with a beaming smile.

Kitty had been for three fittings with Mademoiselle Desmoine so far. Suddenly now the wedding seemed very close, and her heart thudded in her chest as she rounded the top of the narrow flight of wooden stairs to enter the workroom.

A mannequin stood to one side covered with a pristine white sheet next to the bolts of fabrics. Near the centre of the atelier was a round wooden podium raised about nine inches from the floor.

'Now, Miss Underhay, you have the shoes? And you are wearing the undergarments you wish for your wedding?' the dressmaker asked.

'Yes, I have the shoes here.' Kitty held up the small canvas bag containing her brand-new shoes.

'Bien, Madame Treadwell, if you would be so good as to be seated.' Mademoiselle Desmoine indicated the slightly worn black leather armchairs at the end of the room. 'Miss Underhay, you will accompany me.'

She took hold of the mannequin, still shrouded in its white sheet and wheeled it down the length of the workshop to a large area behind another satin curtain. Kitty followed her dutifully. She had changed there before when she had been fitted for something the dressmaker had called a 'toile'.

This, however, would be the first time she would see herself in her finished dress and with the veil and cap. Kitty hoped it would be as lovely as she remembered. There were no mirrors in that part of the workshop and Kitty had not yet seen herself in the gown.

Her grandmother had said she wished to wait until now to see her dress, so it was with some trepidation that Kitty waited as the dressmaker lowered the gown carefully over her head.

Once fastened into the dress she put on her shoes while the seamstress bustled about her making small clicking noises with her tongue as she applied pins in a few places.

'Now we go to the podium so I can pin the hem and you can show your *grandmère* the dress.'

Kitty took a deep breath and gathered her gown so she wouldn't trip as the dressmaker drew back the curtain. Once safely on the podium Mademoiselle Desmoine unveiled a large gilt-framed mirror so she could see herself.

'Oh.' Kitty could only stare at her reflection, for once lost for words. The winter-white satin with the delicate lace trim seemed to elongate her small frame, making her appear a taller, more elegant version of herself.

She glanced at her grandmother to see tears streaming down the older woman's cheeks. 'Oh, Kitty. You look so beautiful. Your mother would have been so proud of you.'

Mademoiselle Desmoine beamed up at her before scuttling about her feet as she pinned the hem. The dress was everything Kitty had hoped it would be. She rotated obediently as the dressmaker pinned and tucked.

'Now we try with the cap.' Mademoiselle Desmoine produced a large flat pale-pink box and moved aside the layers of tissue paper to extract the contents.

Kitty stepped from the podium and bent down so the small ivory-silk headpiece could be pinned to her hair and the long floating lace-trimmed gossamer-like veil spread about her.

'It's perfect. Mademoiselle Desmoine, thank you so much.' Kitty turned to the Frenchwoman.

'Of course. I am pleased you like it. Now, you must remove it very carefully and I will make the final adjustments. You are bringing your matron of honour on your next appointment? We will fit her gown also. The winter cape is also ready.' Mademoiselle Desmoine opened another box and Kitty could see the cape made to match her dress, trimmed with soft white fur around the edges.

'It's so lovely.' Kitty took one last look at her reflection before preparing to return to the dressing area.

'Matt will be quite stunned, I'm sure.' Her grandmother dabbed at her eyes with a lace-trimmed handkerchief.

Kitty changed back into her cherry-red serge dress with a white collar while Mademoiselle Desmoine carefully placed her gown back on the mannequin. Since Matt had seen her covered in mud, battered and bruised and with her stockings in shreds in the past, she was confident that he would marry her even if she arrived wearing a flour sack.

The dress Mademoiselle Desmoine had created though was so lovely she had scarcely recognised herself. It would be nice to surprise her fiancé. Now all she had to do was to prove her father's innocence so that he could escort her down the aisle.

CHAPTER NINE

Kitty and her grandmother took their lunch at Bobby's café near the seafront before they returned to Dartmouth. The café was crowded, and they shared their table with an acquaintance of Kitty's grandmother. Talk was therefore confined to Christmas and the wedding, which was a relief to Kitty and helped to take her mind off her problems.

'Please do remember, Kitty dear, that Millicent is doing you an enormous favour by agreeing to assist you to gain access to Villa Lamora,' her grandmother cautioned later as Kitty pulled her car to a halt outside the Dolphin.

'I know, Grams, and I do understand how tricky this all is.' Kitty did appreciate that her grandmother's friend did not have to assist her, especially given that she disliked Kitty's father. She also knew that Mrs Craven would be unbearably smug and would be queening it over her all afternoon while they were at the villa.

She kissed her grandmother's cheek and waved as she set off again, this time up the hill out of the town to the quiet street where Mrs Craven resided.

Mrs Craven was ready and waiting in her front bay window

looking out for Kitty's arrival. Dressed in her best navy-blue suit with a matching hat trimmed with fur, Mrs Craven made her appearance at the front door.

'Now, Kitty, you will drive carefully, won't you?' she instructed as she entered the car, checking the angle of her hat in the driver's mirror.

'Of course, Mrs Craven.' Kitty managed to suppress a sigh as she turned the car ready to drive back into town to get the ferry across the river.

'I have telephoned Lillie and explained that I need to hand over the paperwork for the ball. I have all the receipts and expenses listed ready for her so she may complete her accounts.' Mrs Craven clutched at the large cream-leather handbag on her lap as Kitty bumped her way onto the ferry.

'Is she aware of Father's arrest? Or that I am accompanying you?' Kitty asked, stopping the engine of her car as the boat began its gentle crossing pulled by the enormous chains on the riverbed.

Mrs Craven peered out through the windshield of Kitty's car as if judging how far they were from the shore. 'I asked her how she was feeling after her poor sister's demise, and she said she was thankful that your father had seen fit to leave the house. I don't know if his arrest is common knowledge as yet.'

The ferry bumped to a halt on the slip and Kitty turned on her engine while the ferrymen secured the boat. 'She declined to see Matt and I yesterday when we called.'

'Well, I suppose it may have been too soon. She did mention that Miss Morrow is firmly convinced that your father is responsible for killing Eliza.' Mrs Craven emitted a small squeak as the boat moved when Kitty drove off the ferry.

'Yes, Miss Morrow is surprisingly vocal in her opinions. Too vocal, if you ask me. I wonder what she is trying to hide?' Kitty put her foot down to get up the steep hill towards Churston.

Mrs Craven turned an interested face towards Kitty. 'You suspect her?'

Kitty shrugged. 'Why not? She had opportunity and motive, and she is a large lady with strong hands. She could just have easily slipped that stocking around Eliza's neck and pulled it tight.'

'My dear Kitty.' Mrs Craven gave a delicate shudder. 'Although I agree you do have a point.'

The broad driveway in front of Villa Lamora was empty once again as Kitty steered her small red car through the gates to park near the front door of the house.

'Leave the conversation to me, Kitty,' Mrs Craven instructed as she exited the car. 'One needs to be tactful in these situations.'

Kitty sighed and closed her car door before trudging after Mrs Craven.

The door of the villa was opened on this occasion by the butler. Kitty recognised him from the night of the ball.

'Mrs Trentham is expecting us,' Mrs Craven said as she swept into the hall.

'Of course, Mrs Craven. Madam is in the drawing room.' A maid appeared as he spoke to take their coats.

Kitty followed the manservant and Mrs Craven along the hallway and tried to look inconspicuous. She really should have chosen a different dress.

The butler led them to a room that Kitty hadn't seen before on her previous visit to the house. Mrs Trentham was seated beside the fire on an old-fashioned brocade armchair, her needlepoint on a wooden frame before her. She set her work aside as they entered.

'My dear Lillie, how are you?' Mrs Craven swooped down on her to greet her with a hug and a kiss on the cheek.

Kitty hung back near the doorway.

'I didn't realise you would have company with you.' Lillie

gave a stiff nod of acknowledgement in Kitty's direction. 'Miss Underhay.'

Kitty took a seat on a straight-backed wooden chair near the door and continued in her attempt to look inconspicuous.

'Kitty has very kindly driven me here. Such a difficulty this time of year to obtain a taxi when one doesn't keep a car and a man of one's own,' Mrs Craven explained airily as she drew off her gloves and seated herself opposite Lillie.

'Hedges will bring tea,' Lillie said as the butler disappeared from the room. 'Thank you for bringing the receipts. I shall be glad to get the charity ball things dealt with before Christmas. Sir Stanford has very kindly offered to assist me with the accounts. Usually Eliza dealt with everything financial for me ready for the rest of the committee.'

Kitty had a hundred questions hovering on the tip of her tongue, but she could see that Lillie was barely tolerating her presence so decided it was better that she remained silent for the time being.

'How very good of him. One often needs a man to sort through such matters. Is Eliza's secretary, Mr Peters, able to help you?' Mrs Craven asked as she opened her handbag to retrieve the promised papers.

'He has been very busy helping the police to sort out Eliza's financial affairs. My sister was always somewhat disparaging about his abilities, but he does seem to have been useful to Inspector Greville.' Lillie glanced at Kitty as she spoke.

'It really is just too distressing, my dear.' Mrs Craven shook her head sympathetically as she passed the receipts over to Lillie along with a small notebook. 'Everything is noted in there for you, and you can see that the ball has returned a very healthy profit for the charity.'

'Thank you, Mrs Craven. Eliza was so grateful for your help, as indeed am I. We had anticipated returning from New York much earlier than we did and, of course, would have saved you all of this work,' Lillie said as she looked through the pile of paperwork.

'Not at all, my dear. It was my pleasure. I think Eliza said in her telegram that Caroline's health was the reason your departure was delayed?' Mrs Craven said as the butler announced his reappearance with the jangle of crockery on a laden tea trolley.

'Yes, the poor child contracted measles just before we were originally intending to sail so we were forced to change our plans.' Lillie nodded her thanks to the butler as he placed the trolley beside her.

Once he had poured tea for each of them, he returned to his duties and the conversation resumed.

'Poor Caroline. She is fully recovered though now, I hope?' Mrs Craven asked as she stirred her tea.

'Oh yes. Thankfully Miss Morrow has a great deal of experience with nursing children through various illnesses. I really wonder what I would have done without her.' Lillie picked up a biscuit and nibbled at the edge.

'You will miss them both when Caroline leaves for finishing school,' Mrs Craven observed.

Kitty hid her smile behind her cup. Mrs Craven was wasting no time in asking the kinds of questions Kitty herself would have liked to ask.

Lillie looked surprised. 'Oh, I couldn't possibly part with Caroline now. Not after what has happened to Eliza. I think it will be for the best if she stays at home with me and Tiny continues with her education. She will still have her season in London of course, in time.'

'Naturally. Shall you stay on in Torquay? Or will you return to London?' Mrs Craven asked. 'Your sister had a house there too, didn't she?'

Lillie set her plate aside. 'I don't really know. There will be all kinds of things to be sorted out and it is so dreadfully close to Christmas.'

Mrs Craven smiled sympathetically. 'I do understand. Let us hope that the police catch your sister's murderer swiftly.'

Kitty held her breath and waited for Lillie's response.

'Oh, but I thought...' Lillie turned towards Kitty, a bewildered expression on her pale face. 'Forgive me, but isn't Miss Underhay's father under arrest?'

'He is assisting the police, but it is very far from certain that he is the culprit. The police enquiries are continuing. After all, he had no reason to kill Eliza. There are several other people with far stronger motives for wishing her harm.' Kitty kept her tone mild and watched as patches of high colour appeared on Lillie's cheeks.

'I expect Inspector Greville will release him soon,' Mrs Craven agreed. 'He has detained the wrong person before in other cases while he investigates and then lets them go.'

Mrs Craven's confirmation of Kitty's statement seemed to throw Lillie into a state of confusion.

'But Tiny was so certain that Mr Underhay was the culprit. I myself *found* him with Eliza's body.'

'Miss Morrow seems very keen to try to implicate my father in this matter. Why is that? Is she hiding something herself? She said she had argued with Eliza just before her death. We only have her word that she left your sister alive and well,' Kitty said.

She was not feeling very kindly towards Miss Morrow just now and had no compunction about pointing the arrow of suspicion firmly in her direction.

'Tiny would have never harmed Eliza. She loved her. She has cared for both of us since we were young girls.' Lillie's eyes were wide, and Kitty could tell that despite her denials the idea had disturbed her.

Mrs Craven finished her tea. 'Kitty does make a good point. There are others who had far more reason to harm your sister. Sir Stanford, for instance.'

'Sir Stanford?' Lillie looked at Mrs Craven.

'I would perhaps be a little careful of accepting all his advice regarding your finances. One can never be too careful, and Eliza did say she was unhappy of late with some of his advice,' Mrs Craven cautioned.

Mrs Trentham placed her head in her hands. 'I feel now as if I may be living in a nest of vipers.'

'We didn't mean to distress you, my dear, just to caution you to remain on your guard until the inspector is absolutely certain that he has the right person under lock and key.' Mrs Craven looked at Kitty.

'Mrs Craven is right, Mrs Trentham. Keep your wits about you and if you see or hear or recall anything that may shed light on whoever killed your sister, please tell the inspector immediately,' Kitty agreed as she set her empty cup back on the trolley.

'Well, that all went rather well I thought,' Mrs Craven remarked smugly a few minutes later when they were safely installed in Kitty's car once more. 'I have a knack for these things.'

'Let us see what becomes of it now that we have sown some seeds of doubt about Father's involvement in the case.' Kitty turned the key to start the car. They had certainly given Lillie something to think about during the course of their visit.

She hoped that Matt and his solicitor were having a similar degree of success at the police station.

* * *

Mr Shillingford was a short, elderly man with a dry tone and wire-rimmed spectacles. He met Matt outside the police station, and they entered the building together.

'Captain Bryant, Mr Shillingford,' the desk sergeant greeted them as they approached the desk. He was familiar with Matt from his many previous visits with Kitty. Mr Shillingford was also a frequent visitor.

'We're here to see Mr Underhay,' Matt said.

'Of course, sir, Inspector Greville said to expect you.' The sergeant lifted the hinged portion of the reception desk to allow them passage to the corridor beyond.

Matt had mixed memories of this area thanks to his own period of incarceration there some months back when Kitty had come to his rescue. He hoped that Edgar was dealing with his captivity in a better manner than he had.

The sergeant led them along the cream painted corridor and down the stone steps to the cells. He paused at the first door and selected a key from the bunch that hung from an iron ring at his waist.

'Thirty minutes,' the sergeant said as he opened the door to allow them to enter.

'That will be ample time. Thank you, Sergeant,' Mr Shillingford said as the sergeant closed and locked the cell door behind them.

Edgar was lying on his bed as they entered. He had his jacket rolled up behind his head and his ankles crossed. A lit cigarette was in his hand, and he looked for all the world as if he were relaxing on a holiday.

'Matthew my dear boy, and Mr Shillingford, I assume? Inspector Greville kindly told me to expect you.' Edgar swung his legs down from the narrow bed and held out his free hand to greet them both.

Mr Shillingford perched himself neatly on the end of the bunk and drew a large notepad from his brown leather brief-case. Matt leaned against the cell wall and waited to see how the interview would progress.

'Captain Bryant has provided me with the gist of the case against you. Shall I go through what I have here, and you can fill in any details that we may have missed.' The solicitor produced his pen and began to read from his notes.

Edgar listened attentively, only stopping the man a couple of times to add a minor detail.

'Hmm, well it does seem to be mainly circumstantial evidence against you, Mr Underhay, at this point. Clearly it is unfortunate that Mrs Trentham found you with her sister's body, but your explanation is one a jury would understand.' Mr Shillingford pushed the wire frame of his spectacles back onto the bridge of his nose.

Edgar sighed. 'I fear I sense a "but" approaching at this juncture.'

Mr Shillingford regarded him levelly over the top of his glasses. 'There are two rather large "buts" unfortunately, Mr Underhay.'

Edgar flicked the ash from his cigarette into a battered small tin ashtray that rested on the tiny wooden ledge beside the bunk. 'I was rather afraid of that.'

'The first issue is the time that you said you went upstairs and your reason for doing so, and the time the servants say that you went up.' Mr Shillingford fixed his gaze on Edgar. 'I would advise you strongly to be completely frank with me, Mr Underhay, or I shall not be in a position to assist you properly.'

'I went upstairs intending to look for Eliza and to find my lighter as I said. Everywhere was in darkness and the door to her room was shut. I didn't bother with the lights as there was enough moonlight coming through the landing window for me to see the way to my room.' Edgar paused and took a pull from his cigarette. 'I went to my room to collect my lighter.'

'Which is unlikely to have taken twenty minutes.' Mr Shillingford's tone was stern.

Edgar stubbed his cigarette out, adding to the pile in the ashtray. 'Very well, yes, it didn't take twenty minutes. I came out of my room and everywhere was still quiet with no sign of anyone else around. Eliza had confided in me while we were on the ship that she thought Sir Stanford was on the take. It occurred to me that since everyone else was downstairs at the ball it would be a good time to have a bit of a snoop in his room. I thought if I could find something incriminating there, it would put me in Eliza's good books.'

'You were in Sir Stanford's room?' Matt could see why Edgar had not wished to share that information.

'Yes, not that I found anything. I suspect he is far too wily a bird,' Edgar said. 'While I was in there, I thought I heard doors opening and closing and the sound of voices. I had to wait until it went quiet before I came out obviously.'

'Did you recognise any of the voices?' Matt asked.

Edgar gave a slight shrug of his shoulders. 'I thought one was Eliza and there was another female voice and then I thought I heard another voice, but I'm not sure if it was male or female.'

'That could have been Miss Morrow quarrelling with Eliza,' Matt said thoughtfully. 'I wonder who the other voice might have been.'

'I can't be certain, I only heard a couple of words.' Edgar looked at Matt.

'There is still the other but.' Mr Shillingford had been making notes during the course of the conversation.

'Fire away, old bean.' Edgar looked as if he were contemplating another cigarette.

'The conversation on the dance floor that was reported to the inspector where you said you could strangle Lady Foxley,' Mr Shillingford read from his notes, his tone dry.

'Ah, yes, that.' Edgar scratched his chin and looked a little sheepish. 'That was a rather unfortunate misunderstanding.'

CHAPTER TEN

Mr Shillingford raised his grey bushy eyebrows. 'I'm sure it was, Mr Underhay, but please enlighten me to the contents of the conversation leading up to that most unfortunate phrase.'

For the first time since the interview had begun Edgar looked slightly discomforted. 'The fact of the matter is, well, I'm rather financially embarrassed just at the moment. A small and temporary shortage of funds you understand.' He paused and glanced at Matt. 'Please don't mention this to Kitty, dear boy.'

'Of course, sir.' Matt knew Kitty would be unsurprised by this news but saw no reason not to agree to his future father-in-law's request.

'Lady Foxley had been most gracious in inviting me to stay. The Imperial is rather expensive, despite my lovely daughter having arranged a generous discount for me. Now I have a man in London who had some rather good tips for me on some stock that was due to come onto the exchange today. I had telephoned him from Villa Lamora when I arrived for a few hints. On our way over I'd had some interesting conversations with Eliza about stocks and shares. She was a very knowledgeable woman. That was when she had confided in me about her concerns about Sir Stanford. Naturally I thought Eliza might be interested in changing her portfolio. I suggested to her that she might care to invest in the stocks my friend had recommended. She refused. She also declined to temporarily loan me any money towards an investment. She said she never mixed friendship and finance.'

'This was the portion of conversation that the witness overheard?' the solicitor asked, his fountain pen racing across the page.

'Yes. I asked her about it. I'd mentioned it earlier in the evening and she had refused. I asked if she had reconsidered her answer. I thought possibly the mellowing effect of a few glasses of fizz might have persuaded her. She said, "No, Edgar." I said then you leave me no choice, meaning that I would be forced to confess to Kitty that I might need a small loan. Something she knew that I wished to avoid. She said, "Do what you will, I don't care." That's when I made the joke about strangling her.' Edgar sighed. 'Eliza was very hard-headed about money.'

'Why did you not tell the inspector about this?' Matt asked.

'Kitty, of course. I would like my daughter to have a few good thoughts about me. If she knew that I was in difficulties, well, it would only reinforce all the negative things my darling mother-in-law has no doubt had to say about me.'

'How did Eliza respond to you saying that you could strangle her?' Mr Shillingford asked.

Matt thought this was a good question.

'She laughed. Looking back now, she seemed distracted. As if something else was occupying her thoughts. I was a little cross that she had refused me a small loan mainly because I didn't wish to distress my daughter so close to her wedding. I made light of my request, however. I hoped that she might yet change her mind before the evening was finished.' Edgar sounded thoughtful.

'I see. Thank you for being so frank, Mr Underhay. I suggest that we make Inspector Greville aware of this statement.' The solicitor regarded Edgar intently as if examining him under a microscope.

'If you think it will help.' Edgar stood and shook the solicitor's hand once more as the heavy sound of the sergeant's boots could be heard approaching on the stone floor of the corridor outside the cell.

Matt went to follow Mr Shillingford out of the cell as soon as the sergeant unlocked the door.

'Remember, dear boy, please don't let on to Kitty about the money,' Edgar said as the metal door swung open.

'Of course, but I shall have to tell her that you have given an explanation,' Matt agreed. Though he was pretty sure that Kitty would be able to work out for herself why her father was reluctant to reveal the background behind his overheard conversation with Eliza.

They were making their way back along the corridor to the front desk when the door of Inspector Greville's office suddenly opened.

'Mr Shillingford, Captain Bryant, most fortuitous. Would you both mind sparing me a moment?' The inspector ushered them inside his small, untidy office. The air was thick with cigarette smoke and piles of manilla folders were stacked haphazardly on every flat surface.

The inspector moved some of the piles from the two wooden chairs in front of his desk and invited them to sit down.

'Thank you, Inspector. Mr Underhay has just provided us with some new information and further context for the conversation heard by your witness. You may care to consider it in your investigation.' Mr Shillingford looked around the untidy office with a slightly distressed expression as he took his seat.

'Oh?' Inspector Greville resumed his seat behind the desk and adjusted another pile of paperwork so that he could see them better. Matt was used to the organised chaos of the inspector's office. If anything he thought it marginally tidier than the last time he and Kitty had called at the police station.

Mr Shillingford apprised the inspector of the contents of Edgar's interview.

'I do wish that man would just take a story and stick to it,' Inspector Greville muttered. 'Begging your pardon, Captain Bryant.' The inspector suddenly appeared to realise Matt's relationship to the man in the cell.

'It's quite all right, Inspector. Kitty and I are both very aware of Mr Underhay's shortcomings.' He was aware that Edgar had spent time in various places of correction in the United States, hence he supposed his nonchalant acceptance of his present incarceration.

'It seems to me that the evidence against Mr Underhay for Lady Foxley's murder is rather flimsy.' Mr Shillingford regarded the inspector beadily through his spectacles.

'My investigation is still ongoing, Mr Shillingford.' Inspector Greville appeared uncomfortable under the elderly solicitor's scrutiny.

'And while it is, I see no reason why Mr Underhay should not be released into the care of Captain Bryant rather than have him occupy your cells. His passport could be retained if you are concerned that he might attempt to return abroad. Although with his daughter's marriage only a week away I think the chances of him attempting to flee the country must be considered rather low,' Mr Shillingford continued.

'Thank you, sir, I shall bear your thoughts in mind. However, I need to follow up a few more things first before I can consider either releasing Mr Underhay or continuing with his detention.' Inspector Greville met the other man's gaze.

'Very well. If you will excuse me, Inspector, I shall return to my office and send you the typewritten transcripts of my conversation with Mr Underhay as soon as my secretary has finished typing them.' The elderly solicitor stood and made his farewells to the inspector and Matt.

Once the office door had closed and the inspector was seated once more, he leaned back in his chair and regarded Matt with a level gaze. 'Well, I have to tell you that there's been a bit of a turn up for the books, Captain Bryant. It seems that you and Miss Underhay were on the money about there being something a bit fishy about that Roger Hemmings.'

Matt was curious to learn more. 'What have you discovered?'

'Well, for starters he's no more a salesman for a valve manufacturer than you or I. The company he purports to represent doesn't exist, not in London or New York. For that matter, neither does Roger Hemmings.' Inspector Greville's moustache twitched on delivering this piece of information.

'I see. Then who is he? And what is his connection to Lillie Trentham and Lady Foxley?' Matt asked. This was a puzzling development.

'This is where it gets very interesting indeed. I made some enquiries and it seems that our Mr Hemmings is in fact in the same line of work as yourself.'

Matt blinked. 'He is a private investigator? But who is he working for? And what is he investigating?'

'I telephoned the Grand Hotel while you and Mr Shillingford were with Mr Underhay and I've asked him to call. He is on his way here now. I thought you might care to be present at his interview,' Inspector Greville said.

'I certainly would. Thank you, Inspector. I wonder that he didn't come clean yesterday when he had tea with Kitty and I at his hotel,' Matt mused. Perhaps the man didn't fully trust them. However, being involved in a murder case must surely have altered the complexion of whatever problem Mr Hemmings had been engaged to solve.

'Let us see if he is more forthcoming when he gets here,' the inspector remarked.

The sergeant rapped on the door of the office a few minutes later before opening it and announcing Mr Hemmings' arrival.

'Please come in and take a seat, Mr Hemmings.' The inspector indicated the vacant chair next to Matt.

The older man undid the top buttons on his dark-grey over-coat and removed his hat before taking his seat.

'I suppose the jig is up?' he remarked as he glanced first at Inspector Greville and then at Matt.

'It would help us enormously, sir, if you could tell us your real identity,' the inspector said.

The man appeared unperturbed by the inspector's request. He dug deep inside the inner breast pocket of his coat before producing a silver card case. He opened it and extracted two printed cards. One for Matt and one for the inspector.

'Roger Harper, private investigator, London.' Matt tapped the corner of the embossed card thoughtfully.

'So, Mr Harper, Hemmings, whatever you're calling your-self, who hired you, and for what ends?' Inspector Greville asked glaring at the card in his hand as if it had purposely insulted him.

'I have been engaged on a case for some time. It's quite a complex one and I am contracted by several companies who have all been affected by the same crime.' Roger looked at them as if he were choosing his words carefully. He named three large firms all operating both in London and internationally. Matt was familiar with the names mentioned and he could see from the gleam in the inspector's eye that he too recognised them.

'Do go on, Mr Harper,' Inspector Greville said.

'It started off as insurance fraud and some suspicious trading in the shares of the companies I have just mentioned. Small at first but then incidents which if they had not been caught in time would have led to very serious failings and severe financial consequences.' Harper's expression was sober.

'They chose not to go to the police?' Inspector Greville asked.

Harper's broad shoulders rose and fell. 'There was no definitive proof of any plot or crime that could be pinned on any one person or group of people. Just a series of events that didn't add up. I was engaged to see if the incidents were linked and if any particular person or group would benefit by any of these actions.'

'I think I am beginning to see,' Matt said. A run on a company's stocks and shares, insider dealing and trading was nothing new. The recent conversation with Kitty's father had been along similar lines.

'The course of the investigation led me to New York and I began to track certain patterns in trading. The stock purchased was always in a few names.' Roger looked at Matt.

'Lady Eliza Foxley's name being one of those?' Matt guessed.

Harper nodded his head. 'Exactly. I needed to find out what Lady Foxley knew about the shares that were purchased in her name and the insurance bonds.'

Matt shifted in his seat. 'I understood Lady Foxley was quite shrewd where money was concerned?'

'Indeed,' Inspector Greville agreed.

'She was quite knowledgeable, but of late she had permitted Sir Stanford to handle more of her financial affairs. He was the one buying, selling and dealing on her behalf. It was clear that she was unhappy about Sir Stanford's actions but didn't know quite what was wrong. When I spoke to her on board the ship, she indicated that she needed to see some of the documents she had here in her house on her return,' Harper said.

'Does he have other clients beside Lady Foxley?' Matt was

interested now in this story of Harper's. It seemed that Sir Stan-ford might have some questions to answer.

'Yes, although it seems that in the last year, they have become fewer in number.' Roger tucked his card case back inside his coat.

Inspector Greville stroked his moustache as he considered this new information. 'And we have heard now from several witnesses that Lady Foxley intended to review her portfolio and go through her finances with Sir Stanford.'

'I did attempt to indirectly warn Lady Foxley once again shortly before we disembarked,' Roger said. 'I had to be careful as I had no desire to alert Sir Stanford. In fact, I wonder, Inspec-tor, if you might continue to refer to me as Roger Hemmings until the case is concluded?'

The inspector nodded. 'My enquiries have indicated that Sir Stanford has some financial difficulties of his own.'

'What of Phillip Peters? Lady Foxley's secretary? Does he have any role to play in her financial affairs?' Matt asked. It seemed clear to him that Sir Stanford had a motive for killing Eliza. But was he acting alone? Or did someone else also have a reason to wish Lady Foxley dead?

Hemmings frowned. 'He's a bit of an odd bod. A very nervous kind of a chap, inexperienced. Lady Foxley found him rather trying, I believe. He mainly organised her social calendar and dealt with her correspondence. I don't believe he would have had sufficient access or knowledge to be involved in the purchase and sale of any stocks and shares.'

'She asked him to ensure the papers were ready for her planned meeting with Sir Stanford while we were at the ball. So he clearly knew where the papers were kept and which ones would be required,' Matt said.

'He has proved very helpful to my officers locating Lady Foxley's will and ensuring her other papers have been made available to us. I have asked that her documents be secured in the safe at Villa Lamora.' Inspector Greville looked at Roger.

'A wise precaution. Now I have a request, if I may, I would very much like to look at the documents regarding Lady Foxley's portfolio? I know what I am looking for and would be able to see if anything was missing or had been altered,' Roger asked.

Matt could see why this would be useful to him. No doubt the papers would confirm his suspicions regarding Sir Stanford. It would also be very helpful to the police.

'It may be possible to allow some access to them, but they are now the property of Mrs Trentham. It would also have to be done under our supervision.' Inspector Greville looked thoughtful. 'Perhaps if the documents were brought here, then Sir Stanford would be none the wiser about your involvement.'

Hemmings nodded his head. 'Thank you, Inspector.'

'I presume, Inspector, that you will also wish to speak to Sir Stanford about his business affairs in relation to Lady Foxley's murder?' Matt asked. It seemed to him that Sir Stanford had far more motive to kill Eliza Foxley than Kitty's father did.

Inspector Greville looked uncomfortable. 'Naturally, I shall have questions to put to him in that regard.'

'Then, as to Mr Shillingford's suggestion, would you be prepared to release Mr Underhay into my charge rather than retaining him here?' Matt asked.

Truth be told he didn't altogether relish the idea of being responsible for Kitty's father. Mainly because the man was quite unpredictable, but he was also certain that he was not Lady Foxley's killer. Kitty would be greatly relieved if her father were a free man. There was enough to worry about with the wedding without Edgar being under lock and key.

Hemmings rose to his feet and extended his hand, first to the inspector and then to Matt. 'I think I should leave at this point. Perhaps you could contact me at my hotel, Inspector, when I can come and view the papers?'

'Of course, Mr Hemmings, and thank you for your co-operation in this matter.' The inspector shook his hand.

Once Hemmings had departed Matt turned his attention back to the inspector. 'Now sir, about Kitty's father?'

The inspector fidgeted in his seat and didn't reply immediately. Matt waited to hear what he had to say.

'You are aware that we have a new acting chief constable?' Inspector Greville sighed as he spoke, the words sounding gusty in the small room.

'Yes, sir.' The former chief constable had retired early pleading poor health. This had been something of a face-saving exercise. Matt and Kitty had been involved in a complex case that had ended with the chief constable's son being tried for murder.

'Our acting chief constable is naturally keen that his position becomes permanent.' Inspector Greville began absent-mindedly arranging various objects in the tiny area of free space visible on the top of his desk.

'Locking up the wrong man for Lady Foxley's murder will hardly help his cause,' Matt remarked in a mild tone. He was aware that the inspector was under pressure to secure a speedy result in the case.

Inspector Greville heaved another sigh. 'Between you, me and the gatepost I agree with you. However, it's a matter of public confidence. The last thing people want as they go about their Christmas shopping is to think a murderer might be on the loose.'

'But a murderer is on the loose, Inspector. We both know that.' Matt could tell that there was something else going on behind the scenes. The inspector was usually a very reasonable man.

'There is also the small matter of my own position. I am

quite content to remain an inspector. My good lady wife, Mrs Greville, however has started to point out rather frequently of late that a promotion to chief inspector might be desirable.' He avoided Matt's gaze.

'Ladies tend to be like that, sir. Ambitious on our behalves.' Matt bit back a smile. He counted himself as fortunate that Kitty wasn't overly concerned with things like social status. Then again, she was concerned that she was regarded and treated as an equal when it came to solving his cases.

'It's an expensive business, marriage, as no doubt you'll discover after next Monday. It's the children you see, school fees, shoes, toys.' The inspector shook his head, his moustache drooping under the financial burden of supporting his wife and all the little Grevilles.

'I am quite prepared to take full responsibility for Kitty's father, sir. From what Hemmings was saying it seems Sir Stanford may have more of a motive for harming Lady Foxley. There is also the question of Miss Morrow's evidence and her determination to accuse Edgar Underhay.' Matt did his best to look sympathetic to the inspector's cause while still pushing for Edgar's release.

The inspector met his gaze. 'Very well. I'll ask the sergeant to bring in the paperwork. He is under your surety, however, and even a hair out of line will see him back behind bars.'

'Thank you, Inspector. Kitty and I are most grateful.' Matt breathed a silent sigh of relief.

'Yes, well let's hope I don't come to regret it,' Inspector Greville remarked as he picked up the telephone to call the front desk.

CHAPTER ELEVEN

Kitty was quite exhausted by the time she delivered Mrs Craven safely back to her home. The return journey had been filled by her companion with ceaseless chatter and speculation about the identity of Lady Foxley's murderer. This commentary was punctuated with squeaks of alarm if Kitty overtook anything or accelerated.

'There is a message for you, Kitty.' Mr Lutterworth was behind the reception desk as she entered the hotel lobby.

He beamed as he retrieved a small piece of paper from the pigeonhole behind him. 'Captain Bryant telephoned for you a moment ago.'

Kitty took the paper and opened it.

Will telephone again later. Your father released into my custody. Lots to tell you. Matt.

'Oh, that is good news. The inspector has released my father.' Kitty smiled happily at her hotel manager, her fatigue fading at finally receiving some good news.

'Splendid news. That must be a great relief with the

wedding so close. Perhaps the inspector has apprehended the real culprit,' Cyril suggested.

'Matt would have said so if he had, but he does say he has lots to tell me. At least Father is out of the cells. I had better go upstairs and let Grams know.' Kitty folded the paper back up and tucked it inside her coat pocket.

Her heart was light as she ascended the stairs to her grandmother's salon with a spring in her step. No doubt her father would have to stay at Matt's house, at least for the time being. Still, at least he would be able to give her away and she wouldn't have to face awkward questions from Matt's family or her aunt and uncle when they arrived.

Her grandmother was dozing beside the fire as Kitty entered her salon. She raised her head as the door clicked shut.

'Kitty, my dear, how was your adventure with Millicent? Did you discover anything useful?' Her grandmother straightened herself up in her chair and blinked drowsily at her.

Kitty explained what they had discovered while she hung her hat and coat on the hooks beside the door.

'Anyway, the best news was from Matt when I came back. Father has been released into Matt's custody. He's no longer in the cells.' Kitty stood in front of the fire and spread out her hands to warm them.

The air had turned colder on her way back to Dartmouth and the short walk from the shed where she kept her car to the hotel had chilled her.

'That is good news. I presume the solicitor and Matthew must have made a convincing argument,' her grandmother said.

'It certainly seems so. Matt said he will telephone me later so I expect I shall discover more then.' Kitty gave her grandmother a tired smile.

It had been a busy day and coming back into the warmth of the hotel after being outside was making her feel as sleepy as her grandmother.

'I shall telephone for some tea. Sit down, Kitty, and rest. You have had quite a busy day,' her grandmother instructed as she rose from her seat to make the call to the kitchen.

Kitty was happy to comply. Her grandmother requested tea and then paused for a moment at the mirror hanging on the far wall of the room to pat her silvery-grey hair back into place before she took her seat opposite Kitty.

'Your great-aunt Livvy is arriving tomorrow. I received a message from her this afternoon while you were out.'

Kitty's aunt, her grandmother's sister, lived in a large and remote house in the Scottish Highlands. Kitty was very fond of her aunt Livvy and was delighted that she was able to come for the wedding. Her aunt's health had been poor during the last year with frequent small but troubling illnesses.

Once warm and comfortable after a nice cup of tea, Kitty must have dozed off herself. She was roused only by the insistent ringing of the telephone on her grandmother's writing bureau.

'Hello?' She struggled to swallow a yawn as she answered the call. Her grandmother had vanished, and Kitty assumed she must have gone downstairs to speak to Mr Lutterworth.

'Kitty, my darling girl,' her father's voice greeted her. 'I'm out of the clink and back at Matthew's house.'

'That's good news. I had a message waiting for me from Matt to say Inspector Greville was releasing you.' Her spirits were lifted by the tone of her father's voice. At least he did not appear too downcast after being accused of murder and incarcerated.

'Matthew is here waiting to tell you all the news. I've promised your policeman friend that I shall be on my best behaviour.'

Kitty smiled to herself. Her father's behaviour could seldom be described as good.

'I'm sure you will be the model house guest. Let's hope the inspector captures the real murderer soon,' Kitty replied.

Her father's chuckle resonated in her ear. 'Absolutely, darling. Now here is your beau.'

He must have passed the receiver over to Matt. 'Hello, old thing, how was your quest with Mrs C? Did Mrs Trentham let you across the doorstep this time?'

Kitty told Matt all that she had learned during the visit and in return he told her about Roger Hemmings and the information he had learned from Inspector Greville.

'It sounds as if Sir Stanford may have questions to answer?' Kitty said thoughtfully.

'Absolutely. I believe the inspector is going to see him tomorrow and while he is occupied the police are going to extract Lady Foxley's documents so Hemmings can take a look at them at the police station.'

'That sounds like a good plan.' Kitty was relieved that it seemed as if there was the prospect of someone else other than her father suspected of the crime.

'The Imperial are happy to continue to store your father's trunks. I saw no point in transferring them here at the moment. He is, of course, welcome to stay here as long as he wishes even after his name is cleared,' Matt assured her.

'Thank you. That sounds like a sensible arrangement.' Kitty hoped her father would be completely exonerated before much longer. She had been looking forward to spending her first few days as a married woman without a house guest, even if it was her father.

Now however, with her father safely installed at Matt's home she intended to have a quiet dinner with her grandmother and an early night.

* * *

Matt and his future father-in-law were still at breakfast the following morning when there was a loud knock at the door. His housekeeper hurried to answer it while Matt finished his coffee and wondered who could be calling so early.

'Inspector Greville for you, sir. Shall I fetch more coffee?'

'Yes, please.' Matt rose to greet the inspector.

Bertie came barrelling in from the kitchen where he had been begging for bacon, to investigate the visitor.

'Please take a seat, Inspector Greville,' Matt suggested as he shooed his dog under the table.

Edgar finished his toast and waited for the policeman to sit down. 'Rather early for a social call, Inspector. I hope this means you have good news for us?'

The inspector's face was grave as he sat down heavily on one of the spare dining chairs. 'I'm afraid not, Mr Underhay. Quite the contrary, in fact.'

'Oh?' Matt resumed his own seat opposite Edgar. 'How so, Inspector?'

'Mrs Trentham was taken violently ill yesterday during the night.'

'Good Lord.' Edgar stared at the policeman. 'Is she all right?'

'She is at the hospital and is still gravely ill.' Inspector Greville had removed his hat and now seemed intent on examining the brim as he spoke. 'It seems, sir, that she has been poisoned.'

'Poisoned?' Matt and Edgar spoke in unison.

'The doctors believe that she may have been given something in her medication. She regularly takes a sleeping powder last thing at night. She has done so for years apparently, ever since her husband was killed.' Inspector Greville looked at Edgar who seemed quite shocked by this turn of events.

'But who would wish to harm Lillie?' Matt asked.

'That is a very interesting question, Captain Bryant. Now, I must ask both of you where you were yesterday evening after you left the police station.'

Bertie nibbled happily on the end of the policeman's boot-lace seemingly unperturbed by the drama that was going on above his furry head.

'Surely, you don't believe I was involved in poisoning Lillie?' Edgar asked, staring at the inspector.

'I have to question everyone, sir, and this incident happened after you had been released from custody. It would be a derelic-tion of my duty if I did not establish that you were not responsi-ble.' Inspector Greville looked at Edgar.

'Mr Underhay and I left the police station by motor taxi and returned here. We telephoned Kitty to tell her of our arrival. I also telephoned the Imperial to give instructions for storing Mr Underhay's trunk. We had supper together and listened to the radio. We were in each other's company all evening,' Matt said.

'Thank you, Captain Bryant.' Inspector Greville had made notes while Matt was speaking in his notebook.

'Surely, it would be more useful to speak to anyone still staying at Villa Lamora. They would have been in a better posi-tion to tamper with Lillie's medication,' Edgar protested.

'There is the possibility, sir, that this had been done at an earlier time and it would be a matter of chance when Mrs Tren-tham took the affected cachet. There is still that period of time you spent upstairs on the evening of the ball before discovering Lady Foxley's body,' the inspector said.

Edgar jumped to his feet, startling Matt's housekeeper who had just entered the room with a fresh tray of coffee. 'Dash it all, man, I've explained all of that already.'

The housekeeper tutted as Edgar apologised and assisted the woman to set the tray down on the table.

'Did anyone at the house know that Edgar had been released?' Matt asked. It struck him that it could be that someone at Villa Lamora was intent on ensuring that Edgar remained firmly in the frame for killing Eliza by harming Lillie.

'Mrs Trentham was informed yesterday evening before dinner when I contacted her regarding her sister's papers. It was imperative that no one accessed the safe before we went to question Sir Stanford.' Inspector Greville looked perturbed as the implications of Matt's question sank in.

Edgar sat back in his seat. 'There you have it then. Someone in that house is determined to see me hang.'

'Perhaps, Inspector, you could tell us exactly what happened at the house when Mrs Trentham was taken ill?' Matt picked up the coffee pot and poured them all fresh drinks.

Bertie raised his head momentarily before lowering it back with a disappointed sigh when he realised that there were no biscuits.

Inspector Greville added cream and sugar to his cup. 'The household dined together at eight. According to Miss Morrow everything was as normal. They had tomato soup, lamb cutlets and prunes and custard before returning to the sitting room for coffee. Mrs Trentham was perfectly well. She was busy with her needlepoint. The household retired at eleven. At around midnight Mrs Trentham rang her bell for assistance, she had been violently sick. Miss Morrow called for the doctor.'

'I presume that the symptoms she was displaying led the doctor to suspect something was amiss?' Matt asked as he collected his own cup from the tray.

'Yes. The doctor arranged for her to be taken immediately to the local hospital where they pumped her stomach and gave her intravenous fluid. He asked questions about what everyone had eaten and drunk. There was a small amount of water in a glass beside the bed. Miss Morrow explained about Mrs Trentham's medication. The doctor had the presence of mind to take the glass and test the remaining contents.' Inspector Greville paused and took a sip of his coffee.

'And the poison was discovered,' Edgar said.

'Yes, sir.' The inspector set his cup back on its saucer.

'Lillie was lucky that the doctor acted so quickly,' Matt remarked.

'Indeed, sir. Any delay at all and she would have died. Fortunately, the hospital is not far away and the doctor is a neighbour.' Inspector Greville looked thoughtful.

It sounded as if Lillie had indeed been fortunate, however she was still very ill. 'What poison was it?' Matt wondered if the inspector had already discovered the source.

'Arsenic. Luckily it was a small amount due I suspect to the size of the cachet and the difficulty the perpetrator must have had in extracting enough usable material. We found an old almost-used container of poison hidden in the cellar. There had been a rat problem a few years ago.' Inspector Greville's frown deepened. 'No recognisable fingerprints, of course. Whoever did this was very clever.'

'Why Lillie?' Edgar asked.

Matt looked at his future father-in-law. 'That's a good question, Inspector. Why was Lillie targeted?'

The inspector took another drink of coffee. 'Mrs Trentham is now a wealthy woman. As you know she inherited the bulk of Lady Foxley's estate.'

'I suppose money might be a motive, but surely if anything happened to Mrs Trentham the only person to benefit would be Caroline.' Matt thought that Miss Morrow might also be mentioned in Mrs Trentham's will but would that be enough to provide a motive for killing her?

'Miss Morrow I think has a bequest and, of course, the charity that Mrs Trentham founded after the death of her late husband would also stand to receive a large sum of money,' Inspector Greville confirmed Matt's thoughts.

'Or perhaps someone wished to try and prevent Lillie from passing something onto the police. Something she'd seen or heard or might discover when Eliza's papers are examined once more,' Matt suggested.

He had scarcely finished speaking when Bertie shot from under the table at the sound of a key in the front door.

'I think Kitty is here, no doubt she may have some ideas on the matter,' Matt said as he rose to greet his fiancée.

CHAPTER TWELVE

Kitty was somewhat surprised to discover the dining room at Matt's house to be fully occupied.

'Inspector, I wasn't expecting to see you here so early,' Kitty said as she petted the top of Bertie's head while the dog sniffed hopefully at her handbag. She hoped this was not a bad omen.

'I'm afraid there has been an unfortunate development in the case, Miss Underhay,' the inspector said as he retook his seat once Kitty had sat down.

The inspector, aided by Matt, told her about Lillie Trentham.

'Goodness, how terrible. The poor woman. Will she recover?' Kitty asked looking around at the men seated at the table.

'The doctor is hopeful, but it is by no means certain,' the inspector said.

'Oh dear, I feel awful. Mrs Craven and I warned her to be careful when we saw her yesterday.' Kitty was quite distressed when she recalled the contents of their conversation.

The inspector's moustache twitched. 'Careful? In what regard, Miss Underhay?'

'Well, Lillie seemed so, well, so blind to the fact that she could still be harbouring her sister's murderer within her own four walls. She told us that Sir Stanford had offered to assist her with her finances and sorting out both Eliza's affairs and the financial matters for the charity.' Kitty looked at the inspector. 'Mrs Craven felt that while she personally found a man's viewpoint useful, she thought Lillie should be a little cautious. Her sister had, after all, been intending to quiz Sir Stanford about his financial advice.'

Kitty hadn't agreed with Mrs Craven about having a man look at the paperwork. In her mind any intelligent woman should be able to understand her own money. Lillie Trentham did not appear unintelligent, just lacking in confidence. Which she supposed was to be expected when she had always been in the shadow of her dazzling older sister.

'Thank you, Miss Underhay. That does throw a different complexion on the case. Until Mrs Trentham regains consciousness, however, we shall remain in the dark about the possibility of her having discovered some information for us.' Inspector Greville sighed. 'I have a constable posted at the hospital, by the way, to ensure Mrs Trentham's safety.'

'That seems a sensible precaution,' Kitty agreed. If someone had attempted to kill Lillie once, then they might well make another attempt.

Inspector Greville rose and replaced his hat. 'I should get off. I'm expected at Villa Lamora.'

Kitty sent Matt an urgent glance. She knew that she would not be permitted to attend during the questioning of the household, but the inspector might allow Matt to accompany him.

'I wonder, Inspector, might I be permitted to observe?' Matt suggested, picking up on Kitty's unspoken hint.

'I can stay with my father,' Kitty offered. Edgar rolled his eyes. She hoped this was at the suggestion that he needed someone to stay with him to prevent him absconding rather than a lack of desire for her company.

The inspector tugged at his moustache seemingly torn by the idea. 'It would be most irregular...' he started.

'Of course, we understand your position, sir, but any help to solve the case quickly must surely help to impress the new acting chief constable,' Matt said quickly.

Inspector Greville sighed. 'Very well. Observation only. Miss Underhay, if you and Mr Underhay could give Villa Lamora a wide berth, that would be much appreciated.'

'Of course, Inspector. Kitty and I shall both be veritable paragons of virtue.' Edgar held up his fingers in a mock salute.

Bertie gave a small whine of agreement.

The inspector looked unconvinced as he led the way out of the room into the hall. Matt followed, giving Kitty a wink on his way out.

'Well, my darling girl, what shall we do to amuse ourselves?' her father asked as the inspector's car drove away.

'Stay out of trouble, like you promised.' Kitty smiled wryly as she spoke. 'Aunt Livvy is arriving later, so I am expected for tea.'

'Then we have most of the day to ourselves.' Edgar smiled at her.

Kitty was struck by an idea. 'Give me a moment.' She left her father in the dining room and went to make a telephone call. She returned after a few minutes.

'Better get your coat, Father. We have a luncheon invitation with a very respectable person who can give you an impeccable alibi just in case there are any more unexpected events.' Her smile widened as Bertie nudged her hopefully with his nose. 'You are invited too, Bertie.'

Her father immediately looked wary. 'Where are we going?'

'A pre-wedding lunch with a guest who can't attend the wedding itself. My dear friend Father Lamb.' Kitty bestowed another dazzling smile on her father and went to find her coat from the hall closet, humming happily to herself.

Father Lamb had been the person who had supported her and her grandmother when they had discovered the terrible truth of what had happened to her mother all those years ago. He lived in Exeter, near the cathedral, and although this time of year was a busy period, he had been delighted to hear that she was to call.

'I suppose a priest would keep me out of trouble,' her father muttered gloomily as he collected his hat.

Kitty's grin grew even bigger as she placed Bertie on his lead ready to put him in the car.

* * *

Inspector Greville was remarkably quiet on the drive to Villa Lamora. Matt wondered if he had perhaps pushed their professional relationship a little too far by inviting himself along. Still, it was done now, and he and Kitty wanted this case solved before the wedding.

The weather was dull and cloudy with a sharp edge to the wind. Matt was glad of his thick overcoat as they waited on the doorstep of the villa for someone to let them in.

'Inspector, please come in. May I ask if there is any more news about Mrs Trentham, sir?' The butler had opened the door and was busy taking their coats.

'Nothing new, I'm afraid. She remains very ill.' The inspector handed him his hat.

The man said nothing but took their things to a nearby cloakroom before returning to lead them along the hall. 'The family are in the sitting room.' The sounds of a piano being played somewhat discordantly echoed down the hall.

Matt followed behind the inspector as they entered. A sullen and red-eyed Caroline was seated at the piano while Miss Morrow was beside her, presumably to turn her pages. Sir Stanford had the morning newspaper open as he sat beside the fire. There was no sign of Phillip Peters, the secretary.

'Inspector, is there any news?' Caro turned around on the piano stool, clearly glad of the opportunity to stop her practise.

'I'm afraid there is nothing new yet, Miss Trentham,' the inspector said.

Matt could see the anxiety in Miss Morrow's plain round face. 'Poor Lillie. Who could have done something so terrible?'

'That is what we hope to determine, Miss Morrow.' The inspector took out his notebook.

Sir Stanford set aside his newspaper. 'First Eliza, now Lillie, where will it end? Are we all in danger if we continue to stay here?' he asked.

'Rest assured, Sir Stanford, we are doing everything in our power to catch whoever is responsible.' Inspector Greville took a seat opposite Sir Stanford. Matt found a chair in the far corner where he could observe the proceedings without drawing undue attention to his presence.

Sir Stanford did not look convinced. 'There's a madman on the loose if you ask me. Targeting women.'

'I'd like to recap the events of last night, if you don't mind.' Miss Morrow looked indignant at the inspector's words, and he held up his hand to prevent her from protesting. 'I am aware, Miss Morrow, that you have already very kindly given me an outline, but I would like to go through things in a little more detail.'

Matt listened intently as the inspector went through the sequence of events provided by Miss Morrow. He reaffirmed the dinner menu and that everyone was perfectly well following their meal.

'Coffee was served in here following dinner?' Inspector Greville looked at Sir Stanford and Miss Morrow for confirmation.

'Yes, we were all in here all evening. Lillie had her needlepoint.' Sir Stanford nodded towards the wooden frame and tapestry workbag that stood to the side of the fireplace. 'I had my paper. Caroline was reading one of her detective books until Peters persuaded her into a game of cards.'

'And I was doing some mending,' Miss Morrow added.

It all sounded quite the domestic picture Matt thought.

'Did everyone retire for the evening at the same time?' Inspector Greville consulted his notes. 'I think you said around eleven, Miss Morrow?'

'Caroline went up first at about ten thirty. Then Mr Peters about five minutes afterwards. I went up just after Peters,' Sir Stanford said.

'Lillie went up just before eleven. I was last to leave. I like to make sure the servants turn off the lamps and see to the fire,' Miss Morrow added.

'Thank you. Did any of you see or speak to Mrs Trentham again after going upstairs, before she rang the bell for assistance?' The inspector looked around the room.

Caroline looked awkward and dropped her gaze to focus on the music pages in front of her. Miss Morrow pursed her lips as if torn between speaking and remaining silent. Sir Stanford frowned. 'I thought I heard voices from the direction of Lillie's room when I went to the bathroom, but it could have been from anywhere I suppose.'

'What time was this, sir?' Inspector Greville asked.

The creases on Sir Stanford's brow deepened. 'I suppose it must have been some ten minutes or so before Lillie rang the bell for help. I hadn't long returned to my room and was still in my dressing gown when I rushed out to her aid.'

He could have been telling the truth Matt thought, or he could have made the story up to cover his own speed at rushing to Lillie's room. The inspector had said that after pressing the bell Lillie had called out, just once, before knocking her lamp from the side of her bed. The ensuing crash and her initial cry had alerted the house.

'Did you recognise the voices at all?' Inspector Greville scribbled busily in his book.

Sir Stanford shook his head. 'I can't even swear one of them was Lillie, but there were two people talking. Actually, thinking about it now, I rather think it was an argument. The tone sounded heated, even if the voices were indistinct.'

'No one else heard anything? Or had a conversation that resembled the one Sir Stanford heard?' Inspector Greville looked around the room once more.

There was a tap at the door of the sitting room and Phillip Peters looked into the room, an anxious expression on his bespectacled face.

'I say, Inspector, I have finished assisting your man. Is there anything further I can help you with?'

Matt paid attention to Sir Stanford to see if there was any reaction to Peter's statement. He fancied that Sir Stanford looked a little discomfited but decided this could have been a trick of the light.

'Thank you, Mr Peters, perhaps you might come and join us. I am attempting to double-check the information from yesterday evening when Mrs Trentham was taken ill.' Inspector Greville waited as Mr Peters scuttled into the room and took a seat on the sofa.

The inspector repeated the questions he had already asked the rest of the group. Peters, however, denied seeing Lillie or hearing any conversation when he went upstairs.

'Of course, my room is the furthest away from Mrs Trentham's. Lady Foxley preferred me to be closer to her side of the landing,' Peters explained.

'I see, thank you, sir.' Inspector Greville consulted his notebook once more. 'Miss Trentham, your room is next to your mother's room with Miss Morrow's room on the other side?'

'Yes, I stopped using the nursery suite years ago.' Caroline picked at the edge of one of the ivory piano keys with her fingernail. Matt noticed her nails appeared bitten down and the quicks around the edges looked red and sore.

'You definitely didn't hear any conversation or an argument from inside your mother's room shortly before she collapsed and called for help?' Inspector Greville pinned the girl with his gaze.

Caroline shuffled uncomfortably, her cheeks flushing.

'I'm sure Caro would have told you, Inspector Greville, if she had heard anything.' Miss Morrow glowered at the inspector.

The inspector merely raised his eyebrows and continued to look at Caroline.

'No... I... I must have been asleep. I was tired,' the girl said defensively.

Matt thought the girl was lying. There was something evasive about her reply and manner.

'Thank you, Miss Trentham.' Inspector Greville made another cryptic squiggle in his book. 'Now, perhaps I could ask you all to cast your minds back to the aftermath of Mrs Trentham calling for help.' He paused and glanced up at Caroline. 'If it's not too distressing.'

'Of course, it's distressing,' Miss Morrow snapped, then appeared to stop and gather herself. 'However, we are all anxious to help,' she continued in a more measured tone.

'Yes, of course,' Mr Peters agreed.

'The bell was pulled alerting the servants, but before any of the staff came upstairs, Mrs Trentham was heard to cry out?' The inspector checked his notes.

'Yes, it was more of a cry than any actual words. Then there was an almighty crash from that side of the house,' Sir Stanford said. 'That was when I went out of my room to see what was happening.'

'Who was first into Mrs Trentham's room?' Inspector Greville's pen was poised over his book.

Miss Morrow flushed. 'That would be me, oh and Caro. We met at the door of Lillie's room.'

'Miss Trentham?' Inspector Greville asked.

Caroline nodded in agreement. 'Yes, Tiny was on the landing in her nightie. I asked her if the noise had come from Mummy's room, and she said she thought it had so we opened the door and went in. It was awful, poor Mummy.'

Tiny placed a meaty arm, around her charge's slender shoulders. 'There now, my love.'

Matt privately thought Caroline did not look as if she desired any kind of consolation from her governess.

'I believe I arrived next, right behind Miss Morrow and Caroline. I could see Lillie was very unwell, so I asked Tiny to telephone a doctor for help,' Sir Stanford said.

Phillip Peters coughed. 'I arrived at that point with Hedges, the butler, right behind me.'

Inspector Greville scribbled furiously as he made notes. 'So, Miss Morrow, you telephoned the doctor from Mrs Trentham's room?'

Tiny nodded. 'Yes, there is a telephone beside the bed. Fortunately, she hadn't knocked it off when she tipped over the lamp.'

'It was all quite confusing. The room was dark as the lamp had broken and there was bits of broken glass being trodden everywhere. I warned Miss Morrow to watch where she was standing in case she cut her feet.' Sir Stanford looked at Tiny.

'I put on the main light when I arrived,' Phillip Peters added. 'I think everyone was so focused on poor Mrs Trentham no one had pressed the switch.'

'The doctor arrived very quickly,' Inspector Greville observed.

'He is a neighbour. He was Eliza's doctor, and he only lives a couple of doors away,' Tiny explained. 'In fact, he came in his pyjamas and a housecoat.'

Matt thought the speed of the doctor's arrival and Lillie having expelled most of the contents of her stomach had probably saved her life.

Caroline looked rather pale now and Matt wondered if he had been mistaken about her not requiring Miss Morrow's support. For all her worldly-wise shell, Caro was still only a young girl, not much older than Dolly.

'It was the doctor's idea to preserve the water glass and cachet wrapper?' Inspector Greville asked.

'Yes, it was. Caroline had the glass in her hand, and he told her to put it down. He said nothing was to be touched. Then the ambulance men came.' Peters looked at Tiny who didn't look pleased at his statement.

'Caroline was in a state of shock. Her mother was collapsed, and everything was confused,' Tiny explained.

'I thought it would get knocked over, like the lamp, with everyone trying to help Mummy.' Caroline swallowed hard as if trying to keep back a sob as she spoke. 'I didn't mean any harm. I just thought Mummy had been affected by something she ate at dinner. She was so sick.'

'Of course you did. What else was the child to think?' Miss Morrow turned on Inspector Greville.

Matt could picture the confusion and chaos there must have been in Lillie's bedroom.

'Thank you all very much. You've all been most helpful. One last question, if I may. Were all of you aware of Mrs Trentham's habit of taking a sleeping draught at bedtime?'

Matt looked around and saw all of them nodding their heads.

'She often spoke of her insomnia. She had suffered from it ever since her husband died. The box from the chemist was next to her bed.' Miss Morrow blinked and pulled out a lace-edged handkerchief to dab at her eyes.

'I see. Thank you.' The inspector closed his notebook and replaced the cap on his pen.

Matt thought he could almost feel the tension in the room dissipate at this action. He was a little surprised that no one there had questioned his presence, but he guessed that it was widely known that he was a private investigator.

Inspector Greville rose from his seat. 'Before we leave, Sir Stanford, would you mind accompanying me to Lady Foxley's study. There are a few questions I should like to ask you about her financial matters. You had offered to assist Mrs Trentham with her affairs, I believe?' Inspector Greville's tone was mild and benign.

'Of course, Inspector. Anything at all that I can do to assist.' Sir Stanford rose and followed the inspector. Matt slipped out of the room after them and they made their way to Lady Foxley's study.

CHAPTER THIRTEEN

Lady Foxley's study was a large square room with dark red walls and matching drapes. Another portrait of a younger Eliza dominated the wall above the Portland stone fireplace. Gilt-framed, it showed Eliza in a more casual pose, sitting on a bench under a tree.

'Splendid picture, done just before her marriage to Lord Foxley,' Sir Stanford said, noting Matt's attention.

The room seemed to reflect Eliza's strong personality. There were two desks. One, in the centre of the room, larger and more ornate, carved in cherry wood. The other, smaller, plainer desk, in the corner, Matt guessed, was where Phillip Peters usually worked. There were a couple of cabinets for papers. Several plush red-leather upholstered chairs with carved frames and button backs. On the mantelpiece were a couple of bronze figures featuring young women in a state of undress and athletic poses.

Sir Stanford looked around the room and sighed before seating himself on one of the easy chairs. 'How may I help you, Inspector?'

'You knew Lady Foxley for many years I believe?' Inspector

Greville dropped into the other chair leaving Matt to take the one behind Peters' desk.

'Yes, both Eliza and Lillie. I first met Eliza not long after her divorce from Lord Foxley, that was a somewhat messy affair. He died only a few weeks after the divorce was finalised and fortunately for Eliza his will still stood. She was a friend of a friend of a friend. You know how these things are. She knew I was a financial advisor and after the war, well, there was a lot of uncertainty, the stock market is an unpredictable beast. She approached me for advice, and I've been assisting her off and on ever since.' Sir Stanford looked unconcerned by the inspector's question.

'Lady Foxley was quite knowledgeable on such things herself, I understand?' Inspector Greville had taken out his notebook once more.

Sir Stanford steepled the tips of his fingers together. 'Yes. She always took a keen interest in her money. Over time she learned a great deal about the markets. She made many of the decisions on where to invest herself. I only advised her from time to time, at her request.'

Matt could tell that Sir Stanford was already preparing some kind of escape clause. By saying that it was Eliza's choice on where to invest, then no blame could come his way if Hemmings was right about the dodgy dealing and money laundering. After all, with Eliza dead, she couldn't contradict him.

'And you have offered Mrs Trentham your assistance too?' Inspector Greville asked.

Sir Stanford smiled complacently. 'Lillie has never been as financially astute as Eliza. Her husband left her very badly off when he died. If it had not been for Eliza's generosity to her and Caroline, then they would have almost certainly been left destitute.'

Inspector Greville's next words echoed Matt's own

thoughts. 'Lady Foxley was very generous towards her sister and her niece.'

'Yes, she was. They've lived with her ever since Lillie's husband died. Eliza paid for all of Caroline's schooling, and Miss Morrow's wages. She spared no expense on the girl. Of course, there were certain rumours...' Sir Stanford paused as if suddenly aware that he may have said too much.

Matt saw Inspector Greville's moustache twitch and a gleam enter the policeman's eyes.

'Rumours, sir?'

Sir Stanford looked uncomfortable. A ruddy tinge had entered his cheeks. 'It was all years ago, when Caroline was little. Probably nothing in it, nothing at all.'

'As you say, sir, probably nothing, but I would like to hear this rumour.' The inspector's tone was firm, and Matt sat up straighter in his seat. He wished Kitty could be there to listen to all of this.

The tinge in Sir Stanford's cheeks grew deeper and he hemmed and hawed before continuing his tale.

'Well, as I said, Inspector, this is just all hearsay, and one doesn't care to repeat gossip. I only heard a whisper of it myself after I'd known Eliza and the rest of the family for quite a few years.' He paused and looked at Inspector Greville before flicking his gaze towards Matt.

'I assure you, sir, anything you say to me will remain confidential. I can speak for Captain Bryant on this matter too. If the information turns out not to be true or pertinent to the case, it will be disregarded.'

The inspector's words seemed to reassure Sir Stanford and he nodded before continuing his story.

'As I mentioned before, there was considerable scandal around the time of Lady Foxley's divorce. He was much older than her and, well, she didn't marry him for love. There were stories of dalliances with other men and wild partying. Around the time that the divorce came through Eliza dropped off the map for some time, socially I mean. It was thought she had done it to let the dust settle, so to speak.' Sir Stanford paused again.

Matt could see the man was lost in his thoughts, clearly trying to get his story straight.

'An understandable move after such a big scandal,' Inspector Greville murmured encouragingly.

'Indeed, no one quite knew where Eliza had gone, some said France, others said Italy or New York. During that time, Lillie gave birth to Caroline. She and her husband had been married for a few years by then. At least, it was claimed that Lillie was Caro's mother.' Sir Stanford met the inspector's gaze.

'You mean Caroline is Lady Foxley's child?' Inspector Greville asked.

Matt took in a breath. He had not been expecting this twist to the morning's events.

'Yes, the story goes that the baby was hers by the man she had been seeing while still married to Lord Foxley. It was the timing I think, Eliza vanished for some six months or so and reappeared after her sister had Caroline. Eliza was a complicated woman, she never cared about conventions for herself. The scandal surrounding the divorce never seemed to touch her and she was very wealthy. She did love her sister though and she has always loved Caroline,' Sir Stanford mused.

'Foxley died you said, didn't he? Just after the divorce and he hadn't changed his will, so Eliza inherited quite a substantial amount of money both in her settlement and then as a beneficiary of his will.' The inspector tapped the end of his pen thoughtfully on his notebook.

Sir Stanford nodded once more. 'Yes, she got the whole kit and caboodle. Houses, money, stocks, jewellery. Foxley didn't have any other family. A distant cousin in Africa, I believe, that's all.'

Matt wondered who the father of Caroline might be if Sir

Stanford's story was true. Was there an unknown person lurking in the shadows after all? Someone who knew both sisters and had somehow discovered he had a daughter? Someone who would want to take revenge for keeping Caroline's birth a secret from him? It was an interesting possibility.

'Do you think either Caroline or Miss Morrow are aware of these rumours?' Inspector Greville asked.

Sir Stanford leaned back in his chair and relaxed his hands. 'The girl, I would say not. Eliza and Lillie would make very sure that no whisper of scandal would touch her. Miss Morrow has known Eliza and Lillie since they were girls. She was with Eliza I believe around the time Caroline was born and went to Lillie straight afterwards. Actually, if anyone knows the truth of it all then it's probably Miss Morrow.'

Matt thought that explained a great deal if it were true. Tiny's protective attitude towards the girl. Eliza's directions to her sister about Caroline's schooling. It sounded as if Miss Morrow would have more questions to answer.

Was it relevant to Lady Foxley's death or Lillie's poisoning however? That was another matter altogether.

'Thank you, Sir Stanford. I think I should speak to Miss Morrow. If you would be so good as to ask her to come here?' Inspector Greville finished his note.

Sir Stanford rose and went to exit the study.

'Oh, and by the by, if you would continue to remain here at the villa until after the case is closed, I would be most grateful,' the inspector said.

Sir Stanford paused, his hand on the ornate brass door handle. 'Of course, Inspector.'

Once he had gone Matt stood and paced about the room to stretch his legs. 'That was a turn up for the books.'

'Indeed, it was. Let us see what Miss Morrow is prepared to tell us on the matter,' the inspector remarked drily.

Matt had just retaken his seat when the belligerent form of Miss Morrow entered the study.

'Sir Stanford said that you wished to see me, Inspector. I feel that I really must protest. I've already told you everything that I know, and Miss Trentham needs me to stay with her. She's just lost her aunt, and her mother has been poisoned. The poor girl is terrified that she might be next.' The woman wrung her hands together as she took the seat recently vacated by Sir Stanford.

'I understand your concerns, Miss Morrow, but information has recently come to light of a rather delicate nature. I wanted to ask you about the matter privately.' Inspector Greville looked at the woman.

Miss Morrow's hands shook, and she pressed them together to hide the tremor. 'I don't think I follow you, Inspector.'

Matt saw a wary look flash across the woman's face as she spoke. Had she guessed what the questions might be about?

'Miss Morrow, you were engaged originally by Lady Foxley and Mrs Trentham's parents when they were young?' Matt thought Inspector Greville had noticed the change in Miss Morrow's demeanour too and was clearly going to take a softer approach to get to the truth.

'Yes, sir, that's right. Eliza was thirteen and Lillie was ten. Their mother was a delicate lady with poor health and their father travelled a great deal with his business. I've been with Eliza and Lillie ever since.' Miss Morrow raised her chin proudly. 'They gave me the nickname Tiny, it was a bit of a joke, since clearly I've never been tiny in my life. My mother said as I were ten pounds when I was born.' She smiled at the memory and Matt could see her guard had dropped a little.

'You remained with them even after Eliza married Lord Foxley, and Lillie married Mr Trentham?' Inspector Greville had resumed his note-taking.

'I went with Lillie as she were younger than Eliza and, well,

Lady Foxley's manner of living was not very respectable at that time.' Miss Morrow pursed her lips in disapproval.

The inspector nodded. 'Yet you returned to be with Lady Foxley after her divorce when she was living more quietly for a while?'

Miss Morrow stiffened. 'Yes, we were in the South of France. She was very distressed by the divorce and needed some support. He treated her terrible he did, it wasn't a love match, but Eliza tried her best to make it work. It were no wonder she needed company after it all ended.'

Matt's eyebrows rose slightly at this fudging of Lady Foxley's affairs.

'Miss Morrow, I think you know what I am about to ask you and before you say anything it is imperative that I know the truth. Eliza is dead and Lillie's life hangs in the balance. I don't know if what happened all those years ago has any bearing on the matter, but it may, and I need to investigate fully. Anything you do say will go no further than this room if it has no bearing on what has happened.' Inspector Greville held the woman's gaze.

She stared at the inspector for a moment and then looked at Matt.

'As the inspector has just said. Whatever you tell us will remain confidential and will go no further,' Matt spoke for the first time.

A single tear escaped and ran down one of Tiny's plump cheeks. 'I think you already know but when Lord Foxley divorced Eliza she discovered she was with child. Obviously, it weren't Lord Foxley's. They had been living separate lives for quite some time by then.' The woman halted to blow her nose before continuing.

'Eliza sent word to me asking me if I would come to her. She had rented a house in France under another name and was living quietly. No one there knew who she was, it was a tiny village at the foot of the mountains. Lillie put it about that Eliza had gone to America. The only people who knew were me, Lillie and Lillie's husband.' Tiny gave another sniff.

'Lillie and her husband took the child?' Inspector Greville asked gently.

Tiny nodded. 'Lillie had been pregnant at the same time, but she lost her baby early on. The doctor told her as she wouldn't be able to have another. She almost died, she haemorrhaged and they had to operate to save her. It sent her into so much despair.' Tiny shook her head and dabbed at the tears now coursing freely down her face. 'Eliza's baby seemed like the answer to a prayer at the time. Lord Foxley died, and Eliza inherited everything as he hadn't changed his will. She were named in it, you see. All Eliza wanted was to see her sister happy and for the baby to have a good life. She knew as Lillie could do that better than her, so they made an arrangement.'

'So, Lillie became Caroline's mother,' Matt murmured. He could see how it had all played out.

Tiny nodded. 'That's right. Lillie came to stay with Eliza when Caroline was born. The doctor didn't speak much English and he didn't know that the woman he examined wasn't Lillie. The baby was registered in Lillie's name. Hubert, Lillie's husband, went along with it all as he could see how happy it made Lillie.'

Inspector Greville blinked. 'I see. Does Caroline herself have any inkling at all that her real mother was Eliza?'

Tiny shook her head vigorously. 'No, none whatsoever. When Lillie took Caroline, she made Eliza promise as she were never to tell her. It was her one condition.'

'Then a few years later Mr Trentham died,' Inspector Greville said.

Tiny gulped and scrubbed at her face with her now sodden handkerchief. 'Yes, sir. It was terrible. They were a happy little family. He doted on Lillie and on Caroline. Nobody seeing them all together wouldn't have known as she weren't his baby. He adored her. She were the apple of his eye. It hit her hard when he was killed.'

'And so Eliza stepped back in.' Inspector Greville continued to make notes.

'Yes. She had always visited. You know, bringing presents. A fancy doll's house, pretty dresses, a pony.' Tiny shook her head more gently, her mouth softening. 'Then when it became clear as Mr Trentham had left nothing but debts behind him, she came to Lillie's rescue. She helped her to set up the charity and paid off Lillie's debts. They came to live here and travelled with her wherever she went.'

'How did Lillie feel about that?' Inspector Greville asked.

Matt wondered the same thing. The two sisters were very different. It must have been hard for Lillie having to trail along after her hedonistic older sister and be incumbent financially upon her. The child she had been raising now suddenly back under the influence of her real mother despite their agreement at her birth.

Had Lillie killed her sister and taken poison herself in a fit of remorse? It was a possibility he supposed.

'On the whole they were all right about it all. They had disagreements, of course, as any siblings would do, and then Lillie would often stay here with me and Caroline when Eliza were off gallivanting.' Miss Morrow gave a defiant sniff.

The inspector sighed and paused for a moment in his writing. 'One more thing, Miss Morrow, Caroline's father, did Lady Foxley ever say who he was?'

Tiny's mouth clamped into a thin, disapproving line. 'Married, that's what he was. Italian, some count or prince. He had a fancy title and a slick tongue. He also had a wife and three children. There was no chance as he were ever going to marry Eliza. She was divorced and he were catholic.'

'Did he know about the child?' Inspector Greville asked.

Tiny wiped her nose again. 'Eliza told him as she lost it. I think as he were glad. His wife had found out you see, and, well, there were a parting of the ways between him and Eliza.'

That rather scuppered his idea that an unknown man could be wreaking revenge on the sisters for concealing the truth of Caroline's birth, Matt thought.

Miss Morrow dabbed at her eyes one more time before tucking her handkerchief away. 'Will that be all, Inspector? I really do want to be with Miss Caroline now.' The woman got to her feet ready to leave.

'Before you go, Miss Morrow, I must ask again, does Caroline herself have any idea at all about the circumstances surrounding her birth?' The inspector looked at the governess.

'No, not all,' Tiny replied firmly.

She sounded very certain, but Matt wondered if she was actually right. Caroline seemed like the kind of girl who uncovered secrets.

Miss Morrow walked to the study door before turning to face the inspector one more time. 'And don't you tell her anything. Some things are best left.'

The door clicked shut behind her and the inspector set down his pen once more.

CHAPTER FOURTEEN

Kitty secured Bertie firmly on the back seat of her car whilst her father took his place, somewhat glumly, in the passenger seat at the front. With the dog safely fastened in, Kitty took her own seat behind the wheel.

'Brr, it's quite nippy today,' she said as she pulled away and set off on the drive towards Exeter.

'I expect you would rather have accompanied the inspector to Eliza's house,' her father observed as she increased her speed on an open stretch of road.

'We're fortunate that he has allowed Matt to go with him. But, yes, you're right, I would have liked to know what questions were being asked.' Kitty glanced across at her father.

'I wish I knew who killed her, and who could have possibly harmed Lillie. Lillie is simply not the kind of person who would harm a fly. It all seems so incredible,' Edgar mused as the car sped along the country road. The ploughed fields were bare and empty, the rich red soil contrasting with the grey of the sky and the green of animal pasture.

'At least the inspector does not seem to think you were involved in poisoning Lillie. That must strengthen the case for you not having harmed Lady Foxley. It seems to me as if there must be more people in the picture now,' Kitty said as she manoeuvred neatly around a slow-moving horse and cart.

Her father seemed to brighten slightly at this. 'Yes, I suppose every cloud has a silver lining and all that. I do hope Lillie recovers. She may be able to shed some light on the matter.'

Kitty hoped so too. 'It must be very hard on Caroline, she's so young, and to have two people close to her harmed, it's quite dreadful.'

Edgar nodded. 'Yes, and she was very close to Eliza. They were kindred spirits in many ways. Caro has quite a rebellious streak, unlike Lillie who is the epitome of respectability.' He chuckled to himself.

Kitty smiled and glanced his way once more. 'What is amusing you?' she asked.

'I was recalling Eliza and Caroline on board the ship. They had been up to some prank or other, playing a trick on poor Tiny. Lillie was not amused. Those two were giggling away all through her scolding.' He shook his head ruefully. 'Eliza was so full of life, such a warm, vital person. I can't believe she's gone.'

'It does seem impossible,' Kitty agreed. Lady Foxley had seemed so vivacious when they had met her on the evening of the ball.

'I'm sorry things have all become so complicated, my darling girl. You have enough on your mind with the wedding without having to play nursemaid to me.' Edgar gave her a tender smile.

Kitty focused on the road and the traffic ahead as they drew nearer to the outskirts of the city. 'It's quite all right. The inspector and Matt will work out who really did it. Just, please stay out of any more trouble between now and Christmas Eve.'

Her father chuckled once more, his laughter rumbling in his chest. 'I shall do my very best, darling.'

Kitty focused on navigating her way through the city streets to the small side street near the cathedral where Father Lamb lived. Everywhere was busier than usual with people shopping at the Christmas market on the green and purchasing last-minute gifts from the shops on the main street.

She managed to find a space further along the street and parked her car at the kerb.

'That was lucky,' she said as she hopped out to retrieve Bertie from the back seat.

Her father got out and stood looking at the hustle and bustle all around him. 'It's been a few years now since I was last here. It brings back so many memories of your mother and me and, of course, Jack.'

Kitty tucked her free hand in the crook of his arm. 'Come and meet Father Lamb, he was a good friend to Jack Dawkins right to the end.'

Jack Dawkins had been the man who had held the clue to what had happened to Kitty's mother back in the summer of 1916. Jack and her father had been close for many years when her father had been younger. Father Lamb had cared for Jack when he was dying and had proved a good friend since then to both Kitty and her grandmother.

Father Lamb's housekeeper beamed at them as she opened the door of the presbytery.

'Good morning, Miss Underhay, Father is expecting you. Go on through to the sitting room, 'tis nice and warm in there.' The plump elderly lady collected their outdoor things and showed them through to the Father's comfortable, if slightly shabby, front room.

'Kitty, my dear, welcome, welcome, and this gentleman must be your father.' Father Lamb's elderly face was wreathed in a kindly smile. 'I was delighted to receive your telephone call, my dear.' He kissed Kitty's cheek and shook hands with Edgar.

A Christmas tree stood on top of a dark-red chenille cloth on a table in the window and every available surface was covered with greeting cards. A small fire crackled in the grate. Bertie wagged his tail happily as he greeted the priest before settling down with a sigh to one side of the fireplace.

The housekeeper reappeared bearing a tray heavily laden with tea things and slices of home-made gingerbread and mince pies.

'Now, my dear, come and make yourselves comfortable and tell me about your wedding plans.' The priest smiled happily as the housekeeper set down the tray and took her leave back to the kitchen.

They spent the next hour discussing the plans for Christmas Eve and Kitty told the priest of the events at Villa Lamora. His expression grew grave when Edgar told him of his own arrest and Lillie's subsequent poisoning.

'Oh dear, and you say that Inspector Greville and Captain Bryant are there now?' he asked.

'Yes, hopefully they will be able to determine who really killed Eliza and why.' Kitty savoured her slice of gingerbread. Father Lamb's housekeeper was an excellent cook.

Father Lamb continued to appear troubled as he sipped his tea and Kitty sensed there was something else weighing on his mind.

'Is there something bothering you, Father?' she asked as she slipped Bertie a tiny sliver of gingerbread.

The priest cast a worried glance first at her father and then at Kitty. 'I was in two minds whether to say anything to you, my dear.'

'What about?' Kitty frowned, a little taken aback by her friend's statement.

Father Lamb placed his cup back on its saucer. 'I was out at a carol concert last night and ran across some other old friends of yours. You'll recall the two young boys who aided you when you ventured into the cellar of the Glass Bottle public house when you were looking for your mother?'

Kitty nodded. She remembered the two boys well and had sent them and their family small Christmas gifts last year to thank them for their help. 'Yes, of course.'

Father Lamb leaned forward in his seat. 'The boys were at the service with their mother. They told me that there are lots of rumours on the streets of the city that Esther Hammett is back. They had heard, of course, what had happened to her brother and how her son had been arrested.'

Kitty's pulse speeded up and she looked at her father for support. 'I thought the police were looking for her after she fled last month?' She still had a couple of sores on her feet from the events of that particular evening.

Father Lamb nodded gravely. 'That's true. I was very troubled by what the boys said so I telephoned the police station this morning and spoke to Inspector Pinch.'

Kitty remembered Inspector Pinch well. He was stationed in the city and had come across the Hammetts and their cohorts many times in the past. She knew he would be very keen to capture Esther.

'Was he aware of this woman having returned to Exeter?' Edgar asked.

Father Lamb sighed and absent-mindedly brushed a few crumbs of pastry from the front of his black cassock. 'He was somewhat evasive initially, but when I pressed him on the matter he said there had been some unconfirmed sightings of her near the waterfront.'

Bertie snuffled noisily around the priest's feet to lick the crumbs from the rug.

'That is quite troubling news if it turns out to be true, Father.' Edgar had been made fully aware by Kitty of all her dealings with Esther in the past. Including the one only a few weeks ago when Esther's son had kidnapped Kitty and she had barely escaped with her life.

'Indeed. I wasn't certain if I should say anything. It is after

all merely a rumour. The sightings have not been verified and
there is no reason to suppose she would venture anywhere near
Dartmouth. Or indeed, near you, Kitty, my dear.' The priest still
seemed troubled, however.

'Thank you for telling me, Father. I would rather know,
even if it is just a rumour. I shall stay on my guard. We all know
that Esther is capable of anything, and she holds sway over quite
a large number of criminals in this area,' Kitty said.

The priest seemed relieved by her reply. 'Just remain alert,
my dear. It may well all merely be just idle gossip, but it is
better to be safe.'

They changed the subject back onto happier matters with a
discussion of Christmas and Kitty and Matt's plans. Before they
knew it the housekeeper called them into the small dining room
for lunch and Esther had almost been forgotten.

After a delicious lunch of omelettes with fried potatoes and
vegetables, followed by a raspberry mousse, Kitty and her father
made their farewells. Kitty promised that she and Matt would
call in the new year and there would be an invitation for Father
Lamb to dine with them once Kitty was settled at Matt's house.

Back out on the city streets, Kitty tucked her hand back into
the crook of her father's arm and prepared to set off along the
road towards her car. Bertie trotted along on his lead at her side.

'Kitty, darling, would it distress you very much if we were to
go to the site of this Glass Bottle public house? I know you told
me it was not far from where Jack once had his shop. If it's too
upsetting for you then, obviously, we won't go. It's just I would
like to see for myself where your mother was found.' Edgar
looked down at her, the brim of his hat shading his eyes so she
couldn't fully read his expression.

Kitty swallowed. She hadn't wished to ever return to the
place where she had finally discovered the truth behind her
mother's disappearance, but she could understand her father's
need to see it.

'No, of course we can go. Although Father Lamb told me that the Glass Bottle itself has now been pulled down. The ruins were quite unstable after the fire.' She fell into step beside her father, and they turned off along the narrow back streets into the poorer area of the city.

Edgar was silent as they made their way past the row of shopfronts where Jack Dawkin's emporium had once stood. The streets were busy with people making their preparations for Christmas. Bertie walked along happily sniffing for interesting scents in every shop doorway.

Kitty couldn't help keeping a watchful eye out for any possible sign that Esther Hammett might be lurking in the narrow lanes. Eventually they reached the corner where the Glass Bottle public house had once stood.

The last time Kitty had seen it the walls had been marked with soot, the windows boarded, and half the roof had been missing. Now the corner plot stood empty. The only sign that a building had once been there was the fragments of brick that littered the ground, barely visible amongst the overgrowth of weeds and brambles.

'It was here.' Kitty shivered as she paused beside her father. Bertie sat obediently at her side.

Her father stood looking at the site for a long moment before covering her gloved hand where it rested on his arm with his own. 'Thank you, my dear, for showing this to me. I know how difficult this must be for you.'

'We should start back for Dartmouth. Aunt Livvy will be arriving soon from Scotland,' Kitty said. Bertie's tail wagged as if in agreement that they should start walking again.

Her father nodded his head slowly. 'Yes, it's time to let go of the past I think.' He gave Kitty a wan smile, and she knew the visit to the site had affected him deeply.

They made their way through the city to where Kitty had left her car and then set off on the return journey to Dartmouth.

Kitty hoped that Matt might have some news for them by the time they arrived at the Dolphin. She longed to know what he had managed to discover during his visit to Villa Lamora with the inspector.

Kitty parked her car near the hotel. There seemed little point in garaging it since she would need to take her father and Bertie back to Matt's home after tea.

'Kitty, my dear, I wonder, I feel a little awkward about coming to tea with your grandmother and her sister. Would you mind very much if I were to take a walk to the church to visit your mother's grave and return in a little while?' her father asked as she unfastened Bertie from the back seat of her car.

Kitty hesitated for a second. She knew that she was supposed to keep her father with her until the inspector agreed that he was no longer a suspect in Lady Foxley's murder. She also knew that relations between her beloved Grams and Edgar were not good.

'Here, take Bertie with you. It will stop him from begging for titbits under the tea table. You know where to go at the church?' she asked.

Edgar took the dog's lead. 'Yes, thank you, my dear. I think I'll call at the florists on the way. It feels right after visiting Exeter today.'

Kitty stood on her tiptoes to kiss his cheek. 'I'll see you shortly then.'

She watched him walk away with Bertie before turning to enter the hotel lobby. If he had the dog with him then he couldn't get into too much trouble, surely. Even so, she couldn't shake the sense of unease that had enveloped her.

She was about to enter the hotel when she bumped straight into Alice, who was on her way out.

'Oh, Miss Kitty, Mr Lutterworth was just looking for you. Your aunt Livvy is here and you'm wanted upstairs,' Alice said.

Her friend had changed out of her hotel uniform and Kitty guessed that she was off home. A sudden thought hit her.

'Alice are you free for a few minutes now?' Kitty asked urgently.

'I were just off home, miss. Why?' Alice asked.

Kitty blushed. 'I hardly even know how to ask this; you will think me quite mad. My father has just gone off with Bertie. He says he intends to call at the florist and then to visit my mother's grave at Saint Saviour's.' Kitty stopped as realisation dawned on Alice's face.

'You want me to follow him, miss? Like they do in the pictures?'

'Well, yes, oh, I don't know. It's a dreadful thing not feeling as if one can trust one's own father.' Kitty wrung her hands.

Alice snorted. 'They don't have a father like you have. Last time he came to visit he almost got you both killed over that stolen ruby business. Leave it with me, miss.' Alice crammed her hat further down on her head to ensure that all of her auburn curls were hidden. Before Kitty could prevent her, the girl hurried away down the street, a determined expression on her thin face.

Kitty sighed. She hoped she was doing the right thing.

CHAPTER FIFTEEN

Upon leaving the villa Inspector Greville provided Matt with a lift into Torquay. Matt had then taken a taxi back to his home in Churston. He was unsurprised to be informed by his housekeeper that Kitty and her father had gone out with Bertie.

'Miss Kitty said as they were calling on a friend for luncheon in Exeter and then going back to the Dolphin as her aunt is expected there at teatime,' his housekeeper informed him. 'She's taken that blessed dog with her too.'

Matt grinned at the note of relief in his housekeeper's voice that Bertie had accompanied Kitty. 'Thank you. I'll take my motorcycle and ride over myself.'

He swapped his thick woollen overcoat for the long brown-leather coat he wore when riding his Sunbeam and swapped his hat for a well-fitting cap. He knew that Kitty's grandmother was expecting them both for tea. If Edgar was attending as well then Kitty would need all the support he could give her.

Inspector Greville had promised to let him know of any new developments in the case or if Lillie's health were to improve enough to tell them anything. It seemed the woman was lucky to have survived the attempt made against her. He halted his motorcycle near the hotel and saw that Kitty's little red car was already at the kerb.

'Captain Bryant, good afternoon. Kitty is upstairs with her grandmother and her guests,' Mr Lutterworth greeted him as soon as he entered the hotel lobby.

'Thank you.' Matt drew off his leather gauntlets and stowed them in the capacious pockets of his coat before taking the stairs to Kitty's grandmother's salon.

The murmur of female voices reached him as he raised his hand and tapped on the door of Mrs Treadwell's apartment. On hearing her call out to enter, he opened the door. Mrs Treadwell was seated on one armchair beside the fireplace and her sister, a slightly younger version of Kitty's grandmother, occupied the opposite chair. Kitty was seated on the sofa beside Mrs Craven. Of Edgar and Bertie there was no sign at all.

'Matt, do take off your cap and coat and come and join us.' Kitty jumped up from her seat and crossed over to greet him.

'Where is Edgar?' Matt murmured as she took his coat ready to hang it on the hooks near the door.

'He's out walking Bertie to the churchyard. Don't worry, Alice is keeping an eye on him,' Kitty assured him.

Matt frowned at this unexpected piece of information, but with the ladies waiting to greet him he felt he couldn't really pursue the matter.

'Kitty said you were with Inspector Greville at Eliza Foxley's house. Has he apprehended the real murderer yet?' Mrs Craven asked as soon as he had greeted them all and taken his seat beside Kitty.

'He has a number of promising leads.' Matt was cautious in his reply. The inspector had gone back to the police station to see what Roger Hemmings had made of the documents they had retrieved from Lady Foxley's safe. If Hemmings' ideas were correct, then Sir Stanford would definitely be a suspect. As, indeed, was Miss Morrow.

Mrs Craven looked doubtful when she heard this. 'Really, the inspector needs to hurry things along before someone else is killed. My maid informed me this lunchtime that Lillie Trentham was in the cottage hospital with a policeman outside her door. Apparently, she was taken in urgently during the night. The doctor attended her in his pyjamas.' Mrs Craven nodded sagely at him, the diamonds in the brooch on her lapel twinkled in the light from the fire in the hearth.

Kitty gave him an apologetic look mixed with amusement. It always amazed him how quickly news travelled in the town. He should have guessed that the news had reached Mrs C by now.

'Mrs Trentham was indeed taken ill unexpectedly last night.' He accepted a mince pie from the laden tea trolley standing next to the coffee table.

'I heard that it was poison,' Mrs Craven said. 'My maid's sister is a nurse at the hospital.'

'You know that I really cannot say anything in that regard, Mrs C,' Matt said.

'Which means, of course, that I'm right.' Mrs Craven smiled smugly.

'That would at least put your father in the clear I suppose, Kitty darling. Your grandmother and Mrs Craven have kindly told me about everything that has happened.' Kitty's aunt smiled at Kitty.

'One would think so,' Kitty agreed.

'Who else could have killed Eliza? Or have wanted to harm Lillie?' Mrs Craven mused before chewing and swallowing a bite of fruit cake.

'That is the question the inspector is asking, Mrs C.' Matt smiled at her.

'I hope he sorts it out before Edgar walks you down the aisle, Kitty dear. One doesn't want a scandal hanging over your head on your wedding day.' Mrs Craven tutted.

Matt was glad that Kitty's aunt and uncle weren't present to hear that particular declaration. Kitty's cousin Lucy's own wedding day had almost been marred by murder during the summer.

'Speaking of Edgar, where is my no-good son-in-law?' Kitty's grandmother asked, looking at Matt and Kitty.

'Father should be joining us shortly; he has taken Bertie for a walk. We have been in Exeter having lunch with Father Lamb. I dropped him off just before I came home as he wished to place some flowers on mother's grave,' Kitty replied.

Mrs Craven exchanged a glance laden with meaning with Kitty's grandmother. Her aunt Livvy remained tactfully silent on the matter.

'Your parents' rooms and one for your aunt are all prepared for tomorrow, Matthew, dear. Rupert and Lucy are expected tomorrow too. By Saturday we shall have quite the party ready for the wedding,' Mrs Treadwell said as she placed her empty cake plate back on the trolley.

'Thank you, it's very kind of you to offer them accommodation and to host them for Christmas.' Matt knew his parents had mixed feelings about his marriage to Kitty. They were old friends of her grandmother but disliked Kitty's modern attitude and her youth. Then again, they had not approved of Edith, his first wife either.

Conversation continued about the wedding and the final dress fittings planned for the next day for both Kitty and Lucy as her matron of honour. Matt saw Kitty taking surreptitious peeps at the time on the clock on the mantelpiece. He guessed she was wondering where her father could have gone.

He was about to suggest to Kitty that he should walk out to find Edgar when the telephone rang.

Kitty jumped from her seat to answer it. 'Thank you, Cyril. Yes, of course. Matt and I will be right down.' She looked at Matt as she replaced the receiver back on the stand.

'Father is downstairs with Bertie. He says he won't come up

if you don't mind as the dog is rather dirty. He found a muddy puddle in the churchyard.'

Matt placed his cup down on the trolley. 'Thank you for a lovely tea. We had better go and deal with Bertie.' He collected his coat and cap as Kitty picked up her outdoor things and they left the room together after completing their farewells.

'I wouldn't have thought there was much standing water in the churchyard. It's on a hill and quite well drained,' Matt said to Kitty as he tugged on his coat as they walked down the stairs.

Kitty's eyebrows raised. 'You know Bertie. He can get into mischief anywhere.'

Matt laughed. 'Much like Edgar.'

Kitty grinned back at him and gave him a playful poke in his ribs as they reached the bottom of the stairs.

Bertie did indeed look rather woeful. He was seated next to Edgar in front of the reception desk. Cyril had thoughtfully spread out an old newspaper for the dog to sit on. A wise precaution given the amount of mud that seemed to be adhering to Bertie's coat.

The dog thumped his tail enthusiastically against the floor as Kitty and Matt approached. This caused Edgar to skip back a step to avoid the mud spatters generated by Bertie's greeting.

'Oh my goodness. Whatever happened?' Kitty stared horrified at the unrepentant Bertie.

'A squirrel and a large, muddy puddle.' Her father looked at the spaniel in distaste.

'We had better take you home for a bath.' Matt looked at his dog. 'Kitty, do you still have those old towels in the car?'

Kitty sighed. 'Yes, I'll spread them on the seats if you'll walk him out.' It was a little annoying sometimes that Matt was unable to transport his dog himself. She had suggested a sidecar for his motorcycle but the horrified expression on his face had silenced any further mention of such a thing.

Edgar handed the leash to Matt and started to examine the

legs of his trousers for mud. Kitty rolled her eyes in despair, and after thanking Cyril for his help, they set off towards her car. As she prepared the rear leather seat ready for Bertie she wondered if Alice had followed Edgar. Had he been to her mother's grave? Or had he been elsewhere?

With Bertie safely secured in the back of the car, a slightly chastened looking Edgar took his place on the passenger seat. Kitty started her car and waited for Matt to pull out ahead of her on the Sunbeam.

'Honestly, he looks as if he's wallowed in the creek rather than in a puddle. He certainly smells badly enough.' Kitty's nose crinkled as the odour of damp dog reached them from the rear seat.

'I'm sorry, my dear. He just saw the dashed squirrel and took off,' Edgar explained. Kitty gave him a sharp glance as she prepared to follow Matt onto the ferry to cross the river. She knew Bertie could still be naughty but how he could get into that state when he was supposed to be on his lead under her father's control, she had no idea.

When they arrived at Matt's house he quickly told her about the revelations of Caroline's parentage. Kitty was surprised but unable to discuss it further as she needed to return to the Dolphin in time to change and dress for dinner with her grandmother and her aunt. She left both Bertie and her father to Matt.

'I'll be over tomorrow, darling.' Matt kissed her farewell. 'My parents and aunt Effie are due tomorrow evening.'

Kitty wasn't much looking forward to seeing his parents again, and his aunt Effie was slightly terrifying. 'I have a dress fitting tomorrow afternoon with Lucy. It'll be nice to see her and Rupert again. It's a shame my aunt and uncle couldn't have come tomorrow too.' She glanced at her father as she spoke.

Edgar's relationship with his sister was strained to say the least and her uncle frequently muttered vague threats about bringing his shotgun when her father's name was mentioned. She suspected that her father was as reluctant to spend time with his sister as Kitty was to see Matt's family.

The dinner her grandmother had planned for them all tomorrow night would certainly prove interesting. Still at least her father was no longer in a prison cell. She supposed that was one good thing.

Alice knocked on her bedroom door early the following morning. Kitty was still rather sleepy from dinner with her grandmother and aunt the night before. Her aunt had insisted on opening a bottle of champagne to celebrate Kitty and Matt's upcoming marriage and it had been late when they had finally retired to bed.

'I followed Mr Underhay,' Alice said as she placed the breakfast tray on Kitty's bedside table with what Kitty considered an unnecessary amount of noise.

Kitty rubbed the sleep from her eyes and sat herself up as Alice whisked about the room, tidying up before opening the curtains to a dull, grey day.

'Bertie was in a terrible state when he arrived back here yesterday. The poor dog looked as if he had taken a mud bath in the creek.' She adjusted her pillows behind her shoulders and made space for Alice to perch on the bed beside her.

Alice poured Kitty a cup of tea before producing her own mug from her apron pocket and helping herself to a drink. 'That's because he did go in the creek,' she said drily.

Kitty blinked at her friend over the rim of her china teacup. Any guilt she had been feeling at asking her friend to follow her father dissipated immediately. The florist and the church were nowhere near the river.

'Where did he go?' Kitty asked. She was suddenly much more awake.

Alice took a sip of her tea and continued her tale. 'I followed behind him for a good way. I hung well back, hiding in the doorways, like they do in the films as he shouldn't see me. He did go to the florist first, on the way like, and bought some red roses. Then he went to the church and put them on the grave.'

Kitty frowned. 'So far, so good. At least he told me the truth about that part.'

'Well, I were going to just go home then as I thought as he would go straight back to the Dolphin, only...' Alice took another sip of her drink.

'Where did he go?' Kitty's pulse was racing. She knew her father well enough to know he had not just decided to go Christmas shopping.

'He went the other way, down round by the market and out to the other side of town,' Alice said.

Kitty knew where her friend meant. That area of the town was much poorer and there were several hostelries there that had a less than savoury reputation. 'Oh, Alice, you didn't go there, did you?' She was concerned she might have placed her friend at risk in some way.

'He went in the first public house, but he weren't inside more'n a couple of minutes. Then he come back out and started walking down toward the creek, but away from the town. I had to duck inside the ironmongers for a minute as he shouldn't see me.' Alice looked pleased at her quick thinking.

'Goodness, Alice, whatever was he up to?' Obviously it was nothing good, Kitty decided.

'I lost him for a minute then realised as he were down by the riverbank at the water's edge. I couldn't get close else he would have seen me. I had to pretend to look at some meat in the butcher's window and try to see the reflection in the plate glass,' Alice explained.

'What was he doing?' Kitty was confused. Why hadn't her

father returned to the hotel? She supposed he could have been avoiding her grandmother and aunt for a little longer, but then why had he visited a public house? He hadn't been inside long enough to have a drink.

'I were about to give up and go home. I thought as perhaps he didn't wish to take tea with your grandmother,' Alice echoed her thoughts. 'Then, as I were about to go this man shows up. A bit scruffy and shifty like. He sidled up to your father and Edgar gives him something from his pocket.'

'I presume this was when Bertie decided the river looked more interesting than whatever my father was up to,' Kitty said with a sigh.

Alice nodded, her auburn curls escaping from under her cap. 'The man had scarce took a step away when Bertie made a dash for a duck that come a-paddling past.'

'Thank you, Alice. I think I have a good idea what my father may have been doing.' Kitty drained her teacup and placed it back on its saucer. She would confront her father at some point, but for now she decided she had enough going on without arguing with Edgar.

Alice's brow cleared as the girl realised what Kitty meant. 'I suppose as there is bound to be racing this close to Christmas.'

'Exactly.' Kitty sighed. 'Now, Lucy is arriving this afternoon and we are going for the final dress fittings.' She wished Alice would have agreed to be her bridesmaid, but her friend had been very firm in her idea that it wasn't proper for a chamber-maid to stand next to a titled lady in the wedding party.

'I shall be pleased to see your dress and Miss Lucy's.' Alice smiled happily at her.

'Perhaps it might be your turn next, Alice. I shall have to make sure you are close by when I throw the bouquet,' Kitty teased. Alice had been walking out with Robert Potter for quite some time now. She knew from things that Dolly had let slip that Alice had started to collect items for her bottom drawer.

'I don't think as that will be for some time, miss. Robert is building his business up first,' Alice remarked primly, although a faint blush had appeared on her cheeks.

Kitty smiled back and refrained from teasing her friend any further. 'I just want my father to stay out of trouble and Inspector Greville to catch whoever killed Lady Foxley and poisoned Lillie before the wedding. I'll feel much easier walking down the aisle knowing the inspector is there as a guest rather than to arrest someone at the church.'

'Let's hope as he has a breakthrough today, miss,' Alice said as she stood and picked up the tea tray.

Kitty hoped her friend was right as the girl went back to her duties leaving Kitty to dress and prepare for the day ahead.

* * *

Matt and Edgar had just finished breakfast when the telephone rang.

''Tis Inspector Greville for you, sir,' Matt's housekeeper announced at the door of the dining room.

'Thank you.' Matt set aside the morning newspaper and went to the telephone in the sitting room.

'Good morning, Inspector, do you have news?' Matt asked as he picked up the receiver from where his housekeeper had placed it beside the telephone.

'Good morning, Captain Bryant, yes indeed. Mrs Trentham is awake. The doctor has said I may speak to her. I've requested that no one at the house is informed of this change in her condition just yet. If she does have any information that might lead to the perpetrator, I do not wish to place her in danger,' the inspector said.

'I understand, sir. May I accompany you? I could meet you at the hospital.' Matt kept his voice low as he was uncertain if

Edgar might be included in the group of people the policeman didn't wish to inform about Lillie waking up.

'Is Mr Underhay with you now?' Inspector Greville asked.

'He is in the dining room. We had just finished breakfast. I can come over on my motorcycle while Edgar remains at the house with Bertie and my housekeeper,' Matt suggested. He knew the inspector did not have to allow him to be present for any of the interviews he conducted so was careful not to sound too forward in his request.

'Very well. I shall set off in the next ten minutes. I'll meet you at the entrance to the hospital,' the inspector agreed.

Matt agreed and replaced the receiver.

'I have to go out for a while. I shouldn't be away very long,' he informed Edgar when he popped back into the dining room.

'A development in the case?' Edgar asked as he fed Bertie the last sausage from the dish.

'The inspector isn't certain. Will you be all right here until I return?' Matt asked.

'Of course, dear boy. I'm sure Bertie and I can amuse ourselves for the morning. Hopefully without involving mud,' Edgar assured him.

Matt hurried away to don his outdoor things and wondered why he didn't feel very reassured by his future father-in-law's words.

CHAPTER SIXTEEN

Matt managed to find a space to park the Sunbeam not too far from the entrance to the hospital. He stowed his gauntlets in the box at the rear of the motorcycle and hurried to the front door. The inspector was waiting for him just outside the entrance.

'Thank you for letting me tag along, sir. How is Mrs Trentham?' Matt asked as they walked through the entrance hall together. Their feet clattered on the tiled floor while nurses in starched uniforms bustled about their work.

'She's still very frail. She's a fortunate woman to have survived. The doctor said we could only stay for a short time.' Inspector Greville started up a flight of stone steps leading to the wards on the first floor.

The uniformed constable seated on a wooden chair outside the green painted door of Lillie's room leapt to his feet as they approached.

'Is there anything to report?' the inspector asked.

The constable shook his head. 'No, sir, no one except the doctor and the nurses have been a'nigh.'

Inspector Greville looked relieved. 'Very well, take a short break and be back at your post before we leave.'

'Yes, sir, thank you, sir.' The constable hurried away, no doubt in search of a well-earned cup of tea.

Matt followed behind the inspector as he opened the door. The curtains of the small cream painted room were open, letting in the insipid winter daylight. Lillie's face was almost as pale as the crisp white pillow beneath her head. Her eyes fluttered open as they approached her bedside.

'Good morning, Mrs Trentham, how are you feeling today?' The inspector's tone was gentle as he took a seat on one of the wooden chairs that had been placed at the side of the bed. Matt sat on the other one next to him.

'I've felt better,' Lillie's voice was faint and raspy as if from disuse.

'I'm sure you have,' Inspector Greville agreed. 'The doctor has told you what happened to you? How you have come to be here?'

A lone tear leaked from Lillie's eyes and ran unchecked down her cheek. 'He said that someone tried to poison me with my medicine.'

Matt reached inside his pocket for a clean white-cotton handkerchief, which he pressed into Lillie's hand.

'Thank you.' She barely seemed to have the strength to raise her hand to wipe her face.

'Can you recall anything of that evening?' the inspector asked.

Lillie's forehead puckered in a faint frown. 'It was very trying. Tiny was cross because I'd changed my mind about Caro. Caro was cross too and kept arguing with me.' She stopped and licked her lips as if her mouth had dried.

Matt poured her some water from the jug standing on the bedside locker and held the glass to her lips. She bent her head forward and sipped obediently. He removed the glass when she rested her head back on the pillow.

'You told Miss Morrow and Caroline that you had decided to send Caroline abroad after all?' Inspector Greville asked.

Lillie made a slight movement of her head to indicate this was correct.

'Did you see anything of Sir Stanford during the evening?' the inspector asked.

'Yes, he seemed jumpy. I can't explain, on edge about something. I think he had argued with Peters.' Lillie's frown deepened as she tried to recall.

'Mrs Trentham, did you argue with anyone yourself in your room before you took your medication?' the inspector asked and Matt guessed he was keen to see if Sir Stanford had been correct about what he thought he had heard.

'Tiny came to see me while I was preparing for bed. She wanted to plead Caro's cause again for staying. I suppose it was an argument.' Lillie's eyelids fluttered shut.

Matt looked at the inspector. He hoped they hadn't exhausted Lillie too much. They waited for a moment to give her a chance to recover from the efforts of answering the questions the inspector had put to her.

'Are you all right to answer a couple of other questions, Mrs Trentham, or would you prefer that we stop and return another time?' Inspector Greville asked.

Lillie opened her eyes. 'I'll try to answer,' her voice was weaker.

'Who had access to your medication?' Inspector Greville asked.

Lillie sighed gently. 'Everyone. It was kept by my bed.'

'And it was widely known that you took it regularly?' The inspector looked at the woman in the bed.

'Yes, it was the last one in the box. I don't sleep well, not since Hubert died. The chemist was due to bring more. I didn't want to run out over Christmas.' Her eyelids closed once more.

Matt could see that the interview was at an end. Lillie had

done her best to answer their questions, but he knew her strength had gone.

Inspector Greville rose. 'Thank you, Mrs Trentham. Please rest. My constable will remain outside for your protection and security.'

Lillie didn't acknowledge their leaving and a nurse bustled in as they left the room. The constable was back in his post beside the door.

'Poor woman,' Matt said as they made their way back along the corridor.

The inspector nodded. 'Yes, let's hope she continues to recover.'

'It seems that all was not peace and harmony that evening though, sir. Miss Morrow said she was last to retire for the evening and she certainly didn't admit to having quarrelled with Lillie.' Matt fell into step beside the inspector as they made their way out of the hospital.

Inspector Greville's face was stern. 'Yes, Miss Morrow is not the most reliable of witnesses.'

'She was very keen to implicate Kitty's father, wasn't she? When Lady Foxley's body was first discovered?' Matt mused. He knew Kitty had wondered why the governess had been so keen to point the finger of suspicion at Edgar. Perhaps she was the murderer after all. But could she have harmed Lillie too?

'I think we need to return again to Villa Lamora,' the inspector said.

* * *

Kitty telephoned Matt's house hoping to alert him to her father's shenanigans. Until he had been officially cleared of suspicion in Eliza Foxley's death and Lillie's poisoning she was keen that the police would have no reason to arrest him again.

'Hello, Kitty, darling.'

She was a little surprised when her father answered the telephone.

'Oh, good morning, Papa, I was hoping to speak to Matt.' She wondered why the housekeeper hadn't answered the call if Matt was unavailable.

'Your chum, Inspector Greville, telephoned earlier as we were finishing breakfast, so he's popped out for a spell. I think there may have been a development in the case,' Edgar explained.

'I see.' Kitty couldn't help feeling a little put out that yet again the investigation seemed to be progressing without her assistance. 'Did he say when he would be back?'

'No idea, darling girl. Has Matthew's family arrived yet?' her father asked.

'I think they are coming towards dinner time. Lucy and Rupert are due any moment now though as I have an appointment at the dressmaker's later.' Kitty glanced at the time on the clock in her grandmother's salon.

'Jolly good. Give them my regards and I expect we shall see you all this evening when Matthew returns,' her father said.

Kitty replaced the receiver feeling rather dissatisfied with the outcome of her call. Much as she was longing to see Lucy again, the excitement about the wedding and the final fitting for her dress, it all was overshadowed a little by the ongoing investigation and her frustration at not being able to take a more active role.

A couple of hours or so later she found herself confiding everything to Lucy as she drove them into Torquay to Mademoiselle Desmoine's shop. Her cousin listened attentively, her eyes wide as Kitty outlined what had happened to Lady Foxley and her sister.

'Oh dear, Kitty, how awful and poor Uncle Edgar,' Lucy said as she exited from the passenger seat of Kitty's car outside the shop.

'Poor Uncle Edgar has been up to his old tricks again.' Kitty told her cousin about what Alice had seen when she had followed him the previous day.

Lucy shook her head in mock despair, the ends of her bobbed chestnut hair swaying gently under her stylish dark-grey felt hat. 'Dear me, what a time you are having.'

Mademoiselle Desmoine was waiting for them inside the shop leaving Lucy little time to coo over the evening purses in the display before they were whisked upstairs. Lucy had sent her measurements ahead and the dressmaker had her gown ready. Emerald-green satin in a style that could easily be worn again as an evening dress.

The colour suited Kitty's dark-haired cousin and there was little to do except to fix the length of the hem and take a little more material in on the bust.

'I do love this colour, Kitty. It's so perfect for a Christmas wedding,' Lucy said as she examined her appearance in the dressmaker's mirror.

'*Oui, ce'est très joli,*' the dressmaker agreed with her mouth full of pins as she made the last adjustment.

Soon it was Kitty's turn and Lucy gasped when Kitty walked out to stand on the wooden podium.

'Oh, Kitty, you look so lovely. Matt is a very fortunate man.' Lucy dabbed at her eyes with her handkerchief.

There was little to do on Kitty's gown and the dressmaker pronounced herself satisfied that everything was done, and the dresses could be collected on Saturday, two days before the wedding.

Once dressed again in her daywear, Kitty linked arms with her cousin. 'Come and have a cup of tea with me and we can have a look in the shops before we go back to Dartmouth. Everything is so pretty at the moment with all the decorations.'

Lucy laughed. 'Well, Rupert has gone to walk Muffy up to the castle, so I expect we won't be missed for an hour.'

Her cousin's little dog always accompanied her cousin everywhere. A notorious thief, Muffy could usually be trusted to misbehave unless some of her energy had been dissipated by a walk.

A walk along Fleet Street looking in the shop windows and a trip into Bobby's café for a cup of tea and a festive mince pie did much to restore Kitty's spirits. The two girls were seated in a corner of the bustling café looking at some embroidered handkerchiefs Lucy had acquired.

'These will be perfect for Mother's Christmas stocking.' Lucy tucked the package back inside her capacious handbag.

'They are really pretty,' Kitty was just agreeing with her cousin when someone bumped against their table.

'Oh, it's Mr Peters, isn't it?' Kitty said in surprise as Lady Foxley's secretary adjusted his glasses and stumbled an apology. He appeared to be laden down with parcels, some of which he had dropped on the floor.

'Um, yes, I...' he began.

'Kitty Underhay, Edgar's daughter, and this is my cousin, Lady Woodcomb,' Kitty said briskly. 'Why don't you join us? It's rather busy in here so you may not get a seat otherwise. Unless of course you have someone you're meeting?'

Lucy helped him to collect his packages and the man blushed. 'Um, no, that is, are you sure? I wouldn't wish to intrude.'

'We were just taking a break from our Christmas shopping and from the dressmaker. Kitty gets married on Monday.' Lucy beamed at the secretary and stacked his shopping tidily to one side of the table.

'Oh yes, of course, your father is giving you away. I mean, he is, isn't he? The police and everything...' Peters ground to a halt as the harassed-looking waitress returned to their table in response to Lucy's summons.

Once Lucy had ordered more tea and the waitress had departed again Kitty turned her attention back to the secretary.

'Yes, the police soon released my father. I'm sure the inspector will get to the bottom of who murdered Lady Foxley and poisoned her sister very soon,' Kitty assured him.

'That's good. Very good. I was glad to be dispatched from the villa to get some last-minute things for Christmas. It's been rather worrying you know, living at the house and, well, you don't know who to trust, do you?' Peters said as he pushed his wire-framed spectacles higher up the bridge of his nose.

'Oh dear me no, I can imagine it must be rather dreadful,' Lucy agreed in a sympathetic tone.

'I keep thinking that it must be one of them. But I mean it's impossible. Unless, of course, well no that can't be right, I mean...' Peters halted again as the waitress returned with a fresh pot of tea and an extra cup.

'Do you have an idea yourself who it might be?' Lucy asked as Kitty poured them all a fresh cup of tea.

Kitty allowed her pretty cousin to direct the questions as she could see from his demeanour that Peters seemed quite taken with Lucy.

'It seems too awful to suspect anyone you've come to know well of doing something so dreadful.' Peters' hand shook as he picked up his cup and he used his other hand to prevent his tea from spilling onto the table.

'And yet the police seem to think it must be someone in the house,' Kitty said as she pushed the plate containing the last mince pie towards the secretary.

Peters' cup clattered against his saucer as he set it down, slopping some of the contents over the side. 'I'm so sorry, my nerves are dreadful at the moment with all of this.'

Lucy dabbed at the spots of tea that had landed on the table with a linen napkin. 'There, no harm done. It's no wonder you are so jumpy with everything that's happened. Had you worked for Lady Foxley for long?' she asked.

Peters shook his head. 'Only for a few months. I used to work as a clerk before for an insurance agency, but I was let go when the company moved its place of business. I saw an advertisement in the newspaper for the position with Lady Foxley and it offered the opportunity to travel.' He paused and sighed. 'I thought I might like to travel. I'd never been anywhere much before.'

'It must have been exciting then going to America?' Kitty said.

'Yes, oh, yes, indeed. I had to learn lots of new things quite quickly.' His face fell again.

'Lady Foxley didn't strike me as the most patient employer,' Kitty said.

The Adam's apple in Peters' throat bobbed as he swallowed. 'No, she wasn't. There were a lot of things I did wrong. I hadn't been anywhere before you see so I wasn't certain. I think she would have dismissed me in the new year.' He bit his lip.

'I'm sure you would have found another job,' Lucy said in a kindly tone.

'I expect I shall have to start looking again soon any way. If Mrs Trentham recovers, she is not likely to require my services. She leads a very different kind of life to Lady Foxley. Much less social. For myself, it's not so bad. I don't need very much to get by. It's just that, well...' He tailed off once more.

'Is there someone else you support?' Lucy asked, her gaze meeting Kitty's across the table.

Peters nodded miserably. 'I have a younger sister. She lives with an old aunt of ours. We lost our parents a few years ago. My aunt is unwell, and Louisa will be homeless if anything happens. I was trying to save enough so we could rent somewhere together.'

Kitty felt quite sorry for the man. It sounded as if fate had dealt him quite a hard hand in life.

'You never know, Mrs Trentham may need to retain you. She will have to take on a lot of her sister's responsibilities,' Lucy remarked as she sipped her tea.

Peters brightened. 'Perhaps.'

'I wish we knew who was responsible for the murder,' Kitty mused.

'You must have some suspicions on the matter?' Lucy looked at Peters, her eyes wide as she returned to her earlier question.

The man fidgeted and the colour in his cheeks deepened under Lucy's bright-eyed gaze. 'I don't really know. It seems impossible. Miss Morrow has always been all right with me, although she is quite controlling about household matters. She sent me out to complete these errands.' He gestured towards the pile of packages. 'She liked to tell Mrs Trentham what to do. Lady Foxley, however, was another matter. She used to poke fun at her. Caroline is just a kid. She surely wouldn't have wished to harm her mother or her aunt. Although...'

'Although?' Lucy asked.

'They kept arguing about her going away to this finishing school abroad. Caro does like to sneak around too. She likes to find things out and then get people into trouble.' His cheeks were crimson now.

'She told her aunt of your mistakes?' Kitty guessed.

The man gave a miserable nod of confirmation. 'Then there's Sir Stanford. I used to work for an insurance company and although I had a very lowly position you learn things.' He looked at Kitty.

'Of course,' she agreed.

'Well, it was some of the papers that I saw. The investments, well they seemed a bit risky to me. Not that it was any of my business. I was only employed to manage her social calendar and correspondence. She managed her financial matters herself. Lady Foxley argued with him about it though, and she was demanding that he go through everything and explain it all to her.' Peters picked up his cup once more and drank the remaining tea quickly as if worried he might spill more if he held the cup for too long.

'He offered to help Mrs Trentham too, I believe, after Lady Foxley died?' Kitty said.

Peters set his cup down and nodded his head. 'Yes, Mrs Trentham didn't have the grasp on money matters that Lady Foxley had.'

'It sounds as if any of them may have had a motive for killing Lady Foxley and for possibly harming Lillie,' Kitty said.

Peters' shoulders slumped. 'That's what I mean. I just don't know.'

Lucy glanced at her watch. 'Heavens, Kitty, we really should get going. Rupert will think I have bought all of Torquay.'

Her cousin waved to the waitress to pay their bill.

'Let us hope the inspector solves this soon,' Kitty said to Peters as she assisted him to collect up his parcels.

'I hope so. Thank you for the tea, Lady Woodcomb, Miss Underhay. You've both been very kind.'

Kitty pulled on her red driving gloves and picked up her handbag as Peters bumbled his way out of the tea room.

'I feel as if I'm part of the investigation team now, too,' Lucy said with a smile as she linked arms with her cousin.

CHAPTER SEVENTEEN

Miss Morrow appeared most put out when Matt and the inspector arrived once more at Villa Lamora. Inspector Greville had driven the black police motor car and Matt had followed on his Sunbeam.

The bell had hardly finished ringing before Miss Morrow was on the step. She had opened the front door to them herself. There was no sign of the butler or the maidservant.

'Back again, Inspector? Captain Bryant?' She scowled at them and gave Matt a deeply distrusting look. 'I hope you have news for us.' She stood aside and grudgingly permitted them to enter the hall.

'Indeed, Miss Morrow. We have just come from the hospital where we have been speaking to Mrs Trentham. I'm sure you will be very happy to hear she is slowly starting to recover,' Inspector Greville said as he handed his coat and hat to the rather harassed-looking young maid who had suddenly appeared from a side room.

'Oh, I see, well yes, that is good news.' Miss Morrow looked flustered by this unexpected turn of events.

There was a clatter of feet on the stairs and Caroline came into view.

'Did I hear you say that mother was better? Is she speaking? May we go and see her? Can she come home?' the girl asked as she hurried breathlessly into the hall.

'She is not to have visitors just yet. She is still very weak. But, yes, she was able to answer our questions.' Inspector Greville gave the governess a meaningful look.

Caroline danced a little jig around the hall. 'Tiny, that is such good news. Mother may be home for Christmas.'

Tiny placed a heavy hand on her charge's shoulder, halting her mid-twirl. 'That's as maybe. It all depends on how well she recovers. If she does come home, she'll need peace and quiet. Not your playing the radio or the gramophone and chattering away ninety to the dozen.'

Caroline looked completely unchastened by her governess' remarks. 'I'm sure Mummy will be fine. It is Christmas after all.' She skipped away along the hall humming a Christmas carol to herself.

'That girl will be the death of me.' Tiny shook her head.

'May we take a moment of your time, Miss Morrow? After speaking to Mrs Trentham, there are a few things I should like to clear up.' The inspector opened the door to Lady Foxley's study as he spoke.

To Matt's surprise the room was already occupied. Sir Stanford was seated at Lady Foxley's desk and the top two drawers were open.

'Sir Stanford, were you looking for something?' Miss Morrow placed her hands on her hips and glared at the man behind the desk.

'I was in need of some stamps. Last-minute correspondence, you know.' Sir Stanford pushed the drawers shut and quickly got to his feet. 'I wasn't aware we were expecting you again so soon, Inspector.'

'Mrs Trentham is recovering. These gentlemen have just come from interviewing her at the hospital.' Tiny glowered at Sir Stanford.

Matt decided that he would not wish to cross Miss Morrow if he were one of her charges.

Sir Stanford, however, seemed impervious to Miss Morrow's ire and sauntered towards the door where they were all standing. 'Oh, that's excellent news. Caroline will be delighted to have her mother home for Christmas.'

'After we have spoken to Miss Morrow, perhaps we might come and find you again, sir?' Inspector Greville remarked as Sir Stanford eased past them to head towards the drawing room.

'Oh yes, um yes, of course,' Sir Stanford said and hastened his steps along the hall.

'Blooming cheek of that man. Stamps indeed. Snooping, that's what he was doing,' Tiny huffed as Sir Stanford disappeared and the sound of the radio escaped along the hallway from the sitting room.

Inspector Greville held open the study door and gestured towards the freshly vacated room. 'Now then a quick chat, Miss Morrow, if you wouldn't mind.'

Tiny marched into the room and took up a stance in front of the fireplace. Matt slipped into the study behind the inspector and quietly closed the door.

'Perhaps you would like to get straight to the point, Inspector. I'm a busy woman with Lillie being in hospital and all the things that need done for Christmas.'

The inspector nodded. 'Very well, Miss Morrow. You told us that you knew nothing of an argument that Sir Stanford thought he had heard on the evening Mrs Trentham was poisoned. Mrs Trentham says that in fact it was you she exchanged words with in her room that night just before she was taken ill.'

A bright spot of colour appeared on each of Miss Morrow's

cheeks. 'I wouldn't have called it an argument, Inspector. Just a frank exchange of views.'

'Whatever you wish to call it, Miss Morrow, the fact remains that you didn't tell us about it. This is not the first time you have omitted to mention something which may be pertinent to this case.' Inspector Greville's tone was stern.

'It was nothing. Lillie kept changing her mind about Caroline's education, that's all. One minute she wanted the girl to stay at home and the next she wanted to follow Eliza's wishes of sending the child away for eighteen months to be finished.' Miss Morrow wrung her plump hands together. 'Caro was unsettled enough after losing her aunt and it seemed to me to be counter-productive to make such a big decision so soon and so close to Christmas. The child would have left for Paris in the new year.'

'You did not agree with Caroline being sent to finishing school? Was this because you would then have been made redundant?' the inspector asked.

'No, certainly not. Lillie would have kept me with her,' Tiny said indignantly.

'Would she?' the inspector challenged. 'Lady Foxley had seemed to think that your role would be done once Caroline left for school. When we examined her papers, it seems there was a note saying she felt it was time you retired.'

This latter statement was news to Matt.

The woman swallowed and licked her lips. 'Well Eliza was mistaken; I had no wish to retire. I've devoted most of my life to her and Lillie and now Miss Caroline. Lillie would never just cast me aside now after everything I've done for them over the years.'

'Why did you not tell us about this conversation? Why deny that it had taken place?' the inspector asked. 'You must realise how suspicious that looks.'

Miss Morrow dropped down onto one of the leather chairs beside the fireplace. 'I wasn't thinking straight. I could see no point in mentioning it especially in front of the others. It had nothing to do with what happened to Lillie. I'd never hurt a hair of her head or Eliza's. They've been like my own daughters to me.'

'You also denied it when asked privately, Miss Morrow. You have deliberately withheld information or attempted to divert suspicion onto others ever since Lady Foxley was killed.' The inspector was clearly having no more subterfuge.

The woman held her head in her hands for a moment as if struggling to compose herself. When she raised her gaze, it was to glare straight at Matt.

'I was convinced that Edgar Underhay had killed Eliza. He was found with her body, and let's face it, everyone knows of his reputation as a ne'er-do-well. I'm sorry if this offends you, Captain Bryant, but it's true. He could still have been the person who poisoned Lillie. He could have tampered with her medicine before he left the house.'

Matt waited for the woman to finish. 'But to what end, Miss Morrow? Edgar had nothing to gain from Lady Foxley's death or from Lillie's. His purpose for travelling back to England was to give his daughter's hand in marriage. He was not on board the ship to seek out Lady Foxley's company. That was pure chance that they met. Plus, from the moment he left the police station he was in my company.'

Inspector Greville coughed, interrupting the discussion. 'Mr Underhay remains under investigation, as does everyone in this household. The only reason I am not arresting you right now, Miss Morrow, is because you are responsible for Miss Trentham until her mother is well enough to return home. I suggest you spend some time thinking carefully if there is anything further you wish to tell us that you have not shared already.'

Miss Morrow stood with as much dignity as she could

muster. 'I assure you, Inspector, that I had nothing whatsoever to do with either Eliza's death or Lillie's poisoning.'

'Perhaps you could ask Sir Stanford to call in when you return to the drawing room,' the inspector suggested, dismissing her.

Miss Morrow departed with a final glare at Matt.

Before anything more could be said between Matt and the inspector there was a tap at the door and Sir Stanford appeared.

'Miss Morrow said you were looking for me?'

'Please have a seat, sir. This will only take a moment.' Inspector Greville gestured towards the seat so recently occupied by Miss Morrow.

Once Sir Stanford was seated the inspector started his questions. 'We managed to speak to Mrs Trentham this morning and she has clarified the discussion you overheard on the night she was taken ill.'

'I presume it was Miss Morrow, judging by her expression when she said you wished to see me,' Sir Stanford remarked with a satisfied air.

'Mrs Trentham also informed us that you had appeared somewhat out of sorts that evening. She thought perhaps you had argued with Mr Peters, Lady Foxley's secretary?' The inspector neither confirmed or denied that it had been Miss Morrow who Sir Stanford had heard in Lillie's room.

Sir Stanford took his silver cigarette case from his pocket and offered it to the inspector and to Matt before selecting a cigarette himself and lighting it after the other men had declined his offer.

'Peters had been snooping in Eliza's private papers. He was engaged as her social secretary and to run Eliza's errands for her. He had no call to concern himself with any of either her or Lillie's financial affairs.' He took a pull on his cigarette and exhaled a thin stream of smoke into the air in front of him.

'And you informed him of this?' Inspector Greville asked.

'Quite right I did. I told him to mind his own business. I reminded him that he was only still in the house at the moment thanks to Lillie's goodwill. Eliza had been on the verge of dismissing him, I'm certain.' Sir Stanford peered at the inspector through the growing haze of cigarette smoke.

'How did Mr Peters take your advice?' The inspector's tone was mild.

Sir Stanford shrugged and tapped the ash from the end of his cigarette into a large crystal ashtray on the coffee table. 'About as well as you might expect. He accused me of not looking after Lady Foxley's best interests and said he intended to speak to Lillie about it.'

'And *were* you always acting in Lady Foxley's best financial interests?' The inspector's moustache twitched slightly.

Sir Stanford leaned forward in his seat and extinguished his cigarette. 'I say, what are you implying?'

The inspector took out his notebook and leafed through it. 'Lady Foxley's financial investment portfolio has been examined by several experts. There seem to have been several very curious purchases and sales of certain shares. The money in the accounts also doesn't quite balance.'

Matt guessed that Mr Hemmings had been among the experts called upon to examine the documents.

Sir Stanford had turned puce during the course of the inspector's words. He started forward in his seat as if eager to physically stand and object to what he was hearing.

'That's rubbish. Those accounts are perfectly in order. Eliza made many transactions herself.'

Inspector Greville regarded him coldly. 'On the surface the books all seem to be in perfect order. It's only when a closer look has been taken that the irregularities become clear. I believe Lady Foxley had her suspicions about the way you were conducting her affairs. I have raised this as a possibility with you before, sir, and you denied it. Now it seems Peters too was suspicious and intended to bring his concerns to Mrs Trentham's attention.'

Sir Stanford gaped at the inspector for a moment before closing his mouth with a snap. 'I think I would prefer not to say anything further, Inspector. At least not without the benefit of my solicitor being present. These are very serious accusations.'

'Indeed, they are, sir, and they also provide you with a possible motive for killing Lady Foxley and for harming Mrs Trentham,' the inspector said.

Sir Stanford stood and raised himself to his full height, a cold expression on his face. 'I think this interview is concluded. Good day, Inspector Greville, Captain Bryant.'

The study door banged shut behind him.

'Well, that was quite interesting.' Matt leaned back in his seat and looked at the inspector. 'What now, sir?'

* * *

When Kitty and Lucy returned to the Dolphin Hotel they discovered that Rupert and Muffy had indeed already returned from their walk to the castle and were waiting for them in the lobby.

'Hello, Kitty, you look jolly pretty today. Looking forward to Monday?' Rupert asked as he kissed her cheek in greeting while Muffy sniffed about her ankles.

'Yes, the dresses look super. We are to collect them on Saturday.' Kitty blushed at Rupert's compliment and her cousin merely smiled and shook her head at her husband's nonsense.

'We stopped off in town for some shopping and tea,' Lucy said as the group made their way along the corridor to a small private residents' lounge that had been made available for all of the family and guests who were staying to attend the wedding.

'Of course,' Rupert said as Lucy and Kitty took off their coats and gloves before sitting on the comfortable velvet-covered sofa near the fireplace. 'Although from the way you said it, Lucy darling, I take it that something else occurred whilst you were out.' He smiled at his wife.

Lucy and Kitty told him of the events surrounding Lady Foxley's murder and Kitty's father's arrest. The smile disappeared from Rupert's face and his demeanour became more serious when he heard of Lillie's poisoning.

'And is the inspector certain that he has cleared your father of any wrongdoing? It would be too awful if something happened to upset your wedding.' He looked at Lucy. 'Ours was eventful enough.'

A shiver danced along Kitty's spine as she recalled the unfortunate death of Rupert's best man hours after the ceremony.

'Obviously until the real culprit is caught, then everyone at the house will be under the same cloud of suspicion. But Father was with Matt when Lillie's medicine was tampered with. Or at least when she took the medication.' Kitty realised that it was still possible that her father could be suspected of leaving the contaminated cachet beside Lillie's bed and ensuring that he had an alibi for when she consumed it.

'Anyway, while we were taking tea at Bobby's café a Mr Peters came by, Lady Foxley's secretary.' Lucy's eyes sparkled as she told her husband what they had learned.

When she had completed her tale Rupert looked at his wife. 'So now you too are part of Kitty's detective team.'

Lucy giggled and swatted his arm. 'Of course.'

'I'm not sure your mother will take the news of Father's involvement in the case as lightly as you?' Kitty remarked.

Lucy's pretty face sobered. 'No, I don't suppose she will. Or my father for that matter. Uncle Edgar is not his favourite person at the best of times. It may be better if we do not mention it unless we have to.'

'I agree, it is only Wednesday so the inspector has time to

make a proper arrest of the real culprit before the wedding,' Rupert said.

'There is one more small matter.' Kitty looked at her cousin. 'I haven't had a chance to discuss this yet with Matt but when I was in Exeter visiting Father Lamb, he said Esther Hammett might be back in the city.'

Rupert sat up at this. Both he and Lucy were very aware of the devastation the Hammett family had wrought on Kitty's life. 'That is most serious. Do you think she may attempt to cause a problem with your wedding?'

Kitty shook her head. 'I think it unlikely. She has a great deal to lose if she is caught. The police finally have enough evidence to charge her with various offences, I believe. That's why she has been gone for so many weeks.'

'Even so, Kitty, please do be careful.' Lucy squeezed Kitty's hand. 'I couldn't bear it if you should be hurt.'

'I promise I shall stay very alert. Now, enough talk of horrid things. We have a Christmas tree arriving for this room tomorrow for us to decorate and the ballroom is being prepared for the wedding breakfast and party.' Kitty smiled at Rupert and Lucy. 'And, you have to tell me more about Daisy's baby.'

Later in the afternoon Matt's parents and his aunt Effie arrived. Kitty's grandmother greeted them and took them to her private salon for tea. Kitty waited downstairs for her fiancé to arrive with her father so she could take them upstairs and make the introductions.

She had changed into one of her new dresses for the occasion, a dark-green velveteen dress with a cream lace collar. On her lapel she pinned her mother's suffrage pin to give her courage.

'Are you all right, Kitty?' Cyril asked from his position at the reception desk as Kitty paced past him for the seventh time.

'Matt is a little late,' Kitty said.

Lucy and Rupert had taken the ferry across to Kingswear to meet an old friend of Rupert's or they would have remained with her until Matt arrived. Lucy was well aware of how anxious Matt's parents made Kitty feel.

'I'm sure he and your father will be here, presently,' Cyril reassured her.

At that Kitty spied Matt and her father strolling along the embankment towards the Dolphin.

'Oh, it's all right, they are here.'

Cyril smiled at her and adjusted the rosebud in his lapel. 'Of course, Kitty.'

'Where have you been?' Kitty asked as soon as the two men entered the lobby.

'Steady on, old thing. I had to see the inspector this morning. I've not long got back.' Matt kissed her cheek.

'You can tell me everything after tea. I met Mr Peters in Torquay this morning,' Kitty murmured in his ear as they made their way up the stairs to the salon, Edgar trailing a little diffidently behind them.

Matt's brows raised at this. 'That sounds like a deal. Now, are you ready?' he asked as they approached her grandmother's door.

'One can never be fully ready,' Edgar remarked drily. 'Especially when encountering family.'

CHAPTER EIGHTEEN

Kitty decided that her father was right after they finally managed to escape in order to prepare for dinner. A couple of hours of her grandmother glaring at her father with her aunt Livvy attempting to mediate and Matt's mother wittering on about the advisability of a goose for Christmas dinner and how she personally considered it a little unwise to get married so close to Christmas. Had Kitty considered the advisability of continuing to work at the hotel after the marriage?

Her future father-in-law had lectured Matt on his choice of career and his aunt Effie had been gossiping away with her aunt Livvy as if they were old chums. It was no surprise that Matt's mother had announced she was getting one of her 'heads' and would need to rest before dinner. Kitty thought she might well develop the same affliction if things continued in the same manner up till Christmas Eve.

She walked downstairs with Matt and quickly told him about her meeting with Mr Peters. In return he told her of the interviews at the villa and gave her more details about Caro's parentage.

'Oh dear, it doesn't seem to be becoming any clearer, does

it? They all seem to have had motive and opportunity.' Kitty frowned.

She wished she could have been present for some of the interviews. Maybe she would have noticed something about the way the answers were given or the person's demeanour. At least it seemed much less likely that her father was about to get rearrested for the crimes.

'I know, darling. It's most frustrating.' Matt kissed her cheek as her father approached them.

'Our taxi is here, dear boy,' Edgar said.

Kitty thought her father looked tired. 'Go and have a rest.' They were expected back to the hotel for dinner, with Rupert and Lucy joining them.

She could only hope that at least with her cousin and Rupert added to the company the atmosphere at dinner would be more convivial and celebratory.

Kitty woke the following morning with her head and mood as dreary as the weather. Dinner the previous evening had been something of a trial. If anything, it had been even worse than the afternoon.

Her father had entertained Matt's parents with somewhat lurid tales of some of his escapades in America. The aunts and her grandmother had set themselves up as a nice gossipy corner and if it hadn't been for Rupert and Lucy, Kitty thought the entire evening would have bordered on being intolerable. Between the dessert course and after dinner coffee she had been giving serious consideration to eloping.

Lucy and Rupert had generously offered to accompany Aunt Effie and Aunt Livvy into Exeter for some Christmas shopping. Matt's mother had taken to her bed with exhaustion and his father had declared his intention of walking to the castle.

Kitty decided that she needed to escape for a few hours. Mr Lutterworth was more than capable of dealing with the setting up of the ballroom and answering any questions from the florist. The Christmas tree for the residents' lounge was to be delivered later and everything was in order for it to be decorated by the guests.

Satisfied that everything was in place, Kitty drove her car across the river and up to Matt's house. She really wanted to spend time with her fiancé and to have a proper discussion about the case. There had to be something they were missing. Perhaps if they reviewed it together, they might be able to see what that thing was.

She was a little surprised when she arrived to discover that her father had also gone out.

'I've loaned him my clubs and he's gone to play a round of golf,' Matt explained as he welcomed her with a kiss.

Bertie sniffed hopefully at her coat pockets, his tail wagging with delight at seeing her.

'Are you sure that's where he's gone?' Kitty asked as she hung her coat on the stand and followed her fiancé into the sitting room.

Matt gave her an enquiring look as she seated herself on one of the stylish black leather chairs. 'Oh?'

Kitty explained what Alice had seen when she had followed Edgar the day Bertie had returned covered in mud.

The corners of Matt's lips quirked upwards. 'You suspect he may be up to no good?'

Kitty sighed. 'We both know that he is up to no good. I suspect it is a spot of betting. There will be several fixtures on Boxing Day and, of course, sporting events this Saturday.'

'That certainly sounds very likely and most like Edgar,' Matt agreed.

Bertie placed his nose on Kitty's knee, and she rubbed the top of the dog's head affectionately. 'Last night I was tempted to suggest we elope. I really did not envisage how stressful this whole wedding caper would become. In my mind I had envisaged a cosy family Christmas with lots of jollity and fun,' she said dolefully.

Bertie sighed as if agreeing with her.

Matt laughed. 'It's only for a few more days, old thing. And it's making your grandmother happy, since your parents eloped and she didn't get to see your mother walk down the aisle.'

'I suppose it's the same in a way for your parents since you told them about your wedding to Edith after the event.' She looked at her fiancé.

'That is very true. I do think Mother is looking forward to it despite all of her complaints.' The dimple flashed in his cheek as he smiled at her.

The black Bakelite telephone on the side table rang, interrupting their conversation and Matt picked up the receiver.

'Inspector Greville, good morning. Yes, I see. A most alarming development. Kitty and I will be right over.' Matt replaced the receiver.

'Has something happened?' Kitty could see Matt was concerned. 'Is it Lillie?' Perhaps Mrs Trentham had taken a turn for the worst. Matt had said how frail the woman had looked.

'The inspector is at Villa Lamora. Someone has attempted to push Caroline down the stairs.' Matt frowned.

Kitty jumped to her feet. 'It's a good thing I drove here.' She hurried into the hall and pulled on her hat and coat once more. Matt followed a little more slowly behind her.

'I don't like this at all, Kitty. First Lady Foxley, then Mrs Trentham, and now Caroline. Who could be holding such a grudge against the family?'

They left Bertie in the hall in the care of Matt's housekeeper and set off through the grey winter morning towards Torquay.

'What exactly did Inspector Greville say?' Kitty asked as she drove along the coast road. 'Is Caroline badly hurt? Did she see who pushed her? Was she definitely pushed?' Questions tumbled from her lips as they drew nearer to the house.

'The inspector didn't say very much. Merely that someone had made an attempt on Caroline's life this morning by pushing her down the stairs,' Matt replied as Kitty turned into the drive of the villa.

'Doctor Carter is here, I hope Caroline hasn't worsened or surely the neighbouring doctor would have been called.' Kitty parked beside the doctor's sleek dark-blue sporty car.

'Perhaps the inspector felt Doctor Carter's opinion would be better,' Matt replied.

The butler answered the bell on their first ring. His usual professional demeanour appearing quite ruffled.

'The inspector is in the drawing room, sir, miss.' He took their coats, and they hurried along the hall to the large, comfortable room at the rear of the house.

They entered to a scene of chaos. Caroline was lying on the sofa with Doctor Carter bent over her shining a light into her eyes. Miss Morrow was sobbing noisily on a nearby armchair. Sir Stanford was pacing about in front of the French windows while the inspector appeared to be attempting to talk to Phillip Peters.

'Goodness me,' Kitty murmured to Matt.

Doctor Carter straightened up as they walked further into the room. 'Captain Bryant, Miss Underhay, good morning.'

'Good morning, is Caroline all right? The inspector said she had taken a tumble down the stairs.' Kitty's enquiry provoked a fresh outburst of noisy sobbing from Miss Morrow.

'It's my fault. I should have protected her, the poor lamb.' Tiny blew her nose noisily into her handkerchief.

'Miss Trentham will have a few bruises but no serious injury, I'm pleased to say.' He gave the wan-looking girl on the couch a reassuring smile. 'A day or so resting quietly and she will be as right as rain.'

'Thank you, Doctor,' Caroline said.

'What happened?' Kitty asked as she perched herself on a stool at Caroline's side.

The girl frowned. 'I'm really not certain. I had gone back to my room to collect my books. Tiny wished me to practise my French work despite it being almost Christmas. Then as I started to go back down, I felt someone shove me hard in the small of my back. I lost my balance and tumbled down the first flight of stairs.'

'Did you see who pushed you?' Kitty asked. She guessed the girl probably hadn't, or the inspector would surely have arrested them by now.

Caroline licked her lips. 'No, I didn't see anyone. The first thing I knew was when someone shoved me. I made quite a noise as I fell. My arms and legs banged against the balustrade, and I think I screamed. Everyone came running.'

'That would account for the bumps,' Doctor Carter said as he closed his medical bag.

'Was everyone upstairs at the time?' Kitty asked.

'I was in my room dealing with some correspondence.' Sir Stanford stopped his marching to whirl around and join the conversation.

'I had gone to my room to fetch more mending, Caroline is very hard on the heels of her stockings,' Miss Morrow said.

Kitty looked at Mr Peters who was seated with the inspector.

'I too was upstairs. I had forgotten to put the spare stamps I got the other day in the study and there were some last-minute Christmas cards that Miss Morrow wished me to post on Mrs Trentham's behalf,' Peters said.

'Well, fortunately, there was no serious harm done, Miss Trentham,' Doctor Carter remarked. 'I must be off, lots to do this time of year. Mrs Carter and I shall see you two at the church on Monday, Miss Underhay, Captain Bryant.' He beamed at Kitty and Matt and with a nod of farewell to the inspector, took his leave.

'You were very lucky not to have been seriously hurt,' Kitty said to Caroline.

Miss Morrow sniffed loudly. 'It's not safe here, not safe at all. Who could have done this?' She looked around the room at Peters and Sir Stanford.

'That is what I wish to find out, Miss Morrow,' the inspector said. 'Who was first to find Miss Trentham?'

'I believe one of the maids was there first,' Tiny said, a frown creasing her forehead. 'She had been cleaning one of the bathrooms and she was just ahead of me on the landing.'

'You were there when I arrived.' Sir Stanford looked at Tiny.

'I think I was last to get there. My room is furthest away,' Peters added.

'Does that seem right to you, Caroline?' Kitty asked.

'I think so. I banged my head when I fell so I may have blacked out for a moment or two. When I opened my eyes, everyone was standing around me and the maid was screaming for Mr Hedges, the butler.'

'And you were quite certain you felt someone push you?' Inspector Greville asked.

'Of course, if she said someone pushed her, they pushed her,' Miss Morrow said in a sharp tone.

'Miss Trentham?' The inspector ignored the governess' outburst and looked at Caroline for confirmation.

'It was definitely a push. It took me by surprise as I was about to step down and it caught me off balance. I was concentrating on carrying my books.' Caroline closed her eyes.

'She needs to go to her room to get some rest,' Miss Morrow

declared. She rose and pulled the embroidered bell pull beside the fireplace to summon the servants.

Within minutes Caroline was supported by the butler and the chauffeur upstairs to her room. Inspector Greville dispatched the constable who had attended with him to follow and remain on guard outside Caroline's room. He prevented Miss Morrow from following after them.

'I think it may be better if you remain here, Miss Morrow,' Inspector Greville said firmly as the woman went to walk out of the room.

'But Caro needs me.' Tiny looked bewildered at his refusal to allow her to leave.

'I would remind you that you are as much a suspect as anyone else in this room,' the inspector said.

The governess sank back down onto her chair, a shocked expression on her face. 'Why would I wish to harm Caroline?' she asked plaintively.

'Why would any of us wish to do so?' Sir Stanford replied with a snap. 'It's ridiculous.'

'And yet Miss Trentham asserts that she clearly felt someone push her down the stairs.' Inspector Greville looked sternly at the group assembled in the room.

'And have you interviewed the servants, Inspector? We are not the only people resident in this house. Perhaps it is one of them who is responsible for all of these mishaps.' Sir Stanford glared at Inspector Greville.

Kitty was certain that the inspector would have considered this possibility when Lady Foxley was killed. He had no doubt revisited it once again when Lillie was poisoned. She supposed a servant with a grudge could have attacked all three women. But why?

'I can assure you, Sir Stanford, that idea has been thoroughly explored and discounted. Many of the servants are of longstanding with the family and none have any motive to harm any member of them.' Inspector Greville was firm in his explanation.

'Then, forgive me for asking, how are we to be protected? It seems there is someone in this house who is attempting to kill or injure the occupants.' Mr Peters shot sideways glances at Miss Morrow and Sir Stanford.

'Peters is correct. One of us could be the next victim. Surely it would be sensible for us to leave the house and stay elsewhere until this person is caught.' Sir Stanford had recommenced his pacing.

'And then whichever of you is responsible could also easily make good your escape.' Inspector Greville looked at Sir Stanford.

Kitty guessed that with the information Matt had given her about the financial shenanigans that Sir Stanford had been involved in, an arrest might be imminent for that gentleman anyway on a different charge.

'For once I agree with Sir Stanford. Like Mr Peters I feel most unsafe, and I have to think of Caroline too. This person has made an attempt on her once, who is to say they won't try again?' Miss Morrow said.

'My constable will remain in the household. He will be stationed beside Miss Trentham's door and will accompany her wherever she goes inside the house.' Inspector Greville looked around the room. 'You will all remain resident here for now.'

The inspector rose and looked at Kitty and Matt. They followed his cue and slipped outside the room. Once they were in the hall and the inspector closed the door, they heard a hum of indignant voices immediately break out inside the drawing room.

'Do you think they are safe, sir?' Kitty asked as they made their way to collect their outdoor things from the cloakroom beside the front door. None of the servants were in sight and they didn't bother to pull the bell to summon them.

'My constable will keep watch on them all and will report anything untoward. The butler here seems a trustworthy man and he is monitoring the servants. There will be a lot of eyes watching their every move until I can determine who is responsible for all of this,' the inspector said as he donned his overcoat, having collected it himself.

Matt assisted Kitty with her coat before shrugging into his own woollen topcoat. 'Do you believe her, sir? Miss Trentham? I mean, I can't think of a reason why someone would wish to harm her.'

Kitty had been thinking the same thought as her fiancé. 'Not unless it is someone who hates the entire family so much that they wish to harm all of them.'

'Exactly, Miss Underhay, but I've not yet discovered any person who might have such a motive.' The inspector put on his hat and rummaged in his coat pockets for his leather driving gloves.

'I can't see that Caro would have a reason to lie.' Kitty took her own gloves from her handbag. 'She doesn't appear to be the kind of girl that constantly seeks attention.'

'Which in itself is troubling, as that adds weight to her assertion that she was pushed.' Inspector Greville frowned. Kitty could see that he was deeply worried about what had just happened inside the villa.

Matt opened the front door, and they stepped outside into the chilly winter air. A gust of breeze swirled around them rattling the dried brown leaves of the beech hedge that bordered the driveway.

'You said that the servants had all been questioned, sir?' Kitty asked as they crunched their way over the gravel the short distance to their vehicles.

'Yes, Miss Underhay. Their backgrounds have been checked and most have an alibi for the time of Lady Foxley's murder. None of them were upstairs at the time Miss Trentham was pushed, except the girl cleaning the bathroom and it is impossible that she could have come from the bathroom, pushed Miss Trentham and then returned to the bathroom in order to leave it once again as the others rushed out after hearing Caroline scream.' Inspector Greville paused at the side of the police car.

Kitty knew he was right. Miss Morrow had definitely seen the maid just ahead of her as she had gone to Caroline's aid.

'I must go to the hospital now and inform Mrs Trentham about this incident. Caroline is her daughter after all, and the doctors tell me that fortunately she seems to be recovering well.' The inspector opened his car door and prepared to get in. 'Thank you both for coming this morning. Mr Underhay is now eliminated from the enquiry following this incident.' The inspector looked at Kitty.

'Thank you, Inspector.' Kitty was relieved that it was now official that her father was not involved in Lady Foxley's murder.

She and Matt stepped aside as the inspector drove away.

'Does that mean that Inspector Greville feels your attendance is no longer required at any interviews since Father is exonerated?' Kitty asked as they walked to her car.

Matt gave a slight shrug. 'I don't know. Your father was technically my client I suppose. I think, however, the inspector is keen to resolve the case as quickly as possible.'

Kitty glanced back at the blank face of the villa and a slight shiver ran through her body. 'He may well like to keep us in the loop then. It's all very strange.'

CHAPTER NINETEEN

Kitty drove Matt back to his house at Churston. The mist had come down over the common while they had been gone and it was difficult to see clearly. The distant sound of the foghorns of the ships in the bay echoed through the damp air.

'Surely Father is not playing golf in this?' Kitty said as she followed Matt inside the house, where they were greeted by an enthusiastic Bertie.

Matt peered into the sitting room as Kitty removed her hat and coat. 'He doesn't appear to be home just yet.'

Kitty's brows raised at this. 'Do you think he is having a drink at the clubhouse?' she asked as she went to warm her hands before the fire still burning low in the grate.

'I suppose he must be. Can you stay for lunch or is your grandmother expecting you back?' Matt added another log to the blaze.

'I think she has arranged for everyone to have a light lunch while they decorate the tree in the residents' lounge, then we are all to attend dinner this evening.' She looked at her fiancé.

Matt grinned. 'Another joyful event.'

Kitty swatted him on his arm. 'I believe Mrs Craven is

joining us this evening too."I suppose we can give our full attention to our wedding now your father is in the clear,' he said.

'That's true,' Kitty agreed. Although, she knew that he would still be thinking about the case. As indeed so would she.

Matt was about to go to the kitchen to check with his housekeeper that there was enough food prepared for Kitty to stay for lunch when there was the sound of whistling and a key turning in the front door.

Edgar entered the hall carrying a large bag of golf clubs and looking, Kitty decided, very pleased with himself.

'Hello, darling girl, have you been here long?' Her father set down his clubs and hung his cap on a peg near the foot of the stairs.

'We've just returned from Lady Foxley's house. Someone has attacked Caroline,' Matt said just before he disappeared into the kitchen to talk to his housekeeper.

Her father's cheerful smile disappeared to be replaced with concern. 'Caro? Who on earth would wish to harm Caro? Is the girl all right?' He followed Kitty into the sitting room with Bertie sniffing happily at his plus fours and argyle socks.

'Doctor Carter has been to see her and says she has suffered no serious harm.' Kitty took a seat on the sofa.

'What happened to her?' her father asked as he moved to the armchair closest to the fireplace.

'Someone pushed her down the stairs at the villa.' Kitty still couldn't make up her mind if Caroline was telling the truth about the incident. She could see no real motive for an attack on the girl and yet she could also see no reason for her to lie about it either.

'Good heavens, how extraordinary. Why though? Do you think whoever killed Eliza and injured Lillie thought Caroline knew something that could identify them?' Her father frowned as he drew out his cigarette case.

'I suppose that's possible but what? Caroline surely would

have said something to the inspector. She has no reason not to.' Even as she spoke, Kitty recalled Mr Peters' comment about Caro always snooping about. Had the girl seen something or heard something that could betray the killer? It might be that Caroline didn't even know that what she knew was important.

Matt rejoined them. 'We have chicken pie for luncheon, so you are welcome to stay, Kitty darling.'

'Thank you.' Matt's housekeeper was a real treasure and Kitty was pleased that the woman had agreed to stay on after she and Matt were married. She knew how to run a hotel but not how to manage a house.

'Father said that perhaps Caroline knew something that could identify the murderer.' She looked at Matt to see what he thought of this idea.

'It's possible, but it seems she must be unaware of it or surely she would have said something to the inspector.' Matt echoed her own thoughts.

Edgar lounged back in his seat. His cigarette held elegantly between his fingers. 'I can't think of another reason why anyone would attack the girl.'

'The only other possibility is someone who hates the whole family for some reason, but the inspector seems to have ruled that out,' Matt agreed.

'And I don't think there can be a financial reason. Caroline won't have made a will, she's too young. I wonder who inherits if anything happens to both her and Lillie,' Kitty mused.

Edgar tapped the end of his cigarette into a small marble ashtray. 'I can answer that. Eliza told me that everything goes to that charity she and Lillie set up. They agreed on the matter years ago when Lillie was first widowed.'

Matt looked at his future father-in-law. 'You seem very well informed on the particulars.'

Edgar waved a careless hand. 'It was a late-night chat in the bar on board the ship. Everyone else had gone to bed and Eliza and I were shooting the breeze, as they say. You know how conversations can take a serious turn sometimes. I told her that everything I own, such as it is, is left to Kitty. She said that she had left everything pretty much to Lillie with a provision for Caroline. I asked as a joke what if anything happened to Lillie, was she as thoughtful. That's when she told me of their arrangements.'

'Speaking of puzzles, you seemed pretty chipper when you came back from the club. Did your golf go well?' Kitty looked at her father.

'I didn't get very far. The fog came down before I reached the seventh tee, so I ventured back to the clubhouse,' Edgar replied in a nonchalant tone.

'I presume it must have been pretty quiet given the weather,' Matt said.

'Yes, indeed, just a couple of fellows in there. I had a whisky to warm myself up and then trotted along back here,' Edgar explained as he extinguished his cigarette. 'Actually, if you'll both excuse me I think I'd better go and change.'

Kitty looked at Matt after her father had made good his escape from the room.

'He's up to something,' she said.

Matt laughed. 'I agree, old thing. Let's hope it's nothing that's going to get him into too much trouble before Monday.'

The rest of the day passed amiably, and Kitty retired to bed later that evening congratulating herself on having avoided any major squabbles between her guests. The hotel was suitably decorated for Christmas and preparations were well in hand for the wedding breakfast. It was strange having so many people to stay while being closed to guests not connected with the wedding.

.   .   .

The fog had cleared overnight again leaving a fresher morning. The news that her father had now officially been exonerated from the investigation had been greeted with relief by her grandmother and her aunt Livvy. Matt's aunt Effie and her aunt Livvy seemed to have struck up quite a friendship and planned their day accordingly.

Matt's parents, along with her grandmother, had mutual friends to call upon to deliver Christmas greetings. Lucy and Rupert intended to visit the Christmas market in Totnes to get last-minute gifts, all of which left Kitty feeling relieved that she could spend her last days as an unmarried woman as she pleased.

There were several of her things still to be packed, ready to be transferred to Matt's home. It would be strange not to call the Dolphin home any more, but she was quite excited by the plans she and Matt were making for the house at Churston. Matt had already promised her a summerhouse at the end of the garden so she could sit out and overlook the sea.

She spent the morning packing up more of her possessions and took her lunch with Mr Lutterworth and Dolly, who were engaged on revamping the hotel's brochures ready for the printers in the new year.

It was quite pleasant, she decided, actually having leisure time and not thinking about the hotel or murders or worrying about her father. She was on her way back to her room to sneak in a few hours reading her latest detective novel when the telephone rang at the front desk.

'Hello, Dolphin Hotel, how may I help?' Kitty answered it automatically. She knew Cyril and Dolly were both busy.

'Kitty, something terrible has happened to Lillie Trentham.' Matt's voice sounded urgently in her ear.

'Lillie? I thought she was recovering well. The inspector said she might even be allowed to return home today?' Kitty was bewildered by this turn of events.

'She's dead. Inspector Greville just telephoned from the police station. He'd not long left the hospital.'

Kitty gasped. 'Dead? But how? I thought she was getting better, and there was a police constable on guard outside her room.' Her mind raced with the possibilities. Had Lillie succumbed to the effects from the earlier poisoning or had someone made a fresh attempt to harm her?

'From what the inspector said it looks as if the poisoner has struck again.' Matt's voice was grave.

'But how? She didn't have any visitors, did she?' Had someone managed to access Lillie at the hospital?

Matt's voice rumbled in her ear once more. 'It seems that she received a box of chocolates from a well-wisher, violet creams, her favourites. They arrived in the post with a little card.'

Kitty shivered as if someone was walking on her grave. 'I don't suppose the card was signed? Not that I expect a murderer to attach their own name to a box of poisoned chocolates.'

'The signature was illegible as one might suppose but since they were her favourite sweets and no one except her immediate family and the other occupants of Villa Lamora knew she was in the hospital, it appears that she assumed they must be from someone there.' Matt's voice held a troubled note.

'Oh dear, poor Caroline. First her aunt is killed and now her mother, plus the attempt on her own life. This is a very nasty affair.' Kitty wondered which of the occupants of Villa Lamora could possibly be behind all of this.

'Inspector Greville is very worried. He's under a great deal of pressure from the acting chief constable to make an arrest and solve the case before Christmas. You know he has his own hopes for a promotion too?' Matt said.

'I take it that's why he is happy to allow us to continue with

our involvement in the case? To bring about a speedy result?'
Kitty could see that would make sense.

Matt gave a slightly grim sounding chuckle. 'I think so. The
inspector is obviously investigating where the chocolates may
have been acquired. The wrapping paper had been discarded so
no chance to try and find a postmark.'

'Oh, that's a pity.' Kitty frowned as she spoke. 'I presume
the inspector will be returning to the house again to speak to
everyone?'

'Yes, he has suggested we might care to meet him there. Are
you free at all to come over?' Matt asked.

'Yes, of course, I'll be right there.' Kitty ended the call and
hurried off to collect her things before calling out to Cyril and
Dolly to let them know that she was going out.

* * *

Matt was ready and waiting when Kitty's little red car pulled
up outside the house. Edgar and Bertie were both snoozing in
front of the fire as he left. Kitty's father had been shocked and
distressed by the news about Lillie and had expressed his relief
that he at least was no longer a resident at the house.

Matt pulled his dark-blue knitted scarf closer about his neck
as he took his seat beside Kitty. The weather had changed from
the previous day with the sea fog having given way to a bright
and crisp afternoon. Whilst the air was drier it was also colder.

'This is a shocking turn of events,' Kitty said as she put her
car into gear and pulled off onto the road.

'I must confess I was taken completely by surprise. I hadn't
anticipated that another attempt would be made on Lillie while
she was still at the hospital.' Matt cracked the window open
slightly and a stream of icy air circulated around the car.

Kitty was well wrapped up in her thick winter coat with a
fur collar around her neck and a delightful dark-green felt hat

with a red band perched on her short blonde curls. 'I agree. I would have thought any further danger to Lillie would have occurred after her discharge back to the house.'

The driveway at Villa Lamora was deserted when Kitty halted her car near the front door. Matt wound up his window. 'The inspector should be here shortly.' He glanced at his wristwatch.

At that the sound of tyres crunching on the gravel alerted them to the arrival of the inspector in his familiar black police car. A uniformed constable was at his side as he got out of the car. Kitty and Matt went to join him at the front door of the villa.

Matt could tell from the grim expression on the inspector's face that he was not looking forward to the task that lay ahead.

The butler answered the door promptly. His expression was equally solemn as they entered the house, wiping their feet on the matting as they walked into the hall.

'The household is gathered in the drawing room, sir, as you requested. Miss Trentham remains in her room. One of the maids is with her,' the butler informed them as he took their coats.

'Are they aware of what has happened, sir?' Matt asked in a low voice as they walked towards the drawing room. The constable who had been accompanying them headed up the elaborate dark oak staircase.

The inspector shook his head. 'I am about to inform them now. My constable will inform Miss Trentham of the news about her mother.'

Kitty remained silent as she followed behind them into the room. A fire burned in the grate but the air in the room was cool. Sir Stanford was seated on one side of the fireplace and Miss Morrow on the other. The secretary, Mr Peters, was seated at a table nearby apparently reviewing some correspondence. The Christmas cards previously displayed on the mantelpiece had been replaced by condolence cards. Matt assumed these were from those who had heard of Eliza Foxley's demise.

The Christmas tree in the corner was the only indication remaining of the festive season. The occupants of the room all turned their attention to the door as they entered. Matt could see Peters had his habitually worried expression. Sir Stanford looked slightly belligerent and Miss Morrow fretful as the inspector approached.

'Good afternoon, I am afraid that I have some very sad news to impart to you all,' Inspector Greville began as Kitty and Matt quietly took their seats at the back of the spacious room.

'What has happened?' Peters asked the question, his eyes wide with anxiety behind the lenses of his spectacles.

'I am very sorry to have to inform you that Mrs Lillie Trentham passed away this morning.'

A collective shocked gasp greeted this announcement. Matt watched the group closely for any sign, however slight, that might provide a clue as to which of them was responsible.

'Caroline, I must go to Caroline. Does she know? Is someone with her?' Miss Morrow rose from her seat. Her round-face pale and distressed.

The inspector held up his hand. 'Please sit back down, Miss Morrow. Miss Trentham is being told the news now. My constable and a maid will remain with her. She will have every care, I assure you.'

Tiny seemed to fall back onto her seat, tears began to stream unchecked down her cheeks. 'This is like a terrible nightmare. I thought, well we all thought, that she was recovering. I knew they had said she might relapse, but not this. We hoped she might even be home later today or tomorrow.'

'Mrs Trentham was indeed recovering well. Her death is as a result of a malicious act against her while she was in the hospital.' Matt was interested to see how the inspector was giving the news.

'You mean she was attacked? Murdered? While under police guard?' Sir Stanford stared at the inspector.

'Murdered?' Peters repeated the word in a horrified whisper.

'My poor Lillie killed in the hospital? How?' Miss Morrow asked.

'Mrs Trentham had received a box of her favourite chocolates in the post from a well-wisher.' The inspector paused and looked at the three suspects.

'Violet creams? She loved them, she could never resist them,' Miss Morrow seemed to speak without thinking of the possible implications of her words.

'Indeed, Miss Morrow, a box of violet creams. The top layer had been tampered with and poison added. Mrs Trentham ate several of them and sadly passed away as a consequence of this. Her constitution had been greatly weakened by the earlier attempt upon her, so she stood little chance of surviving this second attack.' Inspector Greville looked at Tiny.

The woman suddenly seemed to become aware of the implications of what she had said. 'I didn't, I mean everyone knew Lillie loved chocolate and which ones were her favourites. She would buy herself some regularly as a little treat. She only finished her last box a few days ago.' She looked wildly from Sir Stanford to Mr Peters as if seeking their support for her assertion.

Matt heard the distant ring of a telephone from the hallway.

'She did always have a sweet tooth,' Sir Stanford agreed. 'Eliza used to tease her about it.'

The door of the room opened, and another constable entered. He came to the inspector's side and handed him a slip of paper. Matt assumed that whatever it said was of some importance judging by the constable's flushed cheeks and the glint in his eye.

He remained next to the inspector as he read the contents.

'My constable has just taken a telephone call from the police station. We have received information that places one of you very much in the frame as the person who posted the chocolates to Mrs Trentham.' Inspector Greville's eyes narrowed.

A log on the fire cracked and spat a shower of sparks up into the air.

'Mr Peters, you posted several parcels and letters the other day.' The inspector swung around to look at the secretary.

'Well, yes, I met Miss Underhay and her cousin just before I went to the post office but none of those parcels were mine.' Peters blinked owlishly at the inspector, his face now a greenish white. 'Miss Morrow had wrapped them and gave them to me and asked me to take them.'

Inspector Greville nodded. 'Yes indeed, I also have more information. Miss Morrow's fingerprints have been discovered on the lid of the box of chocolates that killed Mrs Trentham.'

CHAPTER TWENTY

Another collective gasp rang around the room as Miss Morrow broke down into noisy sobs of denial. Kitty glanced at Matt and could see that he too looked surprised by this turn of events.

'I would never harm Lillie or Eliza, or anyone. I don't know anything about chocolates. I never sent her anything.'

Inspector Morrow signalled to the constable to escort the weeping woman from the room.

Miss Morrow stood somewhat shakily and looked wildly about the room.

'Miss Underhay, I implore you, go to Caroline and tell her. I didn't do anything. I'm innocent.' Miss Morrow was led away still protesting.

Kitty was left feeling quite shaken by the scene she had just witnessed. Why had Miss Morrow killed both Eliza and Lillie? Was it to keep Caroline close to her? She did appear to be very attached and protective of the girl. Or was she indeed afraid of losing her home and position if Caroline were sent off to school?

'Miss Underhay, may I trouble you to go upstairs to see Miss Trentham? Miss Morrow is correct in one aspect, the girl is bound to be very distressed. She has lost those dearest to her at the hands of the person charged with her care.' Inspector Greville spoke kindly.

'Yes, of course.' Kitty had been about to suggest the same thing herself although she was deeply troubled by what she had just witnessed.

'I'll wait here for you, Kitty.' Matt gave her hand a tender squeeze as she stood to follow the inspector's directions to Caroline's room.

The hum of male chatter followed her as she made her way up the imposing staircase and onto the landing. The other constable was at his post outside Caroline's door, and he stood at her approach as if to bar her way.

'Inspector Greville has sent me to see Miss Trentham. Miss Morrow has just been arrested,' Kitty explained.

A shadow of doubt passed over the policeman's face and Kitty thought he might not let her in. However, Inspector Greville seemed to have anticipated this and called up from the hallway to allow her entry to Miss Trentham's room.

On hearing his superior officer's instruction, the constable stood aside and opened the door. Caroline's room was large and airy. A comforting fire crackled merrily in the small black-leaded grate and the soft furnishings were a mix of soft green and rose. Kitty could see that no expense had been spared.

Caroline herself was seated on a pale-green velour-covered chair beside the fire. She appeared very young and vulnerable in her navy serge pinafore and dark stockings. A detective novel lay discarded on a small rosewood side table. The maid, a young girl in a smart grey uniform with white apron, sat discreetly a little further away, a basket of mending on her lap.

'Miss Underhay, has something more happened?' Caroline's eyes were red rimmed as if she had been crying.

'I'm afraid so, my dear.' Kitty took the other fireside chair opposite Caroline and nodded to the maid to leave them. She waited for the girl to go before proceeding.

Kitty noticed that the girl had her lace-edged handkerchief gripped firmly in her hands as if readying herself for further bad news.

'The inspector has made an arrest for the murder of your aunt and your mother. It seems that sadly your governess, Miss Morrow, is the person responsible,' Kitty said gently.

Caroline's face creased in bewilderment. 'Tiny? But that's impossible. Tiny loved my mother and Aunt Eliza. They were like her children. She would do anything for them. Why would Tiny hurt them? Is it because of me? Because I was to be sent away?'

'Her fingerprints have been found on the box of chocolates received by your mother at the hospital and it seems the parcel was amongst those she gave to Mr Peters to post,' Kitty explained.

'I don't understand. Does that mean that Tiny was the person who tried to kill me by pushing me down the stairs? Why? Why would she do that?' Caroline slumped back in her seat as if unable to take in what Kitty was telling her.

'It seems to be the most likely explanation, although I cannot see why she would have tried to harm you,' Kitty said.

A transient flicker of some undefined emotion crossed the girl's face. 'Perhaps she only meant to injure me, to keep me with her. She didn't want me to go to school, she was frightened that she would be made to retire.' Caro seemed numbed by the idea that her governess was responsible for everything that had happened at the house.

'Perhaps. She does seem very attached to you. But none of this is your fault you know.' Kitty had seen for herself how protective Tiny was towards Caroline.

Caroline dabbed at her eyes with her handkerchief. 'I just can't believe it.'

'I'm so sorry, my dear.' Kitty wondered what would happen to the girl now. She had no clear guardian with her mother and aunt dead and her temporary guardian in custody. 'Is there someone who can come and stay with you? Or someone you could go to? Another relative perhaps?'

Caroline shook her head. 'Aunt Eliza and my mother were my only family. I have the servants here to look after me and I expect Mr Peters and Sir Stanford would at least stay until after the New Year, wouldn't they?'

The girl seemed to have thought things out. 'I expect so. There would be little other choice in the matter until a guardian could be appointed for you. I don't know if there was such a provision in your aunt or your mother's will,' Kitty said.

Caroline sniffed and sat up straighter in her chair. 'I don't know. What will happen if there isn't such a clause? Will I get sent to the school Aunt Eliza had found for me in Switzerland?'

Kitty moved her shoulders, slightly uncomfortable at the question. 'I don't know. I would assume that the solicitor looking after your mother's estate will appoint someone, at least until you are of age. The inspector may know more of this than I do. Perhaps your aunt or mother has some friends who may assist you.'

Caroline shook her head. 'I don't know. Aunt Eliza's friends are not the kind of people who would be bothered with someone my age. My mother had very few friends that I was aware of.'

'Perhaps your godparents?' she suggested. It seemed very hard on the girl and even worse so close to Christmas that she should have no one to care for her.

Caroline dabbed at her eyes once more. 'Yes, perhaps. Thank you, Miss Underhay.'

'I wish I could do more to assist you,' Kitty said.

'You are getting married in a few days. I'm certain you have other things on your mind at the moment,' Caroline replied, a faint wan smile appearing for the first time at the corners of her lips.

Kitty patted the girl's hands. 'All the same, I am at the Dolphin Hotel in Dartmouth if you should require assistance. If I am not free my grandmother or my cousin would be glad to help you, I am certain.'

'That is very kind of you.' Caroline managed another somewhat watery smile.

'Would you like the maid to return, to keep you company?' Kitty asked as she stood ready to take her leave.

The girl shook her head. 'No, thank you. I think I need to be alone for a while. It's a lot to take in.'

'Of course. Remember, you may contact me at any time if you need assistance.' Kitty wasn't sure why she felt so compelled to make the offer. Something about the girl's age and her being alone in the world made her recall how she had felt so many years ago when her own mother had vanished. Perhaps that was why.

'Thank you, Miss Underhay,' Caroline said.

Kitty turned slightly at the door, unsure if she should say anything else to comfort the girl. It had grown dark now outside the house and the curtains had not been drawn. She wasn't sure if there was a distortion in the glass of the windowpane. For a brief moment she thought she saw an odd expression flicker across Caroline's face as it was reflected in the glass.

She left the room and bade good day to the constable. As she made her way back downstairs, she tried to decide what she had seen. Sadness? Fear? A little of those, perhaps. It was when she reached the hall where Matt was waiting for her that she realised it had been triumph.

Matt greeted her with a tender kiss on her cheek. 'Everything all right, old thing?'

'Yes, I think so. Miss Trentham seems to be quite a sensible young woman given the circumstances.' Kitty wondered if perhaps she was a little too sensible. She decided that she was being unkind. It was far more likely that the girl was still in shock.

'Thank you for seeing Miss Trentham.' Inspector Greville joined them. 'How did the girl take the news of Miss Morrow's arrest?'

'She was distressed, as you would expect. It seems she has no one now to take care of her,' Kitty said.

'I shall be speaking to the family solicitor to see if anyone is named as a guardian in either Lillie or Eliza's wills. In the interim, Mr Peters and Sir Stanford are remaining at the house. Mr Hedges, the butler, and the rest of the staff will oversee the running of the home and will care for the girl.'

'Poor Caroline. It won't be much of a Christmas for her,' Kitty said as she glanced back up the stairs.

'No indeed, rest assured that I shall do what I can for her, Miss Underhay,' the inspector said.

'Thank you.' Kitty and Matt left the policeman to continue his work and walked towards the front door. Once more they collected their outdoor things from the cloakroom without bothering the servants.

Kitty paused for a moment to look up at the portrait of Lady Foxley. 'She was so beautiful and full of life. It seems simply awful that both she and Lillie have perished at the hands of Miss Morrow.'

Matt tucked his knitted scarf inside the collar of his coat and came to stand next to her.

'I know what you mean. Come, let's get away from here, it will be dinner time soon and we dare not be late.' He gave her a tender smile, comforting her.

Edgar was out when they returned to Matt's house. Bertie greeted them happily in the hall, his tail wagging with delight at their return.

'There's a note,' Matt said as he looked on the hall table beside the telephone.

'Gone on ahead in a taxi. Edgar,' Matt read.

Kitty fussed Bertie's ears as she looked around for a clock to give her the time. 'Oh dear, are we terribly late?' She presumed that they must be as her father wouldn't willingly seek out her grandmother's company ahead of dinner.

'It'll be a tight squeak. I'll run up and change and then we can go.' He disappeared upstairs so Kitty went through to the sitting room to wait for him.

The newspaper her father had been reading lay crumpled and discarded on the sofa. Kitty picked it up to straighten and fold it, intending to place it in the chrome paper rack until it was needed for kindling.

As she shook out the pages and levelled them up, she noticed a number of the sporting fixtures at the back of the paper had small pencil marks next to them.

* * *

Matt changed for dinner as swiftly as he could before hurrying back downstairs to discover Kitty pacing about the sitting room.

'Could you give me a hand with these cufflinks, please, darling.' He dropped the monogrammed gold cufflinks into her palm and held out his arm for her to fasten his shirt cuffs.

Her nimble fingers made swift work of the fiddly fastenings.

'Thank you.' He was a little surprised by her slightly absent smile and he could see that she had something on her mind.

He pulled on his dinner jacket and ushered Bertie into the kitchen. Bertie gave a long-suffering sigh and settled himself in his blanket-lined basket beside the range to continue his destruction of the wicker rim.

'Is everything all right, Kitty?' Matt asked as he donned his overcoat once more to follow his fiancée out to her car.

He wondered if the afternoon's events had proved too much for her. It had clearly distressed her to see Miss Morrow arrested and he suspected it must have been quite harrowing breaking that news to Caroline.

'Yes, I'm perfectly fine, really.' Kitty started up her car once more and gave him a reassuring glance as she switched on her headlamps ready to drive down to the ferry at Kingswear.

'Something is playing on your mind, I can tell. Was it the events at Villa Lamora this afternoon?' Matt asked as she swung the car off the drive onto the lane.

'That was quite upsetting, but no, I suppose I'm worrying about my father.' Kitty's words took him by surprise. He had thought that with her father having been exonerated from the investigation that Edgar wouldn't be a huge concern any more.

'Oh?' Matt asked.

'I folded up the newspaper he had been reading while you were upstairs. The sporting section is covered with his notations. He is clearly gambling quite heavily.'

Matt was unsurprised by this. Edgar had already revealed the parlous state of his finances. Then, when Alice had followed him, his actions had seemed to confirm that was what he was about.

The set of Kitty's mouth and the determined line of her jaw clearly indicated her disapproval of her father's gambling.

'It's not ideal, but I suppose he knows his own business,' Matt said as they drew into Kingswear and prepared to board the ferry to cross the river.

Kitty looked unimpressed by this statement so Matt decided it would be wise to say nothing further on the subject. He understood why Kitty was worried. Edgar always seemed to swing between poverty and riches. Betting was illegal unless at a course, but bookies' runners were stationed at many friendly public houses. By and large too the police tended to turn a blind eye to the activities unless it caused any trouble.

Kitty managed to park close to the Dolphin when they reached Dartmouth.

'Oh dear, we are a little late,' Kitty said as they hurried into the lobby.

'I'll go in and tell them you'll be there shortly,' Matt offered as they scampered up the stairs towards her grandmother's salon where everyone was to gather for pre-dinner drinks.

Kitty pressed a quick kiss on his cheek and sped up the next flight of stairs.

'Matthew, where is Kitty? We were just about to adjourn to the dining room?' Kitty's grandmother asked as he slipped inside the salon.

'She will be down very shortly. We were delayed in Torquay by Inspector Greville,' Matt explained as his father pressed a cut glass of whisky and soda into his hand.

'Yes, Edgar said you had been called away. Such terrible news about Mrs Trentham, one wonders what will happen to the girl now. It's a bad business.' Mrs Craven was seated in one of the armchairs beside the fire nursing an almost empty glass of sherry. Her cheeks were quite rosy in the firelight.

'Indeed, it was most distressing,' Matt agreed.

His mother pressed her hand to her heart. 'One can't help feeling that this is all a sign. A bad omen, especially so close to your wedding.'

Kitty's grandmother gave her a scathing look. 'Really, Patience dear.'

His aunt Effie snorted and barely succeeded in turning a laugh into an unconvincing cough, while Kitty's aunt Livvy smiled gently.

'Talking of strange omens,' Edgar said. 'While you and Kitty were out, dear boy, I had a gypsy turn up at the door.'

Kitty entered the room as her father was speaking and came to Matt's side to join him. 'A gypsy? That's unusual at this time of year. We usually see them in the spring or the autumn.'

'That's true, they are usually busy at the Christmas markets

at this time, selling their wares there rather than door-to-door,'
Mrs Craven agreed.

'She was selling pegs and bundles of holly. I thought it best
just to buy something, you know, just to avoid any bad luck,'
Edgar said.

Matt saw his mother clutch at her heart once more at the
mention of bad luck.

'She offered to tell my fortune.' Edgar downed the rest of his
drink.

'Did you accept?' Lucy asked from where she was perched
on the arm of the sofa beside Rupert. Muffy as usual was curled
up at her feet. 'I must admit I've always wondered what it
would be like to have that done.'

'Heavens no, I'm afraid I don't believe in any of that tosh.
I've seen rather too many charlatans in my time.' Edgar laughed
and a murmur broke out in the room. Matt thought the men
appeared to agree with Kitty's father while the ladies were more
circumspect.

'So, you didn't get any lucky heather then?' Mrs Craven
asked.

'That would have been prudent,' Matt's mother murmured
hopefully.

'No, it wasn't something she had in her basket. She did say
though that someone close to me was about to marry and they
should take care,' Edgar concluded. He seemed to realise as
soon as he had spoken that this perhaps was not the wisest thing
to say in front of Matt's mother.

'Oh dear.' Matt's mother's eyes had widened at Edgar's
statement.

'Load of old rot. These so-called fortune tellers make up
anything.' Matt's father glared at Edgar.

'Quite so. She probably meant that someone might spill
something on your dress, Kitty, or you could trip going into
church,' Lucy said.

'Well, we all seem to be here so shall we go down to supper?' Kitty's grandmother suggested as Mr Lutterworth entered the room looking very dapper in his evening attire. Kitty's grandmother had invited him to join them once the front door of the hotel had been locked for the night.

Mr Lutterworth gallantly offered Mrs Craven his arm, leaving Kitty's grandmother to somewhat reluctantly accept Edgar's. The dining room looked very festive with garlands and a red and green table setting with roses and fir cones mixed with sprigs of holly.

Matt took his seat beside Kitty thinking how well her dark-red evening gown suited her fair complexion. He noticed Muffy slip under the table and smiled to himself.

Kitty's grandmother had arranged for the hotel's headwaiter to be on duty, assisted by young Albert, the kitchen boy, wearing slightly over-large clothing and a huge smile as he carefully followed his employer's instruction.

Once the leek and potato soup had been served the conversation continued.

'I still feel very uneasy. Murders and then this gypsy,' Matt's mother crumbled her dinner roll into pieces on her plate.

Matt bit his tongue. He was used to his mother and her histrionics. He was aware that his parents, whilst being friends with Kitty's grandmother, did not think Kitty a suitable wife. It struck him, however, that it was a little odd that this gypsy had seemed to know that a wedding was imminent and connected to his home.

'A gypsy?' Mr Lutterworth asked.

Mrs Craven explained Edgar's visitor and her warning. Cyril had clearly missed the original conversation as he had only joined them as they were about to go downstairs to dine.

'A gypsy presented herself in the lobby here today too, peddling her wares. Young Dolly sent her off with a flea in her ear,' Mr Lutterworth said.

'There must be a group of them going about the towns.' Mrs Craven dipped her spoon into her soup.

Matt was unsure. It seemed unlikely that a gypsy would be at the Dolphin in Dartmouth and then across the river and up the hill to his home in Churston all in one day. If there was more than one of them, they surely would have visited all the premises in one place before moving on to the next village.

'Well, I still think—'

Matt's father cut off whatever nonsense his mother was about to say. 'Excellent soup, just the ticket on a winter's night.'

The conversation progressed to food until the next course was served. Roast beef with all the trimmings and Yorkshire puddings, which met with his aunt Effie's approval.

'Has the inspector made an arrest yet, Matthew? You didn't tell us what happened when you went to Torquay?' Mrs Craven asked, looking down the dinner table towards him.

'Yes, indeed he has. It seems that it was Miss Morrow who killed both Eliza and Lillie.' Matt helped himself to mustard.

A ripple went around the table.

'Miss Morrow? Isn't she the governess?' Rupert asked as Muffy emerged from under the white linen tablecloth to sit closer to Lucy.

'She's the woman who accused me. No wonder she wished to divert attention from herself.' Kitty's father looked shocked by the news.

'Why did she do it?' Lucy asked as she slipped a bit of roast beef discreetly to her dog.

Matt gave a small shrug. 'It seems that she wished to remain with Caroline and with both sisters intent on sending the girl away she murdered them.'

'Oh dear, how awful. I really don't think this is suitable conversation for the dining table, Matthew dear,' his mother reproved him.

'Then why injure the girl? I presume she was responsible

for that as well?' Rupert took no notice of Matt's mother's plaintive complaint.

'I suppose she only intended to slightly injure her rather than kill her,' Lucy guessed. 'Then Caroline wouldn't be able to go off to school, she would have to stay at home until she recovered. Didn't Mrs Trentham say how good Miss Morrow had been at caring for Caroline when she was taken ill in New York?' She looked at Kitty's father.

'Yes, she has experience with nursing, I believe,' Edgar agreed.

Matt thought Lucy's suggestion was very plausible.

'It doesn't bear thinking about. That poor child.' Kitty's aunt Livvy shuddered.

'At least the real culprit is now behind bars. Thankfully we shall all sleep more safely in our beds now tonight,' Mrs Craven declared.

CHAPTER TWENTY-ONE

Kitty allowed the dinner conversation to wash over her as the topic was changed from murder to the wedding. She and Lucy were to collect their dresses in the morning from Mademoiselle Desmoine's.

Matt and Rupert were to ensure that the floral bouquets and buttonholes were all delivered and checked, to be stored in the cold room of the hotel. The church flowers had already been sent to St Saviour's. Mr Lutterworth and her grandmother were checking the wedding breakfast arrangements and the arrival of the cake from the local bakery.

She savoured the sweet creamy taste of the trifle that had been provided for dessert and allowed herself to enjoy the evening. For once everyone seemed to be getting along quite well. Lucy's parents were due to arrive the next day and they were all to attend the carol concert at the church on the evening. A lovely festive outing to set the tone for the weekend.

The aunts and Mrs Craven were also very intent on ensuring that the group attended morning service at St Saviour's on Sunday. Matt's mother seemed to feel that this was a good suggestion. By the time they withdrew to the residents' lounge for coffee and petits fours Kitty was in a good mood. The murder was solved, and it seemed that her wedding was going to be everything that she had intended.

The Christmas tree sparkled in the lamplight in the lounge and a trolley loaded with glasses and various bottles was placed next to the other trolley containing all the accoutrements for coffee. Their jobs completed for the evening, the waiter and Albert withdrew, each with a nice tip in their pockets from Matt.

'You haven't yet said where you are to honeymoon?' Lucy said as she took a seat beside Kitty. Muffy trotted across and eyed Kitty's plate, which held a tiny and delicate pale green macaron.

'We thought we would go away in the new year some-where,' Matt said as he came to join them. They had planned just to return to Matt's home immediately after the wedding breakfast since the following day would be Christmas Day.

'That sounds very sensible. You could go abroad in the spring, Paris, perhaps, or Nice,' his aunt Effie suggested.

'I'll leave it to Kitty to choose.' Matt smiled at her, and Kitty felt her cheeks growing warm.

'I suppose you have been to most places already, Matthew,' his father said somewhat dismissively.

Kitty knew Matt had travelled extensively with his previous job for the home office. She, on the other hand, had not really gone far from Devon. At least not in the last few years. As an infant her parents had travelled extensively.

'You could come to New York,' her father suggested.

Kitty smiled at Edgar. 'Now there's a thought.' She wasn't certain if she did wish to visit New York to see her father. Some-times, much as she loved him, the distance between them was a good thing.

Lucy rose to put some music on the gramophone and the evening passed much more pleasantly than Kitty had anticipated.

Matt and her father were due to leave just before eleven in order to catch the last but one ferry across the river. Mr Potter had already taken Mrs Craven to her home in Dartmouth before coming back to collect Matt and her father to transport them to Churston.

'The taxi has returned,' Cyril informed them.

'I'll see you tomorrow evening, darling,' Matt murmured in her ear as the party made their way to the lobby to see the guests off. 'Just, well, be very careful.' His breath was warm on her cheek.

'Of course.' Kitty wondered what had come over him. His mood had suddenly become quite sombre.

'It's this gypsy business. I don't like it.' He kept his voice low so none of the others could hear him.

Kitty's good mood evaporated in a flash and her senses went into alert. 'You think it may have been Esther?' she asked.

'I think it's possible.' He kissed her cheek and disappeared into the cold night air to catch up with her father.

A shiver ran through Kitty that wasn't just generated by the chilly air that had entered the lobby through the front door. Of course, she should have realised. There was every possibility that Esther Hammett was up to her tricks again.

Kitty was woken the following morning by the arrival of Alice accompanied by Lucy in her bedroom.

'I saw Alice with the tray and invited myself along. You don't mind, do you? I brought my own cup,' Lucy said cheerfully as she turned one of the fireside chairs to face the bed. 'I've so missed a good girlish chat since I've become an old married woman.' Muffy who had pattered in beside her took up a spot near the fireplace.

Kitty sat herself up as Alice placed the heavy breakfast tray down beside her. 'Of course not, silly.' She smiled at her cousin.

''Tis a good thing I have the bigger teapot with me and some extra toast.' Alice also smiled as she accepted Lucy's cup before fetching her own thicker one from her apron pocket.

'It's an exciting day today, collecting the dresses,' Lucy said as Alice poured the tea.

'Yes, it will make it all feel more real. I think with this murder investigation I perhaps have been a bit distracted from my wedding.' Kitty accepted her cup and saucer from Alice and settled herself for a comfortable chat.

'Well, that's all done with now, thank goodness. Mr Lutterworth told our Dolly this morning as it were that governess woman who done it.' Alice passed a cup to Lucy before pouring her own drink.

Lucy gave an exaggerated shiver. 'Such a beastly thing to have done, and to people who have been so good to her.'

Kitty frowned. 'Miss Morrow had been with them a very long time. She knew all their secrets and she seemed to love Caroline as if she was her own child. Now the poor girl is all alone in the world.'

'Well, enough of thinking of all that now. You'm getting wed on Monday.' Alice had perched herself in her usual spot on the end of Kitty's bed.

'I hope the dresses are done and there are no problems with the flowers,' Kitty said.

'We shall see the flower arrangements tonight at the church. Aren't they putting them in today so they can use them for the carol concert and the Sunday service?' Lucy asked as she took a sip of her tea.

'The vicar asked me, and I was delighted to oblige. It

seemed to be sensible.' Kitty set down her cup and helped herself to toast. She had seen no reason why her arrangements of white Christmas roses with evergreen shouldn't be enjoyed by everyone and not just for her wedding.

'Alice dear, are you sure you wish to assist us when we dress for the ceremony? I feel so awful that you are not joining us as part of the wedding party,' Lucy asked, slipping her dog a corner of her slice of toast.

Alice had stoutly declined to be a bridesmaid but had offered her services to dress their hair and get them ready for the church. Something she had done in Yorkshire when Lucy had been the bride and Kitty her bridesmaid.

'I'm looking forward to it.' Alice's tone was firm, brooking no argument.

Kitty reached out and squeezed her friend's hand. 'We are very grateful for your help, Alice.'

''Tis my pleasure. I'm looking forward to seeing you in your gown. It sounds lovely.' Alice had provided Kitty with several pictures taken from various bridal and her beloved film magazines. She had seemed to believe that the weddings of famous actors and actresses would show the latest fashions.

'You have been really helpful when I was choosing a design,' Kitty said.

Her friend blushed at the praise.

'Yes, you have such a good eye for these things,' Lucy agreed.

Kitty placed her butter knife back on her plate and looked at her companions. 'There is just one tiny thing.'

The other women looked at her.

'It's probably nothing but I'm telling you both just so that you can stay alert. Please don't let Grams or the aunts know. And especially don't let anything slip in front of Matt's mother,' Kitty said.

'Darling, whatever is it?' Lucy looked alarmed.

'You'll recall that I was told by Father Lamb that Esther Hammett was thought to be back in Exeter. The police are aware. The business yesterday of that gypsy woman turning up at Matt's house and also here at the hotel, well, it could have been Esther. It all seems too much of a coincidence.' Kitty felt better for voicing her fears out loud.

A frown creased Alice's forehead. 'Our Dolly said as a woman had called at the hotel. Nerve of her, she come to the lobby instead of a going round to the kitchen door. Dolly got rid of her quick smart. Told her as we were closed as the family had a special event on.'

'What did the woman look like, did Dolly say?' Kitty asked.

'She didn't take much account of her I don't think. She said as she were a gypsy, big woollen shawl around her and a wicker pedlars' basket with holly and mistletoe and such in it.' Alice was clearly trying to recollect what her sister had told her about the encounter.

'She could just have been part of a number of women calling at various establishments to sell their wares.' Lucy finished her tea.

'It's possible, but better to be careful. Matt was concerned about what she said to Edgar when she called at his house.' Kitty appreciated her cousin's attempt to reassure her.

Realisation dawned on her cousin's face. 'Oh, the warning about the wedding?'

Kitty nodded.

Alice finished her own drink and replaced her cup on the tray. 'We'll keep our eyes peeled; don't you fret. Wretched woman. Anyways time's a ticking, Miss Kitty. You'd best get going if you wants to collect your wedding dress.'

Lucy let out a squeak of alarm when she looked at the time on Kitty's clock. 'Heavens, I shall fly and leave you to dress. I'll meet you downstairs. Come on, Muffy.' She hustled herself and her pet out of Kitty's bedroom.

Alice collected the breakfast tray and prepared to return to her duties. 'I'll tell our Dolly to keep an eye out too, miss. Can't be too careful, that Hammett woman is capable of anything.'

Torquay was busy when Kitty drove her little red car along the seafront towards the main shopping area looking for a place to stop near the bridal shop. The air smelt of ozone where the high tide had splashed seaweed over the wall onto the pavement beside the road. Everyone was out and about in the pale wintry sunshine looking for last-minute gifts.

She finally managed to park in a spot vacated by a grocer's van near to the shop. Mademoiselle Desmoine had everything boxed ready for them to collect, including her veil and the fur-trimmed capes she had promised.

One of the young girl assistants helped them to carry everything to the car and installed the boxes safely on the rear seat.

'I hope the boys have collected the flowers from the florists,' Lucy said as she retook her place in the passenger seat.

Kitty hoped so too. Everything so far had gone according to plan. 'Matt said that Father intended to move out of the house to the Imperial today too.'

'Oh, that's good. I suppose he didn't wish to still be at the house after the wedding. It would have been a trifle uncomfortable.' Lucy giggled.

Kitty joined in with her cousin's laughter. 'No, I expect he would feel a bit of a gooseberry.'

The traffic was slow as they drove back along the coast road to make their way towards Paignton and up onto the Dartmouth Road.

'That looks like that chap we met the other day, Mr Peters,' Lucy remarked. 'With a young woman.'

Kitty turned her head to glance briefly in the direction her cousin had indicated. 'So it is. It looks as if Miss Trentham is with him.'

A blast of a car horn from somewhere behind her forced her attention back to the road.

'I expect a walk by the sea might help soothe Miss Trentham's mind,' Lucy said, still craning her neck in an attempt to see where the couple had headed.

'Poor girl. It must be hard seeing everyone else preparing to spend time with their families when everyone she loves has been taken from her,' Kitty mused.

Lucy turned back around in her seat as Kitty picked up speed as the traffic began to thin. 'At least Mr Peters is being kind to her. I suppose having a sister of a similar age he is used to knowing what to do to help.'

Kitty thought her cousin made a good point. Caroline had certainly had a rough deal in her life. Eliza had given her in secret to Lillie at birth and then the girl had lost the man she knew as her father while still a young child. And now both her aunt and her mother killed by her governess. What was to become of the girl?

They drove back to Dartmouth and Lucy helped her to transport the wedding gown and other paraphernalia up to Kitty's room. Matt and Rupert had delivered the flowers to the kitchen cold store and had taken the aunts and Kitty's grandmother out on some mysterious errands.

Mr Lutterworth informed them that Matt's parents were in the residents' lounge taking a morning coffee. Lucy excused herself to collect Muffy from where her little dog had been out with Mickey, Kitty's maintenance man.

Kitty took a deep breath and decided that she really should go and join Matt's parents at least for a while in an attempt to improve her relationship with them before the wedding. After all they were soon to be her in-laws.

'Good morning,' Kitty greeted them cheerily as she entered the lounge.

'Kitty, my dear, have you and Lady Woodcomb collected the dresses already?' Matt's mother asked as Kitty came to sit on one of the empty seats next to them.

'Yes, all done and safely stowed away upstairs,' Kitty replied.

'I do hope they have done a good job. One never can tell sometimes with dressmakers.' Patience took a sip of her coffee. She made no offer for Kitty to join them.

'I'm sure it will be fine. It's only for one day after all. Well, a few hours really. We didn't make so much fuss in our day, did we, Patience?' Matt's father added.

'No, indeed. Matthew's first wife merely wore her best suit, or so I'm told. Still, it was wartime,' Patience agreed.

'Of course your parents eloped, didn't they? Quite upset your grandmother was at the time.' Matt's father looked at Kitty.

'Yes, sir, they married in London.' Kitty had often wondered how Matt had managed to be born to such a couple. His father was a brusque former military man and Matt's mother was one of life's pessimists, determined to worry or find fault with everything and everyone.

'Your father seems quite a character.' Matt's father stroked his moustache dubiously.

Kitty thought that 'character' was probably being generous. 'My aunt and uncle, Lucy's parents, are arriving later today. It will be nice having everyone together before the wedding.'

'Your aunt is your father's sister, I believe?' Patience asked.

'Yes, they own Enderley Hall, just outside Exeter. Aunt Hortense is a great gardener. My uncle works in manufacturing. They would have been here sooner but my uncle does a great deal of work for the government and had several meetings to attend.' Kitty would be pleased to see them both. She was very fond of Lucy's parents. In the short time she had known them they had always been very kind to her.

'I believe Effie knows your uncle from when she was a girl.' This was as close to anything approving that Matt's father had ever said to Kitty.

'She said that when I met her at Lucy and Rupert's wedding in Yorkshire.' Her first meeting with Aunt Effie had been quite an ordeal but it had ended well, and Matt's aunt had even approved of the match enough to pass on the family engagement ring, which was now on Kitty's finger.

'Jolly good.' Matt's father picked up his newspaper and Kitty guessed the conversation was at an end. Patience seemed disinclined to talk further so Kitty reassured herself that she had tried her best.

'Begging your pardon, Miss Kitty, but you'm needed for a moment.' Dolly was at the door of the lounge.

Kitty rose quickly and made good her escape.

'Dolly, you're a lifesaver,' she murmured once she was out of the room.

'Our Alice said as you was worried about that gypsy woman who was here yesterday,' Dolly said, stopping at the front desk in the deserted lobby.

'Yes, Matt was concerned in case Esther Hammett might be up to her tricks again,' Kitty said.

Dolly's expression was troubled. 'I've done a bit of asking about this morning while you were out.'

Kitty sensed that she wasn't going to like what the girl was about to tell her. She knew that Dolly knew a lot of tradespeople in both Dartmouth and the other nearby towns. 'Do go on, Dolly.'

'Well, according to all the tradespeople there aren't no gypsies encamped anywhere near here at the minute. There was a group near Cockington, but they moved on a week or so ago. The nearest ones here about are in Exeter for the market.'

Kitty's stomach somersaulted at the news. She had been pushing her bad feelings about Esther to one side while she tried to focus on the wedding. It seemed now, however, that Matt had been right to be concerned.

CHAPTER TWENTY-TWO

Kitty barely had time to reassure a concerned Dolly that she would stay alert to any possible threat from Esther when Matt arrived.

'Your father has moved to the Imperial this morning.' He kissed Kitty's cheek. 'And, the bouquets and buttonholes are in the cold store ready for Monday.' He looked at her with a puzzled frown. 'Is something wrong? Were the dresses all right?'

'The dresses are perfect. No, you were right to be suspicious about the gypsy. Dolly has checked.' She quickly told him what her young assistant had learned.

Matt's mouth hardened into a grim line. 'May I use the telephone? I think Inspector Pinch should be informed.'

Kitty nodded and he dialled Exeter Police Station using the telephone on the reception desk. Dolly returned to her work in the office.

Rupert and Lucy, accompanied by Muffy, joined them at the end of the call. Matt told them what Kitty had learned.

'Oh dear, darling.' Lucy looked concerned. 'We shall all be on our guard.'

Kitty had to admit she felt somewhat better about Esther knowing that so many people were intent on protecting her.

'Let's go out for lunch, Mother and Father will be here in a couple of hours and it would be nice to have a little time together before they arrive,' Lucy suggested.

'Why not?' Matt agreed.

Kitty thought it sounded better than making conversation once again with Matt's parents at the luncheon table so made no objection to the plan.

The rest of the day passed pleasantly. Her aunt and uncle arrived from Exeter and Kitty's worries about Esther Hammett gradually subsided. After high tea, everyone prepared for church and the evening's carol concert.

Since the evening was dry and crisp, it was agreed that they would walk through the town to the church. The lights were on along the embankment and around the edge of the boat float. Kitty rested her gloved hand in the crook of Matt's elbow and enjoyed the feeling of being surrounded by her friends and family as they walked.

The ancient wooden church door was open as they arrived with warm yellow light spilling out onto the path. The service was usually well attended, and the pews were filling rapidly as they entered the church.

Kitty was pleased to see her flowers had been carefully arranged and added an extra touch to the church. A large Christmas tree covered in carved wooden and painted ornaments stood to one side near the ornate stone font. Beside it stood the nativity set. The stable with the animals, the shepherds, angels, the kings and with Mary and Joseph. The manger remained empty, waiting for the arrival of the baby Jesus on Christmas Day.

Kitty found herself seated beside a little girl of around seven who was accompanied by her mother, with Matt on her other side. All around them was the cheerful buzz of friends and neighbours catching up on news and wishing each other a Merry Christmas.

The little girl had her head tilted to one side as she studied the nativity scene and the Christmas tree.

'Father Christmas is coming on Monday night,' she informed Kitty.

'Yes, on Christmas Eve. Not long to wait,' Kitty replied, amused by the child's excitement.

'P'raps he'll bring baby Jesus then as well.' The child looked at the empty manger.

Kitty tried not to laugh. 'Have you asked for something for Christmas?'

The girl heaved a big sigh and peered up at Kitty from under the brim of her red knitted hat. 'Dad says if I'm good then I might get a dolly, but my brother, Jack, says I'll probably get a lump of coal.' She looked away to stick her tongue out at a slightly older boy seated on the other side of her mother.

Kitty assumed he was probably her brother. 'The church looks very pretty tonight.'

The child nodded. 'Yes, Mother says as a lady is getting married here on Monday. I wanted to come and see but everybody is busy that day 'cause of Father Christmas.'

Kitty smiled. 'Well, I'm the lady that's getting married.' It felt odd saying the words out loud in the church where she would be taking her vows.

The girl looked at her with interest. 'Will you have a new dress? All pretty like?'

Kitty nodded. 'Yes.'

The girl seemed to think about this for a minute. 'That's good. P'raps Father Christmas will bring you a baby then.'

The music started for the first carol and as they all rose to sing Kitty smiled to herself at the note of approval that had been in the child's voice. She hoped that Father Christmas wouldn't bring her a baby, not for a while at least.

The girl's words played on her mind throughout the concert, and she found her gaze constantly drifting to the nativity set and the empty manger. At the end of the concert, she walked with Matt through the crowd to find the rest of their party outside the church.

'A most delightful service. It reminded me of the ones we usually have at Enderley,' Lucy's mother said as she snuggled down into the large fur collar of her coat.

Kitty suppressed a slight shudder when she remembered the events of last Christmas at her aunt and uncle's home. Matt looked at her and she could see the amused twinkle in his eyes.

'Let's start back, it's grown much colder while we've been in church,' her aunt Livvy said as she accepted Mr Lutterworth's arm.

As they made their way back through the town to the Dolphin, Kitty tried to shake off the uneasy feeling that had settled on her during the concert.

Kitty woke the following morning after a restless night. The evening had passed pleasantly enough after they had returned from church. They had played games and there had been dancing to music from the gramophone. There was no reason why she should have tossed and turned all night.

Her head ached as she dressed for morning service and went downstairs to join the others for breakfast. Matt was to meet them at the hotel before they set off for church once more. Alice was also meeting them at the church with Dolly, since both sisters had the day off.

The bells were ringing as they once again braved the cold air to walk through the town and up the hill to St Saviour's. The sun appeared fleetingly from behind the clouds and a stiff breeze was blowing in along the estuary.

'You look a bit peaky this morning, old thing. Are you

feeling all right?' Matt asked her as they drew closer to the entrance of the church.

'I've had a bad night's sleep, so I've a bit of a headache today.' Kitty forced a wan smile of reassurance and hoped the aspirin she had taken earlier would start working soon. She couldn't help feeling that there had been something she had missed at the previous night's carol service. Something important.

'Perhaps you should rest this afternoon. Tomorrow will be a busy day.' He placed his hand tenderly over hers where it was resting on the crook of his arm.

Dolly and Alice greeted them with wide smiles, and they all made their way inside the church. Kitty was a little surprised to see Inspector Greville already seated on one of the pews. He seemed to be unaccompanied by Mrs Greville or any of his children.

'Good morning, Inspector. I hadn't anticipated seeing you here today,' Kitty said as she joined him.

'Inspector Pinch passed on the word about Esther Hammett. I thought it would be prudent to be here this morning as I knew you all planned to attend,' the inspector murmured. 'Just to be on the safe side.'

Kitty was touched by his thoughtfulness. 'Thank you, Inspector. That's very kind of you.'

'My pleasure, Miss Underhay. You can never tell with that family what they might have planned.' His moustache twitched. 'The word is that son of hers is due to stand trial in the new year.'

Kitty had encountered Esther's son during their last big case. No one had been aware of his existence before, and Kitty would have been glad never to have encountered him at all.

'Has a guardian been found for Miss Trentham?' Kitty asked.

'The secretary and Sir Stanford are staying with her at Villa

Lamora until after New Year. It is then planned to send her away to school as her mother intended,' Inspector Greville said.

'How is Miss Morrow?' Kitty felt compelled to ask about the elderly governess. She had appeared so devoted to Caroline. It still felt shocking that she could have killed Lillie and Eliza.

'Alternating between proclaiming her innocence and wailing about Miss Trentham being alone for Christmas,' the inspector remarked drily as he picked up his hymn book ready for the start of the service.

She wanted to ask more questions, but the service started so she was forced to turn her attention to her own hymn book instead. The inspector's words played in her mind as they listened to the lesson and the readings. Her gaze kept finding the empty manger in the nativity scene.

As the service finished, and people began to exit from the pews Kitty turned back to the inspector. 'I was wondering, all that business about Caroline's birth?'

Inspector Greville appeared startled by her question. 'What of it, Miss Underhay?'

'Well, obviously Lillie and Eliza and Miss Morrow were all party to what happened, but didn't Sir Stanford hint that he knew or had heard whispers of something?' Kitty asked.

The inspector frowned. 'Yes, that was what he said, but I'm not following you, Miss Underhay.'

'What is it, Kitty?' Matt asked.

'It may be nothing, but I think we need to revisit Villa Lamora, Inspector,' Kitty said.

'The case is closed, Miss Underhay.' Inspector Greville glanced around the almost empty church.

'Is it closed if the real culprit is still at large?' Kitty asked.

'I don't quite follow...' the inspector said.

'Please, Inspector Greville, indulge a bride-to-be. If I'm mistaken, then no harm is done. Miss Morrow is still in your custody, and I can get married tomorrow knowing that all is well.' Kitty placed her hand on the inspector's coat sleeve. Her heart pounded and she thought for a moment that he would not acquiesce.

Inspector Greville raised his eyebrows but agreed to Kitty's request. They made their excuses to the rest of their party and hastened down the street to where the inspector had parked his black police motor car.

'Please can we hurry, Inspector,' Kitty asked once they were all inside the car. 'I have a very bad feeling about the occupants of that house.'

Matt looked at her curiously as the inspector started his car and, once across the river, he upped his speed along the road towards Torquay. To her relief the inspector didn't ask her to elaborate on why they needed to return to the house, and quickly. She had only just begun to fit all the pieces of the puzzle together herself.

They pulled to a halt on the gravel drive of Villa Lamora and hurried to the front door. The butler answering their ring appeared startled to see them all back again so soon.

'Miss Trentham is in the drawing room,' he replied when Kitty asked Caroline's whereabouts.

She declined his offer to take her coat and hurried along the hall, her heels clicking on the tile floor. Matt was at her side with the inspector close on her heels. The scene as they opened the door was one of domestic bliss. Caroline was engaged in a card game with Phillip Peters, while Sir Stanford was engrossed in the Sunday paper beside the fire.

'Inspector, Miss Underhay, Captain Bryant, good morning, is something amiss?' Sir Stanford struggled upright in his chair, setting aside his paper. Wariness settled on his features.

Caroline's gaze locked with Kitty's and she saw that odd gleam in the girl's eyes once more. Triumph, excitement?

'We're sorry to disturb you all but Miss Underhay wished to

see you. An unresolved question about the case,' Inspector Greville looked at Kitty.

She was aware that the inspector was placing a great deal of trust in her, allowing her to re-enter the house under his auspices. It was very possible that she was about to make an almighty fool of herself.

'Miss Underhay?' Mr Peters had also focused his attention on her.

'Sir Stanford, you indicated to Inspector Greville that there was a rumour relating to Lady Foxley about the time she spent abroad after her divorce?' Kitty looked at Sir Stanford, who had retaken his seat.

The older man glanced at Caroline uncomfortably. 'That is correct, but I really couldn't say to its veracity or indeed where it had come from.'

'She was out of society for some eight months or so?' Kitty asked.

Sir Stanford nodded.

Kitty saw that flicker of undefined emotion on Caroline's face once more and was certain now that her theory was correct.

'Inspector Greville, through some dreadful machination from the real killer I am very much afraid that you may have arrested the wrong person for the murder of Lady Foxley and Lillie Trentham.'

Peters placed his playing cards down on the table and she noticed his hand shaking.

'I don't understand.' Sir Stanford turned to the inspector.

'The real motive behind these murders was revenge. Revenge for a wrong done a long time ago. Right from the start we thought Lady Foxley's murder seemed very personal. When did you learn that it was Eliza that was your mother and not Lillie?' Kitty looked directly at Caroline. 'Was it when you were ill in New York, just before you sailed back to England?'

Everyone turned and stared at Caro.

The girl's expression changed. An array of emotions crossed her face, fear, then triumph, swiftly followed by hatred. 'I heard them talking, Mother, Aunt Eliza and Tiny. I heard everything. Aunt Eliza had convinced Mother it would be best for me to go away to school. She said that I was the daughter of a lady and should have those advantages. Mother said that she had given up those rights when she gave me to her. Tiny was trying to stop them from arguing.' Tears sprang up in the girl's eyes and ran freely down her pale face.

'Caroline?' Sir Stanford stared at the girl.

'That was when you decided to make them pay, wasn't it? All of them, for keeping the truth from you for all those years.' Kitty fixed her gaze on Caroline, her voice remained stern.

'Miss Trentham?' Inspector Greville asked.

'My whole life was a lie, don't you understand? Everything. Everything I ever knew about myself. Daddy wasn't my daddy. Mother wasn't my mother and Aunt Eliza, well, she didn't want me, did she? I was only brought out when it suited her, to amuse her, like a kitten or something.' Caroline was working herself up into a frenzy now. Her voice rising as she crushed the playing cards she was still holding in her hand.

'So you killed her,' Kitty said.

Peters gasped, instinctively drawing back from the card table and away from Caroline.

'I'd gone upstairs to try and talk to her. She was changing her stocking. She wouldn't listen to me when I told her she should keep me with her. Aunt Eliza made some absurd comment on how I'd soon learn how to be a grown-up if I went to that stupid school. I told her that I knew the truth, that she was my mother. I wanted to know about my father. She laughed at me; said he hadn't wanted to know. I had the stocking in my hand.' Caroline's shoulders shook and she buried her face in her hands.

Sir Stanford and Mr Peters stared at her in horrid fascination.

'And your mother?' Matt asked.

'I had found the old container of weedkiller in the cellar when I was looking to see if I could sneak a bottle of wine without Hedges noticing. There wasn't much left, but I thought there would be enough. I put some in the cachet. I'd read about how to do it in one of my detective stories.'

'But that didn't work?' Kitty said.

'I had a little left that I'd hidden so I put some in the chocolates. Mummy loved violet creams. The lid of the box was an old one from Miss Morrow's room. I swapped them over as I knew it would have her fingerprints on it. She deserved to hang. I trusted her and she lied to me more than anyone.' Caroline raised her head and glared at Kitty.

'Two of them for the price of one,' Sir Stanford murmured.

'And Sir Stanford would probably have met with some kind of accident too, wouldn't he? You knew that he was aware of your secret.' Matt looked at Kitty for confirmation of his theory.

'I hate all of them. Whispering their nasty little secrets and lying to me about everything. He would have hung around after money like he did with Mummy and Aunt Eliza.' Caroline eyed Sir Stanford with real malevolence in her gaze.

Inspector Greville placed his hand on Caroline's shoulder. 'I've heard enough. I think you had better accompany me to the police station, Miss Trentham.' He produced a set of handcuffs as the girl began to wriggle like a wild animal in his grasp.

Once she was secured, he led her from the room with the girl still crying and ranting.

'Kitty, I think I had better aid the inspector to get her into the car. Will you be all right here?' Matt asked.

She nodded and her fiancé hurried from the room. Kitty sank down on the end of the sofa, barely aware of the two men still sitting in shocked silence.

Sir Stanford rose somewhat shakily to his feet and crossed over to where a decanter of brandy stood on a small trolley. He poured three glasses, and after giving one to Mr Peters, he pressed one into Kitty's hand.

'Drink, my dear girl. I rather think you may have just saved my life.'

Kitty's teeth chattered a little on the brim of the glass as shock set in.

'How did you know? That it was Caro and not Tiny?' Phillip Peters asked.

'I couldn't see why Tiny would have harmed Caroline. I know there was an idea that the fall was only intended to hurt her enough so that she shouldn't be sent away, but Tiny wouldn't ever have harmed her. Not on any account.' Kitty felt the reviving warmth of the brandy hit the back of her throat.

'I see,' Sir Stanford said.

'I was at the church carol service yesterday evening and there was a little girl and I started thinking about families and there was the empty manger.' Kitty wasn't sure if either man knew what she meant. She wasn't really explaining herself terribly well.

Sir Stanford, however, seemed to understand her chain of thought. 'You thought of a baby who had a parent that wasn't the parent everyone thought.'

Kitty smiled at him. 'Yes, I rather think that was it, and then Mr Peters had said how Caro loved to snoop about finding out secrets. It all started to come together.'

'She threw herself down the stairs to make sure she would not be suspected when Lillie was poisoned. She knew her mother loved violet creams. She often shared them with Miss Morrow.' Phillip Peters looked horrified. 'I felt so sorry for her too. I kept thinking of my own sister – they are almost the same age – and how she must feel being suddenly all alone in the world.'

Matt re-entered the room. 'The chauffeur has gone with the inspector to take Caroline to the police station. I expect he will release Miss Morrow now.'

Kitty put down her glass. 'I think we should telephone for a taxi.'

'Mr Hedges has done it already. It should be here shortly.' Matt held out his hands to help her to her feet.

'Thank you again, Miss Underhay,' Sir Stanford said as Matt placed his arm around Kitty's waist and prepared to lead her from the room.

She wondered if he would still thank her when Mr Hemmings had delivered what she suspected would be a rather damning report on Sir Stanford's financial shenanigans. She suspected the police were not quite finished with Sir Stanford just yet.

'Please be kind to Miss Morrow when she returns. She has been through a dreadful ordeal, and she loved Caro so much.' Kitty was glad of Matt's support as she said her farewells and they walked out of Villa Lamora and past Eliza's portrait for hopefully the final time.

CHAPTER TWENTY-THREE

Matt sat beside Kitty in the back of the taxi taking them back to his home at Churston. He was glad of the cold air circulating inside the car through the gap in the window beside him. Kitty was snuggled up next to him, her head resting lightly on his shoulder.

He couldn't help but feel relieved that the puzzle of who had killed Lady Foxley and her sister and why was now finally solved. The issue of who could have pushed Caroline on the stairs had troubled his mind too but, until Kitty had spoken up, he hadn't realised why.

'I wonder if they have saved some lunch for us,' Kitty said. 'I'm really rather hungry now and I suspect we are too late to join everyone at the table.'

'We can telephone from our house and let them know what has gone on. There are some cold cuts in the larder and a very good cheese if you would care to dine privately,' Matt suggested.

A private luncheon at home sounded infinitely preferable to him instead of the event he knew Kitty's grandmother had planned for them.

'That does sound rather lovely. I expect Bertie will be pleased to see us.' Kitty lifted her head and the corners of her mouth tilted upwards. 'We had better save some room for tonight anyway. Grams has a very nice roast lamb dinner organised.'

Kitty's grandmother had arranged a formal dinner for everyone followed by champagne and dancing. Alice, Robert Potter, Mrs Craven and several of their other close friends had been invited to join them that evening in a pre-wedding celebration.

'It should be quite the affair. Your father has already arranged his taxi,' Matt said.

'Then a quiet lunch together now with just the two of us sounds lovely.' Kitty's smile widened.

They let themselves into the house to be greeted by a happy and enthusiastic Bertie. He seemed to have destroyed a yellow duster in their absence, judging by the remnants scattered all around the hall and kitchen.

'Oh dear, that looks like another one to replace,' Kitty said ruefully as she collected up the pieces.

Matt was used to his dog's destructive tendencies. 'Don't worry. There are plenty more pieces in the rag bag which can be used as dusters.'

Kitty took off her outdoor things and telephoned her grandmother to assure her they would be at the hotel in good time for dinner. She apologised for missing lunch and reassured her grandmother that all was well.

In the meantime, Matt went to the kitchen and prepared them a hearty meal of bread, butter, cheese, ham, pickles and apples.

'This looks lovely, thank you.' Kitty settled into her seat at the table with a contented sigh.

He poured them both a small glass of cider to accompany their meal.

'To us.' He held up his glass to chink it against Kitty's.

'To us,' Kitty agreed.

Matt took a sip from his drink and looked at his fiancée across the table. 'I have a small wedding gift for you.'

Kitty looked up from where she had been applying butter liberally to her bread and stared at him in surprise. 'A gift? For me?'

Matt couldn't help grinning at her. 'I was going to give it to you after the wedding but after this morning I think you should have it now.' He rose from his seat. 'Wait there for a moment.'

He disappeared into the sitting room to retrieve the small package he had prepared for her.

'Matt,' Kitty protested as he placed the small brown-paper parcel in front of her.

'Open it.' He wanted to see the look on her face when she saw the contents.

Kitty pulled the string and opened the package to reveal a silver card case with the monogram *'KB'* engraved on the lid.

She looked at him, confused.

'See what's inside,' Matt instructed.

Kitty opened it up to see that the card case was full of printed cards. She took one out and gasped as she read it.

'"*Mrs Kitty Bryant, Private Investigator, Partner, Torbay Private Investigative Services.*" Oh, Matt!'

He could see that she was momentarily overcome and, unusually for Kitty, temporarily lost for words.

'I can think of no one else that I would rather have both as my wife and as my business partner.' He reached across the table to take her hand.

'Thank you, Matt. That is really the loveliest present in the world.'

. . .

Kitty woke on Christmas Eve morning to find Alice, Lucy and Muffy all in her bedroom. A small trolley laden with breakfast things was set up beside the fireplace and the two girls were merrily chattering away while Kitty rubbed the sleep from her eyes.

'Today's the day, Miss Kitty.' Alice beamed at her as she set out the tea things on a small round table.

'We thought a good breakfast would be just the ticket. We don't want you fainting at the altar,' Lucy said as Muffy sniffed hopefully at a silver lidded dish that Kitty guessed contained bacon.

'Everyone else is already up and about getting ready. We thought as you should enjoy a bit of a lie-in as your last day as a single maid,' Alice said as she set out plates and cutlery.

'This is so kind of you both. What a lovely idea.' Kitty felt quite tearful as she looked at her cousin and her best friend's efforts.

She had to admit after consuming a cup of tea and a plate of bacon and eggs she did feel somewhat more ready to face the day. Alice cleared away and went to prepare a bath for Kitty, while Lucy disappeared to sort out her own appearance. Muffy followed happily along behind having had a good breakfast from the titbits passed down from the table.

A peep through the window revealed a dull grey day with a hint of sunshine to come. She couldn't help feeling relieved that the rain had held off.

'Your grams says as she'll be along shortly afore your father gets here to take you to the church,' Alice said when Kitty had emerged from her bath ready to submit to Alice's ministrations with her hair and her wedding gown.

There was a tap on the door and Lucy entered dressed in her dark-green satin gown, carrying her white fur-trimmed cape.

'Oh, Kitty, you do look lovely.' Lucy admired Alice's handiwork as the maid secured the Juliet cap and veil carefully on top of Kitty's short blonde curls.

Alice stepped back to scrutinise Kitty's appearance. 'I think as you'll do,' she said, before whisking out a cotton handkerchief to dab at her eyes.

'Stop it both of you or I shall cry too,' Kitty teased, aware that she was close to tears herself.

'I had best get a move on, miss. I've to get my own glad rags on and meet our Dolly. I'll see you at the church.' Alice slipped out of the room.

Another tap at the door a moment later brought Kitty's grandmother bearing the bouquets for both girls to carry. Lucy's posy was a smaller version of the white roses and green myrtle Kitty had chosen. Like Lucy, her grandmother was clothed in a festive green for her dress and hat.

'Your father has arrived and is waiting for you downstairs, Kitty. The rest of us are about to set off for the church. Rupert has already gone ahead to meet Matthew.' She paused, then said softly, 'You look beautiful. Your dear mother would have been so very proud.' She kissed Kitty's cheek and Kitty breathed in the familiar lavender scent her grandmother always wore.

'Thank you for everything, Grams.' Kitty had her mother's suffrage pin tucked inside her dress as her something old in order to keep her mother close to her during the service. Lucy had loaned her a pair of pearl earrings for something borrowed, her gown was new, and a blue ribbon had been sewn inside her dress for something blue.

Her grandmother dabbed her eyes, then left leaving Kitty and Lucy together. The faithful Muffy had been left with Mickey, Kitty's maintenance man, who had promised to ensure the dog behaved at the church.

'Are you ready, Kitty dear?' Lucy asked.

Kitty took a deep breath and nodded. Together the girls made their way down the broad oak staircase to the lobby where

Kitty's father, resplendent in his grey morning suit, was waiting for them.

Lucy went out to get in the car taking her party to the church, while Kitty had a moment alone with her father.

'I have your silver sixpence.' Edgar bent and slid the tiny coin into her satin shoe before straightening to look at her. 'You look so much like my darling Elowed. I wish with all my heart that she could have been here today.'

Kitty blinked back tears at the emotion in her father's eyes.

'I know that I haven't always been here for you, dearest girl, when I should have been, but you have always been in my heart. I'm sure that I know what your answer will be, but I believe the convention is that I am supposed to ask if you are quite certain about marrying Matthew?' A wry smile tugged at the corner of his mouth as he posed the question.

'I've never been more certain of anything in my life,' Kitty assured him.

'Then I couldn't be happier for both of you.' Her father placed her hand on the crook of his arm. 'Shall we, my dear?'

Kitty's heart raced as she and her father travelled the short distance to the church. The bells were ringing, and a small crowd had gathered outside near the doors. Lucy was waiting for her at the church door wearing her cape and Kitty spotted the small girl in the crowd who had been seated beside her at the carol concert.

Alice and Dolly stepped forward to take Lucy's cape and Kitty's, straightening her veil and dress ready for her to enter the church.

The first notes of the wedding music reached them, and she heard a shuffling of feet and a drop in the hum of conversation from the congregation. Her pulse speeded up and her mouth dried.

'I believe that is our cue,' Edgar said as Lucy took her place behind her as she entered St Saviour's to marry Matt.

. . .

Afterwards when they were signing the register Kitty could only remember the tender expression on Matt's face as he had turned to see her walking towards him. Her heart had been so full that everyone else had seemed to disappear.

The register duly signed they made their way out of the church to the joyous clamour of the bells announcing their marriage. Her engagement ring now sat snuggly above a narrow band of gold on her wedding finger. A matching band was on Matt's hand.

Her uncle had engaged a photographer to record the occasion, so they posed together on the small piece of grass near the doors. She was surprised by how many people had come to see the wedding. It felt as if all of Dartmouth had stopped by.

She glimpsed Inspector Greville, along with Doctor Carter and his wife, and wondered where Mrs Greville had gone. Mrs Craven, wearing the most impossible hat, was with her grandmother and her aunt Livvy. There were employees from the hotel and tradespeople from the town that she had known all her life.

Mr Lutterworth had produced rice and he and Dolly scattered it over them for luck as the crowd drew nearer to surround them. Matt turned away momentarily to greet a well-wisher.

'I've a little something for luck,' a vaguely familiar female voice suddenly sounded close to Kitty.

Something in the tone of the comment caught her attention. An icy shiver seemed to chill her to the bone. She whirled around to see a gypsy woman, shrouded in a woollen shawl carrying a wicker pedlar's basket approaching her.

'Matt!' Kitty could barely manage to speak as she locked eyes with Esther Hammett. The woman's mouth twisted in a semblance of a smile as she plunged her hand into the basket.

Time seemed to stand still as Kitty caught a glimpse of

something metallic hidden under the posies of holly and heather.

'Oh no you don't.' Alice sprang forward from the crowd. She snatched Aunt Effie's silver-headed ebony walking stick from her hand and hit Esther hard over the head. Caught unaware, the woman dropped to the floor, the contents of her basket spilling out as she fell.

Aunt Effie shrieked and wobbled and was caught by Kitty's uncle. Mr Lutterworth and Inspector Greville pushed their way forward through the crowd, which had surged even closer at the commotion.

'Up you get.' Inspector Greville dragged the dazed-looking Esther to her feet with Mr Lutterworth securing her other arm so she couldn't flee.

''Tis a gun she's got in that basket.' Alice indicated the contents of the basket now strewn across the flagstones. Dolly clung onto her sister's arm steadying her.

A gasp rang out from the crowd. Matt placed his arm protectively about Kitty's waist shielding her from the now captive Esther.

Kitty's stomach rolled when she saw her friend was right. A revolver had indeed been hidden under the posies. Her uncle swooped to pick it up from the floor.

'Here, Inspector, I'll take care of this until you can send a constable to collect it.'

'Are you all right, Kitty?' her father asked as he realised what had just happened.

Matt's mother had collapsed against his father, her hand pressed to her bosom. 'I knew there were bad omens.'

'Oh, do stop wittering, Patience.' Aunt Effie glared at her as Alice passed her cane back to the elderly woman.

Esther had recovered her wits and started screaming abuse at Kitty as Inspector Greville wrestled a set of handcuffs onto her before dragging her away from the wedding party.

'Kitty, my love?' Matt's gaze met hers. She saw relief mingled with concern at what had almost happened.

'I am perfectly fine thanks to Alice and her quick wits.' She smiled at her friend who looked shaken now the import of her actions had begun to sink in. It was a good job Alice had reacted as quickly as she had, or Matt may have been a widower for a second time.

'I saw her at the last minute.' Alice frowned. 'Thank heavens as she's been took care of.'

'You were terribly brave, my dear.' Kitty's father dabbed at his forehead with his handkerchief.

'Well, it seems that our married life is going to be as eventful as our single life.' Matt's own smile widened, and the dimple flashed in his cheek once he realised that Kitty was indeed unscathed.

'It would seem so, Captain Bryant.' Kitty's own expression matched his.

'Then let's get back to the Dolphin and start our next adventure together, if that's all right with you, Mrs Bryant?' Matt teased.

Kitty blushed. 'Absolutely,' she agreed.

A LETTER FROM HELENA

Dear reader,

I want to say a huge thank you for choosing to read *Murder at the Charity Ball*. If you did enjoy it, and would like to keep up-to-date with all my latest releases, just sign up at the following link. Your email address will never be shared, and you can unsubscribe at any time.

www.bookouture.com/helena-dixon

This book is very special as it marks the closure of some story threads that were started with the very first book in the series, *Murder at the Dolphin Hotel*. It also sets the scene for many more new and exciting mysteries for Matt and Kitty to solve. I can't wait to share those with you.

I do hope you loved *Murder at the Charity Ball* and, if you did, I would be very grateful if you could write a review. I'd love to hear what you think, and it makes such a difference helping new readers to discover one of my books for the first time.

I love hearing from my readers – you can get in touch on my Facebook page, through Twitter, Goodreads or my website.

Thanks,

Helena

KEEP IN TOUCH WITH HELENA

www.nelldixon.com

facebook.com/nelldixonauthor

twitter.com/NellDixon

ACKNOWLEDGEMENTS

Thanks as always to everyone in Torbay who has given me information, support, and sight of documents and pictures. Your help with my research is invaluable and I'm so grateful.

My thanks also go to my family for their help with my research and their unstinting support.

Love to the Tuesday morning zoomers, and my writerly pals in the Coffee Crew.

Special thanks to my lovely agent, Kate Nash, my incredible editor, Emily Gowers, and all of the team at Bookouture who work so hard to make these books the best they can possibly be. I appreciate all of your hard work so much. Thank you.

Made in the USA
Coppell, TX
06 May 2023

16502231R00152